GHOST BOY

He was alone in the house, and it was dark. He was only eight. When he heard the noises from the back of the house, William tried to ignore them. It was a sneaky, scratchy sort of noise that started out on the back porch but now sounded as if it were *in* the house. When he couldn't stand it anymore, he nearly burst through the front door to freedom. Outside was better, even though it was almost midnight. He was going to go to the bar where he knew his mother was . . . she might be a little mad at first, but she would get over it. She had to.

William didn't walk very far before he realized it was going to take longer to get to Goldy's than he'd thought. The bar was on the other side of town, and it began to seem like a bad idea to be out so late alone.

When the car pulled up alongside him, William looked at the friendly face at the open window.

The driver scolded him in a friendly way, "Son, what are you doing outside at this hour?"

William shrugged, "My mom's at Goldy's. That's where I was going, but I think I changed my mind. I'm gonna be in trouble."

"No, you're not. Hop in and I'll take you home. No one has to know a thing."

Gratefully, William ran around to the other side of the car and got in. "Really, you won't tell?"

"Not a word. I promise."

ghost boy
JEAN SIMON

ZEBRA BOOKS
KENSINGTON PUBLISHING CORP.

ZEBRA BOOKS are published by

Kensington Publishing Corp.
475 Park Avenue South
New York, NY 10016

Zebra and the Z logo Reg. U.S. Pat. & TM Off.

First Printing: April, 1994

Printed in the United States of America

Prologue

This had happened before. Sometimes he felt small, and something in him struggled to break free. In the past he'd always been able to push it down, but this time it bubbled to the surface, ready to pop open like a poisonous, festering wound, and he was too small to fight it. The hate was growing out of control—denied for too long, so that it had been allowed to grow and strengthen. Now it was going to burst free, and he knew there was nothing he could do to stop it.

The little girl who taunted him was homely, with kinky red hair and freckles the size of coins. Unaware of her own ugliness, she was one of those kids who had the talent to sense the exact point of weakness in others, and knew how to use it.

"You missed a spot," she said on this bright afternoon. She pointed at the bench he was sanding in preparation for a fresh coat of paint.

"You could get fired if you screwed up such an easy thing." Then she snickered and danced away from him, not really afraid but keeping her distance nonetheless.

He kept his head turned away from her as he worked, pretending not to hear.

His hands trembled. His fingers itched to slap her, to strike the smugly superior expression from her face.

She was a child, years younger than he was, but already well-schooled in the fine art of savagery.

"My mom says your job isn't much better than a janitor here," she continued, venturing closer in her desire to make sure her words struck home. "Having some kind of title doesn't change anything." She scrunched her face up in a mask of disdain, freckles melding together over her nose.

He stopped what he was doing, at last, and looked at her.

An icy calm had slipped over him, and his hands no longer trembled. He'd never experienced anything quite like it before, but he savored it. He realized he didn't feel quite so small anymore.

Let her come a little closer, he thought. She was like a bird, venturing near to peck at the seeds of her cruelty, but ready to take flight from him at any moment.

He hadn't seen another person in almost half an hour. The school bell had rung long ago, the other children were gone. He'd stayed in this room because he had things to do that often

6

kept him for two or three hours after the others had left. He usually worked in peace.

Until today, when she'd walked by and had seen him alone in the room.

Probably no one knew she was here. Eyes darting around the room, he took in the long workbench, the metal lockers against the far wall. There was a row of windows, but the view outside revealed an empty playground, the swings hanging limp on their chains.

There was no one to see.

His calm remained, and he backed away from the workbench, deeper into the room to lure her away from the door.

"You'd better go home now," he said softly. "You'll get in trouble if you're late."

This was a calculated risk, but he was gambling that her stubbornness would drive her to do the exact opposite of what he suggested.

It worked. She came forward, her shoes clattering on the worn tile of the floor. The shoes were white, with big bows instead of laces, and made so much noise on the tiles that he thought they must have little metal studs on the soles, like tap shoes.

"I won't get in trouble," she sneered. "I can do whatever I want. My parents never get mad at me. I can—a-a-a-ck!"

He'd reached out and grabbed her around the throat with one hand, his strong fingers digging into her soft flesh and cutting off her words. She was left only with a newly terrified expression, her mouth twisting as she fought to scream.

He was no longer small.

He didn't pull her to him immediately. Instead, he held her like that with one hand. Her shoes barely touched the floor, her hands dug at his wrist, trying to make him loosen his grip on her.

It was fascinating to watch, the way she struggled on the end of his arm, like a fish just reeled in. She was much lighter than he'd expected her to be—or maybe it was his fury that made him strong.

"You shut up," he hissed, giving her a little shake.

It felt good to say this out loud at last. He'd thought it so many times, but had never before been in a position to actually utter the words.

He did pull her to him then, caution taking over. He held her pressed to his chest, his hand still on her throat, his other arm around her in an uncompromising embrace.

Still no one outside the windows. And no one had walked past the doorway in a long time. But to be sure he wasn't observed now—because it was too late to go back, he could never adequately explain his actions—he dragged her to the door and closed it softly, then flipped the latch.

Her struggles increased, as though she fully realized at last how hopeless her situation was. She'd been frightened before; now she was in a death-panic, fighting him as a drowning person fights the undertow that sucks with relentless strength.

Ineffectually.

He almost laughed at how easy it was to hold her. Her bones felt fragile, like twigs. He was sure he could snap her neck with very little effort.

"Now who's stupid?" he whispered, his mouth near her ear. He gave her a little shake. *"Now* do you want to call me names? What's the matter? You always have so much to say. Always running off at the mouth. You don't have such a big mouth now—do you?"

She made a desperate noise deep in her throat, a trapped whimper that pleased him because he recognized it as a sound that had come from him many times before, during those times when he'd been locked up and helpless in the dark basement, being punished.

How nice to know that for once *he* was the one doing the punishing, and it was someone else who was frightened and alone.

But there was no more time to explore the taste of this victory, no matter how much he might want to drag it on. Every moment he stood here with this girl in his arms increased his risk of discovery. Even with the door locked there were still other people in the building.

Now what to do? He couldn't release her. As soon as he took his hand from her mouth she would begin shrieking.

The decision came easily enough. He looked

down at her kinky red hair with distaste. What made her think she was so special?

She deserved whatever she got.

Still, he might have backed down, even as unpleasant as the consequences of her telling on him was sure to be, if there had been anything in her to elicit his compassion. He wasn't an unfeeling person. To the contrary, he often took extra time to help others, and always enjoyed having done some good.

But this girl. She had touched a raw nerve in him, and then, seeing the hurt she'd caused, had gone out of her way to inflict more pain.

He looked down at her, tilted her head up so he could look into her eyes. What he saw there sealed her fate. She was glaring pure venom at him. Fear—yes, that was still there. But more than the fear he saw her continued belief in her own superiority.

Only a few minutes had passed since he'd grabbed her. It felt like an eternity. He couldn't wait any longer.

He moved the hand that was over her mouth only slightly, just enough so that it covered her nose as well. Her eyes widened, and he pressed her head hard against his chest, holding her so that he wouldn't have to look at her while her life ebbed away.

She flopped against him but he held her tightly for one minute . . . two minutes. There was a clock high up on the wall with a second hand that seemed to drag, taking forever to make a full circle. He was aware of every second, and of those uncovered windows that might at any moment be his undoing.

Even after she fell limp in his arms he kept her mouth and nose covered, not wanting to take any chances. Her head flopped loosely and he let himself look at her face again. Her eyes were open. The pale blue irises already seemed dulled, as though covered by a thin film.

He couldn't take her out of the room yet. He'd have to wait until later. For now he needed a place to hide her, and his eyes went immediately to the rows of metal lockers.

Perfect. No one ever used them anymore. They were kept mainly for storage, and there had been talk lately of getting rid of them entirely because they were an eyesore.

Dragging the body with him, he opened several lockers until he found one that was nearly empty. It contained some small boxes that probably held outdated supplies that no one at the school knew quite what to do with. At any rate, there was plenty of room inside for one small girl, and he pushed the body into the locker. An arm poked out, but he managed to get it in and then closed the locker door.

He stood back to look. Good. A casual observer wouldn't notice a thing. He wished he could lock it, but there was no way or time to think more about it.

He left the room. Casually, hands in pockets, he strolled down the hallway. Later, when it was dark, he would come back and move the body to a better place here on the school grounds. His first thought had been to somehow get the body as far away from the school as possible, but on further reflection he dismissed that idea. To try to take a body anywhere, even under cover of darkness, created a greater risk than he wanted to take.

No, better to just move the body to another place in the school building, a place that wouldn't immediately be associated with him.

Surprisingly, he was neither frightened nor appalled by what he'd done. A part of him wondered at this, but he didn't allow himself to dwell for long on his lack of remorse. A dark, gleeful corner of his soul celebrated the path he'd taken. This part of him had always been there, but only now did it grow and strengthen, having been fed a complete and satisfying meal.

Once outside the building he walked, almost whistling at the perfection of this day. Someone greeted him, and he raised one hand and returned the wave. And why not? He was a well-liked guy. Most people treated him with the respect he deserved.

The dark thing deep in his soul straightened his spine and put a smirk of satisfaction on his lips.

He did move her body as soon as he was able, but by then he realized what a chance he was taking in doing so. The school would almost undoubtedly be one of the first places the police would look, once contacted. Still, he felt compelled to get her away from the one room where people would first think of him as being connected to, and he'd thrown the cold body over his shoulder and carried it to the space below the school's stage. That space was so dark and full of dust that it wasn't even used as storage, and he felt he was buying a little time by selecting it as a hiding place.

It didn't work out that way. Once the police were called it didn't take them long to find the little girl's body.

He'd barely gotten out of the building himself before two police cars pulled up and the search began, prompted by the girl's worried parents. The police didn't see him, but the encounter was too close and he found his heart beating heavily with delayed shock as he let himself melt into the small, curious crowd that gathered across the street.

"Does anybody know what's going on?" a thin woman with pink sponge curlers in her hair asked.

"Don't know," her companion replied, "but they brought the principal with them. I saw him get out of that first police car. D'you suppose he's done something wrong?"

"That straight arrow?" a man with thick, wire-rimmed glasses snickered. "Not a chance. I saw a light on in there awhile ago. Probably someone noticed and called it in, and they're checking it out, just as a precaution."

"Which light?" the thin woman asked.

The man lifted one hand to point. "That one over—hey, it's out now. I'm *sure* I saw a light on in there, before the cops arrived. Maybe I should tell them about it. Maybe there was a prowler."

The three discussed this possibility at great length.

As he stood close to this little group of observers, he began to sweat. He'd had to turn a light on to move the body, but it hadn't occurred to him that the light would be seen from the outside. Stupid mistake. He should have thought of it. Mistakes like that were what got a person caught.

Still striving to remain inconspicuous, he strained to listen to what was being said. The man and the two women, obviously neighbors by their easy familiarity, were still trying to decide whether to go across the street and tell the police what they knew.

"Tell 'em," the second woman urged. She nudged her friend, and they exchanged knowing looks. To the man she added, "Maybe when they smell the beer on your breath they'll take *you* in for questioning."

The women snickered, but their companion paled and seemed torn between righteous anger and caution. He glared at them through his glasses. So he'd had a couple after work. Was that a crime? The neighbor stalked off, headed

14

back to his own house, mumbling under his breath about people who couldn't mind their own business.

It was going to be okay. No one else was saying anything about seeing a light on at the school, and certainly no one was coming forward to point an accusing finger.

Then all hell broke loose across the street. He watched, hypnotized, as more police cars arrived, sirens screaming and lights flashing this time, and a half-dozen officers tumbled from the cruisers almost before they'd come to a complete stop. Spotlights were aimed at the school building, a yellow do-not-cross tape was stretched and held in place by sawhorses.

The body had been found. Surprisingly fast, he thought, a little shiver of fear bringing his shoulders up.

The straight-arrow principal staggered from the building, supported himself against a tree, his face drawn into a mask of misery. What an act.

Then the wailing parents; at least their grief was genuine.

A shocked and silent crowd watched as an ambulance arrived and, sometime later, a small figure was brought out on a stretcher. Covered. That meant death.

He'd seen enough. He faded into the night, away from the rapidly growing group of observers, without having spoken to anyone.

It had been so easy.

One

Libby spilled coffee on the front of her blouse and swore as the spot spread over the fabric. The blouse was pink; the wet coffee darkened it to deep red, like blood.

The morning wasn't starting off well, and there were definite signs that things were going to get worse. Spilled coffee was only a small part of it. She placed her mug on the countertop and tried dabbing at the stain with a dishcloth. It didn't help.

"Mom! Joely is wearing my shorts."

"They aren't yours. These are mine."

Two girls charged into the kitchen, the smaller one in the lead. She took refuge behind her mother, nearly knocking Libby over in the process. For a moment the girls ran around her, until Libby reached out and grabbed the nearest arm. It happened to belong to Tess, the fifteen-year-old, who immediately protested.

"You always take her side!" Tess shouted, still trying to reach her sister. "It's not fair."

17

Libby held onto the girl. "I'm not taking anyone's side. I'm trying to stop you both from running around like a couple of wild animals until I figure out what's going on. Joely—stop that right now."

Joely had taken advantage of the fact that her older sister couldn't reach her, and was making faces. She stopped when caught, but didn't try to deny that she'd been doing it.

The girls sulked, but at least they were standing still, and Libby took this moment to catch her breath. She would be late for work if she didn't leave the house soon, but she couldn't leave until the problem was resolved. If she did, Tess and Joely would continue the fight after she was gone and there was no telling what would happen then. Last time, the consequences had involved broken dishes.

This wasn't an easy time for any of them, and Libby tried to show a little more patience now than she might have in the past. Only six months divorced, she'd moved her daughters to this small city almost a hundred miles from their home partly out of a need to put distance between herself and painful memories, but also because, reentering the work force after several years of being away, she'd had to face some harsh realities. One of those was that she was a woman in her late 30s, trying to compete with sharp, energetic recent college grads, and although she'd always considered herself capable

18

and organized, her ego had taken a beating during the experience.

Moving to Cielo had been a matter of necessity, but at least the town wasn't completely strange to them. It was her ex-husband's hometown, and Libby and the girls had been visiting—along with the now-absent Brandon Gregory—regularly for the past fifteen years. Libby had even made some friends in town over the years, and one of them, Francine Curtis, had helped her find the job she now held and a house to rent. True, her former mother-in-law lived here in Cielo, and she and Libby had never had a great fondness for each other, but so far they'd managed to avoid any contact.

Living in Cielo, one hundred miles inland from the California coast, was cheaper than in the cities, so it didn't matter quite so much that the job paid only a couple of dollars above minimum wage. She could get by, if she managed her money carefully.

But, despite her relief in finding employment and a place to live before her savings had been completely drained, all was not going smoothly. The girls were going through a difficult adjustment period in these summer months before the new school year would begin. They bickered constantly, and complained often and loudly about having been forced to leave their friends behind.

Libby tried to remain calm. She might *feel* hysterical on the inside, but she'd become an expert at hiding it.

"Tess," she said, keeping herself between her daughters, "you gave Joely those shorts three months ago because they were too small for you."

"I didn't—"

"I was there," Libby interrupted. "I'm a witness."

"Well, you're wrong. They're mine and I want them back."

"You can't have them," Joely shouted. Tears were threatening, making her eyes look large and luminous behind her glasses. "I have hardly anything to wear. You have tons of stuff."

Libby looked at the clock on the kitchen wall. This dispute was going to have to be resolved quickly. "Tess, you gave those shorts to Joely. They don't fit you anymore, you have no use for them—and that's the end of it."

"You always take her side!" Tess cried. "Every little thing she wants, she gets. The *baby*."

"I'm not a baby!"

"All she has to do is turn on the tears and you cave in. She's got her act all worked out, and you fall for it every time." Then Tess burst into tears of her own and ran from the kitchen. A door slammed with enough force to shake the walls.

Unbuttoning her blouse, Libby struggled for control. This was too much. She had to go to work, but felt like she was abandoning her children by doing so. They obviously needed her. They'd never fought this viciously before the divorce, but if she was going to take care of them that meant tending to the material needs as well as the emotional ones. Child support helped, but it wasn't enough for the three of them to live on, not with both girls growing so quickly that the shorts in question would probably be too small for Joely as well within a few months.

Libby sighed. "I have to change and go to work," she said. "Finish your breakfast, okay, Joely? And do the dishes for me—I don't care when, just so they're done before I get home."

Joely's lip began to tremble. "As soon as you're gone Tess is going to rip these shorts right off me."

"I'll tell her not to." Libby walked to her bedroom, pulling the blouse from her shoulders. What was the time? She was going to be late, and though it wouldn't be by more than a few minutes, it also wasn't going to be the first time.

Joely followed her into the bedroom.

"That won't do any good," the little girl pouted. "Tess hates me. Why can't I have my own bedroom? She closes the door and then I'm not supposed to go in there, but it's my bedroom, too. She's probably doing something to my stuff right now, for revenge."

Libby selected a new blouse, one that matched the skirt she was wearing, and removed it from the hanger. "I couldn't afford a three-bedroom house, honey. This is the best I can do for now. Things will get better, I promise. Once I get the car paid off, that'll make a big difference, and

21

there are only six payments left on the refrigerator. We just have to tighten our belts for now."

"I don't have any belts. Tess has all the clothes, she always gets the new stuff and I get the leftovers."

"Yeah, I know . . . it's the pits."

"It sucks."

"Joely!" But Libby had to turn her back to button her blouse, so her daughter wouldn't see that she was trying to hide her smile. Joely Gregory, at eleven, had the appearance of an angel, with her delicate features and straight blond hair cut in a pageboy. Even a mild swearword coming from those cupid's-bow lips was too ridiculous for Libby to be angry about. She looked at her watch. "Now I really do have to go," she said. "What are you going to do today?"

Joely shrugged. "I dunno. Maybe the library."

"Isn't there anyone you can play with? What about that girl who was here a couple of days ago? Rachel? What about her?"

"She's mean to me."

"She didn't seem mean. You two were having a lot of fun." Libby tucked the blouse into her skirt.

"Yeah, for a while. But then she got mean. She always has to do everything she wants to do, she'll never do anything I want to do. She's bossy. And she thinks she's so great because—"

"I get the message," Libby said. Then, because she couldn't stand the misery any longer, she pulled Joely into an embrace. Holding the child tightly to her, Libby lowered her cheek to the top of Joely's head. "School will start in—what? About seven weeks? Then you'll meet more kids and it won't seem so bad. It's always tough getting started in a new place. It takes time." They stayed like that for a minute, then Libby released her daughter. "If you want to come to the doctor's office at about noon, we can have lunch together," she added.

Joely's expression brightened. This was a treat rarely offered because Libby usually used her lunch break to run errands, and the proposal was especially sweet to Joely because Tess wasn't invited.

She nodded, and wondered how she could casually mention her lunch plans to Tess later.

Having smoothed things over to the best of her limited abilities, Libby drove to her job at Dr. Tim Kyle's office in the heart of downtown Cielo. She was about ten minutes late, but she'd gotten lucky; Dr. Kyle himself wasn't there yet, so no one had to know that she hadn't been at her desk promptly at eight-thirty.

Libby clung to the belief that things really would get better for her and her daughters. Sometimes this belief was the only thing that kept her going. If she thought it would always be this difficult, that the girls would always be at odds and her nerves would forever be this frayed, she'd be a candidate for a nervous break-

23

down. But all she had to do was get through the summer, then Tess and Joely would be in school, they would make friends and get involved in extracurricular activities, and maybe they wouldn't be so inclined to go after each other out of boredom and frustration.

Libby stood beside her desk and slid open the heavy glass window that separated her office area from the waiting room. The day's patients would begin arriving soon, and Libby, as the office manager, would have to keep things running smoothly. She didn't mind. It was better than sitting around with nothing more to do than answer a telephone, as had been the case with some of the jobs she'd held in the past, before she'd gotten married and before the girls had been born. At least here she had the chance to show off her skills. She was organized and disciplined once she sat at her desk and got to work, and she kept order almost entirely on her own. The only help she had was a nurse who could watch the desk if necessary but didn't know much about the filing system or bookkeeping. Those responsibilities were all Libby's, and she was also the one to take the flack if something did happen to go wrong.

So far she'd been lucky. She was becoming indispensable to the doctor, and that was just how she liked it. Her personal life might be in a shambles, but no one could say her work suffered because of it.

The front door opened with a jingle of the

little bell overhead. Dr. Kyle crossed the waiting room and entered the office with his usual air of preoccupation.

"Good morning, Libby," he said. "What do I have?"

Libby pulled her appointment book out from the side drawer of her desk. "Mrs. Stefanos at nine-fifteen, for her arthritis again. Then Bobby Waverly—that cast is ready to come off. After him a Miss Lionel. She's a new patient; she didn't want to tell me what the visit was for."

Dr. Kyle nodded as she spoke. He lifted his white lab coat from a hook on the wall and slipped it on.

Libby continued to outline the day for him. Dr. Kyle listened, asked a couple of questions which Libby answered, then indicated his approval of the scheduling. He liked to keep enough time between appointments so that he could give each patient plenty of personalized attention. Libby had to always keep this in mind when scheduling, and she appreciated his thoughtfulness. Dr. Kyle didn't rush his patients through like they were on an assembly line.

Sometimes Libby couldn't help wondering about the man.

Tim Kyle was handsome, in his early forties, with a few strands of gray in his light brown hair and thoughtful brown eyes that often seemed focused inward. There were deep lines between his brows and around his eyes, but whether these were laugh lines or frown lines

25

was impossible to tell. He was a man who kept his emotions to himself in front of other people. In the several weeks since she'd come to work for him, Libby had found him to be a pleasant boss and a well-liked doctor, but a man who kept the world at arm's length.

Dr. Kyle went into his office, and Libby got up from her desk to make a pot of coffee. As she poured water into the top of the coffee maker, the bell on the door jingled. Mrs. Stefanos entered, a few minutes early for her appointment.

"I'll be right with you," Libby called out.

The day was beginning in earnest now. In addition to the arriving patients, the phone would ring and Libby would have to field the calls to determine which ones were the most urgent, and schedule accordingly. She would also have to run interference, soothing those callers who insisted they had to talk to the doctor personally. Nine times out of ten those calls were about minor aches and pains, and Libby had to see to it that the doctor wasn't disturbed unless it really was important.

She pushed the "start" button on the coffee maker, and wondered how things were going at home with Joely and Tess. There'd been no time to say goodbye to Tess, but any attempt to do so would most likely have been greeted with stony silence anyway.

More than anything, Libby wished there was something she could do to smooth the way for her girls, to get them safely through the minefield of their first summer away from their father. But it was rough going, and there were bound to be some mistakes along the way, some damaged spirits that, if not too badly mangled, would begin to heal with time.

In a perfect world, Tess and Joely would understand that Libby'd had no choice in the disruption of their lives. She'd gone through her own sleepless night of pain, the difference being that she tried to keep these dark trips into despair to herself. With the light of morning she always forced herself to smile and make breakfast, referee arguments and provide as calming an influence as she could. The girls had enough to worry about. They didn't need to see that their mother also sometimes felt like the world had dropped a big load of manure on her head. She kept up a sunny front for their sakes, but the backlash to this was that Joely and Tess thought she was unfeeling. They blamed her, and that wasn't fair.

"Will the doctor be seeing me soon?" a querulous voice asked.

Libby turned away from the coffeepot and faced the elderly woman who stood at the open window. Her fingers were twisted and painful-looking, the knuckles huge.

"In just a minute, Mrs. Stefanos," Libby told her. "Are the hands bad this morning?"

"No worse than usual, I suppose. Nothing seems to work for long anymore. I build up a resistance to the pain pills, then he puts me on something else and it works for a little while. I've been hearing talk lately about injections, I'm going to ask the doctor about it . . ."

Libby listened sympathetically, letting her concern show on her face. This always made Mrs. Stefanos feel better, to know that someone was genuinely interested. There was no more time for Libby to think about Joely's shorts or Tess's door-slamming. For the next few hours, at least, her mind was going to be on doing her job.

Two

Joely pushed her glasses up with one finger and took a deep breath before entering the sanctity of the bedroom. She'd waited long enough. It was *her* bedroom, too, and no one could keep her out.

Fully expecting Tess to attack her the moment she stepped into the room, Joely was surprised when her sister only looked at her, rolled her eyes heavenward, and turned her attention back to the magazine she was reading.

"You can have the shorts back if you really want them," Joely said timidly, one hand on the doorknob in case she had to make a hasty escape. "I can wear my cutoffs."

Tess didn't crack a smile, but looked over the magazine at her sister. "And what am I going to do with shorts that don't fit me anymore? Keep 'em . . . I don't care."

Joely ventured farther into the room. Her bed was the one closest to the door, against the wall, and she sat on the edge of it. "Then why did you make such a big deal out of it?"

"I don't know." Tess tossed the magazine aside.

Her bed was on the other side of the room, but because the bedroom wasn't that large to begin with there was less than three feet of floor space in between. It was a room that would have comfortably accommodated twin beds, but the sisters each had a full-sized bed. Because Libby hadn't wanted the girls to have to give up any of their precious possessions, furniture that had once been divided into two separate rooms was now squeezed into this too-small space. The closet was filled to overflowing, and out-of-season clothing was stored in boxes in the basement.

Joely had put posters up on the wall above her bed, and her collection of stuffed animals rested against her pillows. She'd taken her little corner of the bedroom and made it her own.

Tess's space reflected the four-year difference in their ages. She had posters on her wall as well, but instead of pictures of kittens and unicorns, hers were of TV stars and Heavy Metal bands. Not that Tess particularly liked Heavy Metal music, but she liked the posters and she'd particularly enjoyed the glazed look that had come over her mother's face when she'd first tacked them to the wall.

Nor did Tess have stuffed animals. On her chest of drawers at the foot of the bed was a small stereo, and beside that her collection of tapes. She wanted a CD player, but her mother had told her they wouldn't be getting one in the near future, especially when it would mean replacing her favorite tapes with CDs.

Money. It was always money, or the lack of it, that spoiled things. Tess knew it was also the reason she'd jumped all over Joely this morning over a pair of shorts that she had, in fact, given to her sister. But she was worried, because school would be starting and she didn't know if she'd be getting any new clothes for the year. This latest frustration, added to the many others of the past year, had sent her on a rampage. Her anger, as usual, had gotten away from her almost before she'd known it was happening. She'd lashed out at Joely as an easy target. But she *couldn't* start out at a new school in clothes that were leftover from last year. Didn't anyone understand that? She was going to be a sophomore, there were certain things she had to have if she was going to fit in. She had a little money saved from her own part-time job, but she'd only had the job for a couple of weeks, and what she'd saved wasn't going to be enough to get the things she would need.

She blamed her parents for all of it.

"Are you going to work at Mrs. Coddington's today?" Joely asked. She swung her feet so that her heels banged against the bed frame.

"It's Thursday, isn't it?" If not as angry as she had been, Tess still felt sulky.

31

"Yeah."

"Then I'll be working at Mrs. Coddington's."

"I wish I could have a job."

"No you don't. You think you do, but that's only because you don't know anything."

Joely considered this. "If you don't like it, how come you do it?"

"For the money. And because it's the only kind of job I can get for now. If you're under sixteen you can't work a real job, because of the laws. You can only do stuff like babysitting . . . and what I'm doing."

"Can I go with you sometime, just to see what it's like? I won't get in your way."

Tess opened her mouth to say something nasty, but then stopped before the words came out. She'd had her fill of being mean for one morning, and the truth was most of the time Joely wasn't so bad. She could be a pest, but she was only eleven years old, so being a pest sort of came with the territory. And it was much too easy to hurt Joely. Sometimes that gave Tess a perverse satisfaction, but only briefly. She usually felt guilty afterwards, because Joely was one of those kids who could look like a puppy being kicked when she was sad, sort of pathetic but still loving at the same time. No matter what Tess did, no matter how mean she acted, Joely was always ready to forgive at the slightest word of encouragement. Always eager to hug and make up. More than once Tess had wondered if this was a calculated move on Joely's part, if the

32

younger girl knew that, if she just let her bottom lip tremble and hunched her shoulders in as though afraid of being struck, she could make Tess feel like a shit.

Which was pretty much how Tess felt right now.

"Maybe sometime," she said in response to Joely's question. "But not today. It's laundry day and I'll be too busy to have you hanging around."

Sensing a softening of Tess's attitude, Joely got up from her bed and ventured toward her sister's stereo. Testing the waters. She didn't go so far as to touch it—that would be pushing her luck—but she did stand dangerously close.

Tess watched her with narrowed eyes, but didn't say anything.

"I might go find Rachel today," Joely said finally.

"I thought you didn't like Rachel."

"She's not so bad if she doesn't get bossy. If she does, I'll come home. I can always watch TV."

"You shouldn't be inside watching TV on a beautiful summer afternoon," Tess said. "God, listen to me—I sound just like Mom. Do what you want. I'm leaving in a few minutes." She got up and went to the closet to get some clothes. She'd put on shorts and a tank top first thing this morning, but old Mrs. Coddington didn't approve of skimpy clothing at her house. No matter how hot it was, Tess had to wear slacks and a blouse with nothing less than short sleeves. Not even a skirt was allowed, for God's sake, and in the middle of summer.

She turned to warn Joely not to dare touch her stereo, but found that she was alone in the bedroom.

Joely walked away from the house, thinking that there were some things about living in Cielo she really didn't mind. Being able to go anywhere she wanted was one of them. When they'd lived in the city she hadn't been allowed to go anywhere by herself, and if her parents were going out and Tess wasn't going to be around to watch her, Joely'd even had to bear the indignity of a babysitter. She'd hated that, but fortunately it hadn't happened often.

In the city her parents talked about kidnappers, perverts, stuff like that, and were always warning her against the dangers of talking to strangers. She hadn't even been allowed to go to the beach by herself, even though the ocean had been so close that sometimes you could actually smell it, drifting inland on a breeze.

In Cielo there apparently were no strangers, and Libby had explained that if she was going to be at work all day she wanted to know that her girls could safely be on their own for a few hours.

The bad thing about being in Cielo, though, was that Joely did miss her father. She didn't completely understand why he couldn't move here, too. Cielo was *his* hometown. They wouldn't even know about this place if it weren't for him; yet here they were, and he was in the city, living in an apartment by himself.

Joely understood about the divorce, but still thought he could get his own place here, or stay with Grandma Gregory, his mother, in her big old house. Joely had even mentioned this to him once, when they'd been packing to relocate, but he'd said something vague about his work being in the city and about not feeling comfortable in a small town anymore. He'd also promised to visit them often, but so far he hadn't been here once in all the weeks since they'd moved.

To Joely this was a betrayal that she was finding it hard to cope with.

Head down, looking for rocks to kick at on the sidewalk, Joely walked east toward Cielo's small mall. Here she was more likely to run into some of the kids she'd met lately, and she watched the side streets hopefully. The sun was already high overhead, and beat down on her relentlessly. It was going to be another hot day, but there was no public pool and Joely wasn't allowed to go to the river less than a mile away.

Finding no one of interest, Joely finally gave up and headed for the library. If she couldn't find anyone to hang around with, the library was always a welcome substitute. There she could lose herself in the books, and the librarian always made her feel welcome.

The more she thought about it, the more the library seemed an excellent place to be on this hot summer day, and Joely quickened her pace. Sometimes there was even a pitcher of iced tea that the librarian shared with whoever came in.

So, of course, that was when Joely ran into Rachel Fletcher and two of her friends.

Rachel was twelve, but would be in the same sixth-grade class as Joely in September. She was a tall girl with tiny breasts growing on her chest, and once she'd lifted her shirt and shown Joely and some other girls that she was wearing a new training bra. It hadn't looked like all that much to Joely, but the other girls were impressed so Joely had gone along with the crowd and made the same noises of admiration.

"Hey, Gregory," Rachel called when she spotted Joely about to go into the library. "We were looking for you. What're you doing?"

Joely reluctantly veered away from the library and walked to where the other girls were waiting. Rachel's companions were Maria Rafael, a skinny girl whose dark eyes always seemed to flutter nervously, and Alice Moriarty, whose father was a lawyer in town and was said to be thinking of running for mayor. Joely felt awkward around these girls, but was careful to keep her feelings to herself. If she showed her vulnerability, Rachel, as the natural leader, would be on her like a coyote on a wounded rabbit. And the other two always followed Rachel's example.

"I was just walking around," Joely told them.

Rachel lifted one eyebrow. "I bet you were going into the library."

"I was not." Joely frowned at her, to show she wasn't intimidated.

"Sure you were. That's why you have to wear glasses—you read too much. Don't you know it's not good for you? Don't you know boys don't like girls who wear glasses?"

Joely didn't see what difference *that* made. She wasn't interested in boys, so if they didn't like her glasses that was their problem. But she did understand that Rachel had a lot of friends in town and could make things difficult for her if she chose, so Joely bit back the smart response that had immediately come to her lips. As she did so, she noticed that Maria looked uncomfortable, as though she also didn't care for Rachel's attitude. Not uncomfortable enough, however, to say anything in Joely's defense.

"I was going to walk to the river," Joely said, changing the subject. "I might even take my shoes off and wade in."

"I thought you weren't allowed to," Rachel sneered.

"No one'll find out. My mom works all day, she doesn't know where I go."

"Better not," Maria warned. "The current can get really strong, and you won't even know it until it sucks you under. A boy drowned there last summer."

Joely looked at Maria. "Really?"

"Yeah, and his family moved away afterwards,"

Maria said breathlessly, "because they couldn't stand to be in town and have to see that river all the time. Their hearts were broken."

Rachel snorted. "That's not why they moved. The kid's father got a chance to go into business with a partner in some other city. I know because my mom was friends with their next-door neighbor."

Joely, who'd been lying about going to the river anyway, was glad for an excuse to abandon the idea. Growing up near the ocean had given her a healthy respect for water, which she knew could seem calm but be bubbling with activity just below the surface.

"Well . . . what are *you* guys doing today?" she asked.

Alice spoke up first. "We're going to rent a movie and watch it at my house. My dad's at work and Mom's gone shopping with some friends so she won't be back for hours. Want to come?"

"What are you going to rent?"

"*Night of the Living Dead,* "Rachel said. "Think you can stand it?"

"You can't rent that," Joely said. "It's rated R."

Rachel waved a hand in the air. "They don't care. I rent whatever I want all the time. How about it, Gregory? We pull the drapes shut so the room is almost dark. It's more fun that way. You coming or not?"

Joely looked at the three faces before her. Her

mother was expecting her for lunch, but if she turned down this invitation she would be forever branded a coward. "Sure," she said, sounding braver than she felt.

Rachel grinned triumphantly. "Great. And tonight, after midnight, we're all going to sneak out of our houses to go to the cemetery on the edge of town."

"What?"

"Sure. We've done it before, haven't we?" Rachel looked at the other girls. Maria and Alice nodded uncertainly. "It's really spooky," Rachel continued. "There's no lights or anything, and I've heard stories about people who went there and never came out again. So, are you with us, Gregory . . . or are you afraid?"

Joely looked at all three faces and found no salvation. Maria, maybe, looked sympathetic, but again she wasn't saying anything.

"No, I'm not afraid," Joely said softly in a voice that quaked only a little. "I'll go."

Three

Libby wiped down the surface of her desk with a paper towel from the bathroom, then lifted the framed photograph of herself with Tess and Joely, cleaned under that as well, and put it carefully back in place.

Helen Crandall, the LPN who also worked in the office, mostly tending to the patients' simpler needs as they waited in one of the examination rooms for their turn with the doctor, passed by Libby's desk without saying anything. When Libby had first come to work for Dr. Kyle she'd considered Helen an ally. The nurse had been friendly and helpful, always willing to answer questions, and Libby had considered herself lucky to have Helen on her side. Something had changed, however, and Helen's friendliness gradually turned cool. She was still polite, but that was all, and Libby had no idea what had caused the change in attitude.

"You want a last cup of coffee before I clean

the pot out?" Libby asked as Helen bent to pick up a scrap of paper from the floor.

Helen straightened. "No, thank you," she said.

Even after a long day Helen's white uniform was crisp, and hung on her thin frame without a wrinkle. The clunky white shoes she wore didn't do a thing for her skinny legs, Libby thought, then regretted her lack of charity. Helen couldn't help that she was in her forties, and had the flat-chested, sexless appearance of a woman who'd probably looked exactly the same way since she was in her teens.

It was five o'clock. The last patient of the day had gone a half hour earlier.

Still hoping to break through the icy exterior that Helen was presenting to her, Libby said, "It's nice that Dr. Kyle keeps reasonable hours, and doesn't work himself to death as so many doctors do. That's another advantage to being in a small town, I suppose. Is that why he took over the practice here by himself, rather than going in with the other doctors at the clinic by the hospital?"

Helen, who'd already gotten her purse and was preparing to leave the office, stared at Libby. "Those doctors are most interested in how much money they can make. Dr. Kyle cares about *people.*"

"Oh, I know that," Libby said hastily. "What I meant was—"

It was too late. Helen was gone, disapproval wafting behind her like cheap perfume. Libby shrugged. She tried, but it seemed Helen was going to find fault with anything she said. She closed her desk drawers, threw the paper towel she'd been using into the wastebasket, and emptied the small amount of coffee left into the sink.

Dr. Kyle came out of his office. "An interesting day, I think, Libby," he said. He went to the waiting area and began straightening magazines and picking up the well-worn toys he kept on hand for his younger patients.

"I'll get to that, Dr. Kyle," she told him.

"Oh, I don't mind. I'm used to picking up after myself. A man living alone can't wait around for someone else to clean up after him, or he'd end up wading through the debris." He pulled the blinds shut against the late afternoon sun, throwing the room into semidarkness. He'd removed his lab coat and was in his shirt and tie. "Is Helen gone already?" he asked.

Libby fished her purse out from under the desk. "Yes, just a minute ago. I think I said something wrong again. She wasn't happy with me."

Dr. Kyle smiled. "Don't worry too much about Helen. She always gets over it. Oh, I almost forgot—Debbie Lionel will be coming in tomorrow morning at ten-thirty. Can you juggle things to make room for her?" He came and stood expectantly beside her desk.

Putting down her purse, Libby looked through the appointment book. A long strand of light-brown hair fell forward and she brushed it back behind her ear. Ridiculous, having long hair at her age, but it was a small vanity and Libby hadn't been able to bring herself to cut it off to a shorter, more practical length.

Brandon had loved her long hair, which might be part of the reason . . .

Libby forced her thoughts away from her ex-husband. What Brandon Gregory had or had not liked about her was no longer relevant.

She concentrated on tomorrow's schedule. "Shouldn't be a problem. I can move Mr. Ross back a half hour, he won't mind. Will that be enough time?"

"Should be. She'll be coming in with her parents to talk to me."

Libby nodded, and made a pencil notation in the book. The mysterious Miss Lionel—one of the first patients that morning—had turned out to be a pregnant seventeen-year-old who'd sat trembling in the waiting area and jumped nearly a foot in the air when Libby called her name. Libby didn't know much more about the case than that, but the girl had seemed much calmer when she'd left the office almost forty-five minutes later. That she was coming in tomorrow with her parents was a good sign, Libby thought. A young girl shouldn't try to make such important decisions about her life without her family's support.

"Is she going to be all right?" Libby couldn't help asking.

"Oh, I think so. She's a smart girl, she'll make the right decision for her particular situation. What makes me mad is that she wasn't on birth control in the first place. These kids don't think until it's too late—they go for the moment, then expect someone else to bail them out of trouble. And not just the girl; the father of her baby should have had enough sense to pick up a couple of those condoms they're passing out at the schools." He shook his head in anger.

Libby couldn't hide her surprise. She'd never heard the doctor speak harshly about any of his patients before, even though there'd been times when she'd have felt him justified in doing so. But he'd probably treated many unwanted and neglected babies during his career.

With the last of business taken care of, they turned out the lights and walked together to the front door. There was a back door to the clinic, but it opened to a rather dingy alley and was rarely used. The parking lot was next to the building, empty now except for Libby's Ford Escort and the doctor's BMW.

He didn't usually walk her to her car. Most days the doctor seemed distracted, and even if they did leave the building at the same time he would walk on ahead of her and get into his car before she'd gotten halfway across the parking lot. He seemed to be hanging back today, though, as if wanting to talk. Libby didn't mind. She missed adult company. Her only good friend in town was Francine Curtis, but her time with

44

Francine was limited because Libby felt her time after work needed to be spent with Tess and Joely. Sometimes there was the opportunity to chat with the people who came into the clinic, but usually those conversations were cut short by the responsibilities of her job.

"How are your daughters getting along?" he asked as they walked together. "Has the change been difficult for them?"

"It's been an adjustment," Libby admitted. "But I think they'll be okay. Tess has a job, so at least she's not moping around the house all day. It forces her to get out."

"That's right . . . she's helping Mrs. Coddington out, isn't she?"

Alma Coddington had been the office manager at the clinic, the job that Libby herself now held, for thirty years. She'd retired reluctantly a couple of months earlier for two reasons: She had an adult son who was suffering from a degenerative disease and needed her attention, and she was in her seventies and couldn't put retirement off any longer.

Libby knew how difficult it had been for Mrs. Coddington to leave the clinic. She'd stayed long enough to show Libby around the office and tell her how things should be done, and even now she stopped in twice a week or so, just to—under the guise of saying hello—look around and make sure Libby wasn't making any changes she wouldn't approve of. It was a little stifling, this scrutiny, but Libby felt certain the visits would taper off with time, and maybe eventually come to a stop.

"I wasn't sure I wanted Tess to take that particular job at first," Libby admitted. They'd reached her car, but Dr. Kyle didn't act like he was in a hurry to go anywhere. He leaned slightly forward as she talked, taking in everything she said with the same small frown he wore around the office. "I think part of me didn't want to admit she was ready to be working four afternoons a week," she added. "I'd like to keep her young forever, because all too soon she'll be going away from me. Do I sound overly protective? I don't mean to . . . it's just that now that I'm divorced, the girls are all I have."

"It won't stay that way. You're an attractive woman, Libby. I find it hard to believe that some man won't come along who'll recognize your fine qualities."

Libby found herself blushing, something she was sure she hadn't done in a long time. Was he flirting with her? Or was this just his bedside manner, soothing the hurts of the walking wounded?

"That's not really what I'm looking for," she said. "It'll be a long time before I'm ready for another relationship." Libby looked away from him and brushed her hair out of her eyes. The wind had come up since this morning, and even as she brushed one strand away another was blown into her face.

46

"Famous last words," he teased.

"Maybe. I suppose I sound like every other recent divorcée—so burned by the experience that I've sworn off men forever. But I'm not bitter . . . it's just that I've been married since I was nineteen, and this is the first time in a long time I've been fully in charge of my own life. I like the feeling, even with all the problems of trying to figure it all out. I like . . . being the boss." She giggled a little. Until she'd said the words out loud, she hadn't realized that's how she felt.

But it felt right.

Dr. Kyle seemed about to say something more, but at that moment Libby spotted Joely across the street, walking slowly with a group of girls about her own age. She lifted a hand and called to her daughter.

Joely said something to her friends, then jogged across the street to where Libby waited. Dr. Kyle greeted the girl, then said goodbye to Libby and unlocked his car door.

"You were supposed to meet me for lunch," Libby said as she opened her car door for Joely. "What happened?"

"Oh . . . I forgot, Mom. Sorry. I was with my friends."

"Did you eat?"

"Yeah, we had microwave popcorn and pizzas at Alice's house."

"Sounds nutritious. Who's Alice?"

As they drove out of the parking lot Joely described her afternoon to Libby, leaving out those details she knew her mother wouldn't appreciate. Like the name of the movie they'd rented, and their plans for a midnight rendezvous. She'd hoped the other girls would forget that idea, but after shrieking their way through the scary movie—twice—Rachel had been especially enthusiastic. Joely was beginning to feel trapped.

Libby looked at her watch as they waited for a light to turn green. "I'm going to drive by the Coddingtons' house and see if Tess needs a ride home. This is about the time she's usually leaving there." She turned her head just enough to glance at her daughter. "I see you're still wearing the shorts. Was there any more trouble about that this morning?"

"No trouble," Joely said.

"Good."

Tess was almost out the front door when Mrs. Coddington called her back. The shrill voice cut through Tess like a knife, making her pull her shoulders up against the chills that ran up her spine. She closed the door and dutifully returned to the kitchen, the direction from which the voice had come.

"Yes, ma'am?" she asked, standing in the doorway.

Mrs. Coddington was an energetic woman who looked a decade younger than her seventy-some years, but when she was displeased she gave out a look that could crack cement. "I told you an hour ago that this dishwasher needed unloading," the old woman said. "Were you going to leave without doing it?"

"I forgot," Tess admitted. "There was an awful lot to do today. And Coach seemed restless, so I read to him longer than I usually do."

Mrs. Coddington looked less stern. "He does like it when you read to him. Well, all right . . . you can go. I'll unload the dishwasher myself, it's not like I haven't done it a thousand times before. Can you be here an hour earlier tomorrow? I have some appointments and want to leave the house early."

"Sure, no problem," Tess said.

"All right, I'll see you tomorrow. Don't forget your purse again. I don't know how you can be so careless about it."

"I won't," Tess said.

She left the kitchen, looking back over her shoulder once to see if Mrs. Coddington was watching. She wasn't, and Tess headed straight for Coach's bedroom, where she'd left her purse and would have forgotten it if not for the reminder. It was the second time this week. She *was* careless, and she was beginning to think she'd just stop bringing it with her entirely. If she didn't have it, she couldn't very well forget it.

At the threshold to Coach's bedroom, Tess stopped. The drapes were open as she'd left them, the TV in the corner showed a local news

49

program. The remote control was on the dresser next to the bed, where Coach Coddington could reach it easily if he decided he wanted to change the channel, although he never did.

"Hi, I just came back for my purse," she said softly, speaking in the hushed tones she always used in this room.

He was in his wheelchair by the window, facing away from the television—a wasted, withered shell of a man, the shadow of what he had once been, according to what she'd heard. Illness had drained him of dignity as well as strength, and as always Tess dreaded the time she had to spend with him.

He didn't acknowledge her. He never did. Mrs. Coddington had told Tess that he could speak if he wanted to, but so far she'd not heard him utter a sound. She read to him in the afternoons, and when he grew tired of listening he turned his face away, the slack skin of a once-large man hanging loosely over the collar of his shirt.

Tess edged into the room, trying to read his profile. Sometimes, driven by something only he knew, he would glare at her with an expression of such anger that Tess would have to make up some excuse to leave the room. She never knew what would bring it on, but the mood always seemed to leave him quickly and inevitably when she returned he would again be indifferent to her.

Her purse was on a chair just inside the door,

and Tess reached for it. It was on its side, a floppy cloth bag that zipped shut and had a strap long enough for her to slip over her head and one shoulder so that it could swing at her side without her having to use her hands to hold it.

The purse was open, its contents half spilled out.

It had been closed when she'd put it on that chair shortly after arriving this morning. Tess was sure of that, and she hadn't touched it in the hours since. Sometimes she brought a candy bar or something else to snack on in case she got hungry after the meager lunch Mrs. Coddington provided, but she'd brought no such thing today and had had no reason to go near her purse.

She looked up. Coach was watching her. He'd turned his wheelchair slightly, and so silently that she'd been unaware of it until this moment. His watery blue eyes drilled into her, his mouth forming a crooked smile. He looked older than his mother; most of the time he looked barely alive. This was the first time she'd seen him smile, and it was not a pleasant sight.

Tess snatched up her purse and left the room quickly. She let herself out the front door, determined to get out this time and unsure whether she'd be coming back. She didn't like snoops, and the fact that he was sick didn't excuse the man's behavior as far as Tess was concerned. She couldn't get out of the house fast enough.

She'd just closed the door behind her when her mother's Escort pulled up to the curb, and Tess hurried to it. Joely was in front, but she leaned forward so that Tess could squeeze into the back seat.

"Good timing," Libby said. "How'd your day go?"

Tess didn't answer. She sank into the seat and watched the Coddington house recede in the distance as her mother drove.

Libby looked in the rearview mirror. "Hon?"

Joely had turned completely around in her seat to stare at her.

"It was the same as always," Tess said when she realized they weren't going to leave her alone. "Coach Coddington sits in his wheelchair and watches TV. If he starts leaning too far to one side I straighten him up, and sometimes he drools and I have to wipe it."

"Oh, uk," Joely said.

Libby frowned in the mirror. "Tess, that's cruel. The man can't help it."

"I know. I'm sorry. Sometimes he points to let me know what he wants, but most of the time he just lets me do the stuff his mother has told me to do. She has everything scheduled out, practically every minute, but today I read to him a half an hour longer than I was supposed to because he seemed to like it. Sometimes it calms him down."

"Why do you call him Coach?" Joely asked.

"That's what he used to be, at the high school here in town. Everyone calls him that, even his mother."

"It's probably a fond memory for him," Libby offered. "Something from the past he can cling to."

"What's wrong with him?" Joely asked. She was full of curiosity about the invalid her sister cared for.

"Mrs. Coddington told me, but it was some big long name I don't remember."

Libby said, "The tragedy is that he used to be a healthy, active man. He was the coach at the Cielo school for over twenty years, then he was struck down with this thing. Think how you'd feel if you slowly started losing control of your body, if at first you could get by with a cane, but then even that wasn't enough and you had to be put in a wheelchair. Then his wife left him and his mother had to take him into her home, and she's not a young woman herself. From what I understand, his mind is still intact, which makes it worse, I think. You're probably the only bright spot in his day, Tess."

"That's a pretty awful day when Tess is the bright spot," Joely said, then quickly turned and sat down in her seat in case Tess decided to try to hit her.

But Tess didn't have it in her to retaliate against her sister for that last crack.

"Tess?" Libby persisted. "I hope you keep

what I've told you in mind when you're around that poor man."

"I try," Tess mumbled.

They drove the last few blocks home in silence, a subdued, thoughtful little group.

When they got there, Joely retreated immediately to her bedroom and was surprisingly forceful in staying there when Tess tried to get her to leave. She wasn't in the mood to be bullied, and neither did Tess feel like forcing the issue. She left Joely alone and went to the kitchen to help Libby with supper.

Once alone, Joely turned her dilemma over and over in her mind, examining it from all sides, looking for a solution. There was none that she could see. Rachel, Alice and Maria fully expected her to sneak out of the house after everyone else was asleep tonight and meet them. This planned trip to the cemetery, instead of being abandoned as something that could get them all grounded for a very long time if they were caught, had grown large and out of control, fed by their fears and strengthened by secrecy.

Joely ate very little supper, prompting Libby to feel her forehead with the back of her fingers and remark on her paleness.

"I'll probably just go to bed early," Joely said, pulling away from Libby's concern.

"She *must* be sick," Tess commented.

Joely crept back to her bedroom, her stomach flip-flopping nervously. Maybe she really was coming down with something, she thought hopefully as she hunkered down under the sheets. If she was, that might be an acceptable excuse for not going out later.

Except that Rachel would never believe her, and would make her life a living hell forever afterwards.

After an hour or so Tess came into the bedroom, and, after banging around for awhile, finally settled down. Joely listened from her side of the room as the house grew quiet around her. The TV in the living room went off, Libby did some things in the bathroom that separated the two bedrooms, then she too went to bed.

Outside, the summer night had sounds of its own that Joely usually found comforting. Tonight, though, the crickets that sang their evening song seemed to be beckoning to her, reminding Joely that she had an appointment to join them in their nocturnal activities.

She rolled over restlessly, keeping an eye on the digital clock on Tess's desk. The green numbers seemed to be taking forever to change.

Four

Rachel stepped out from behind the tree as soon as she saw Alice approaching. Her sudden appearance caused the smaller girl to let out a little squeak of surprise. Rachel grinned.

"You scared me to death!" Alice hissed, holding one hand against her chest.

"Where's Maria?" Rachel asked. "She was supposed to be coming with you."

"Her mother wouldn't let her spend the night at my place. I talked to her on the phone at nine, and she said she's coming."

"She'd better. If she doesn't show I'm gonna—"

But then Maria was there with them, slightly winded and with hair that looked like it'd been slept on and not combed.

"You're late," Rachel said.

"I couldn't stay awake, so I set my alarm for eleven-thirty. Then I had trouble getting out of the house. My mom was still up watching TV. I had to climb out a window!"

Alice was shifting nervously from foot to foot. "Now what?" she asked.

"We wait for Joely to get here," Rachel said.

"What if she doesn't come?"

"She'll come. She won't have the nerve not to."

"Why did you tell her we'd done this before?" Alice asked.

"Because I figured if we told her that, she wouldn't be able to say no," Rachel said.

She looked around. They were standing in front of the iron fence to the cemetery, a fence that was only four feet high and easily scaled. Security had never been a problem here, so the only thing they had to watch out for was the occasional patrol car that might cruise by. But even that was unlikely, because the officers on the Cielo Police Department night shift were known to spend most of the evening in the all-night coffee shop at the other end of town.

Beyond the fence they could see some pale headstones, but the night was too dark to see more than a few feet ahead. Night bugs that had been chirping before the girls arrived fell silent, but an owl hooted somewhere overhead, and off in the distance they heard music. The nearest houses were less than fifty feet from the edge of the cemetery; most likely the music was coming from one of them. The trees grew thick and tall in this part of town, creating shadows that moved around their feet and danced according to the command of the gentle night wind.

Alice and Maria stood close together.

"Are we really going to leave her here?" Maria asked timidly.

"You bet we are!" Rachel said, a glint of cruelty in her eye. "It'll be funny, and maybe it'll teach her not to be such a whiny baby all the time, moping around with that long face she puts on when she wants some attention. I'm sick of her."

"Joely's not so bad," Alice said, standing up to Rachel in a rare display of spirit. "I kind of like her."

Rachel turned the full blast of her fury on the smaller girl. "Then maybe you'd like to stay out here with her!" she snapped.

Alice backed down. "No," she whispered, shrinking into herself. "I guess not."

"Good. She should be getting here soon, and you better not warn her what we're going to do."

Joely stood at the back door of the house, ears strained for any sound that might mean that either her mother or Tess were awake. She heard nothing except the soft ticking of the clock on the kitchen wall.

Still, she didn't step outside. The night, like her fear, seemed a living, pulsing thing, and she had no real desire to go out into it even though she knew there was no way she could avoid doing so. Rachel, Maria and Alice were waiting for

58

her, probably at this very moment putting her down in that special way they had—or that Rachel had, at any rate. By agreeing to meet them all at the cemetery tonight Joely had hoped she could prove herself, that she could at last do something that would raise their opinion of her, and force them to treat her better.

She slipped quietly outside, being careful not to let the door slam behind her. She closed the screen, but left the heavier door slightly ajar, so there would be no chance that she wouldn't be able to get back in later. Then, trying not to think too much about what she was doing, Joely walked away from the house.

The first few blocks were easy, because her way was guided by streetlights. Too soon, however, the gravel road turned and grew dark, heading to where she knew the cemetery was located. It wasn't far, a half mile at most, but it seemed an eternity before Joely spotted the outline of the tall iron gate that was the designated meeting place.

If she'd harbored some small hope that the others wouldn't be there, that fate or their parents would have kept them in, those hopes were dashed when Joely saw the three girls standing near the gate.

"You came. I'm surprised," Rachel said when Joely stopped a few feet in front of them.

"Of course I did," she said. "I had a little trouble getting out, is all. I had to be real careful."

Rachel snickered. "Oh, that's right—you live in

that tiny little house where everybody practically sleeps in the same room. I didn't have any trouble sneaking out. I have the whole upstairs to myself. I just have to go down the back stairway, and no one can hear a thing."

"What do we do now?" Alice asked, looking around fearfully.

"We go in," Rachel said.

She walked toward the gate and pushed it open with both hands. It made a loud creaking noise, a scream of protest. The sound was so eerie that even Rachel hesitated, the gate halfway open, and looked over her shoulder at her friends. Their expectant faces fueled her courage. She turned and opened the gate the rest of the way.

"Come on. We have to go all the way in, or it doesn't count."

The other girls entered the cemetery behind Rachel. Not one of them would have gone in alone during the day, much less at night, but there was strength in numbers and together they were able to do the unthinkable.

At first Joely was truly afraid, and her heart galloped in her chest until she thought the others would hear it and say something.

The tombstones were all different sizes and shapes. To her left Joely spotted a tall marble structure with the figure of an angel on top, and by leaning close to it she could read the inscription beneath the angel's feet. It marked the grave of a woman who'd died over thirty years earlier, a length of time almost too great for Joely to comprehend.

Curiosity, that indefinable thing that Joely had been accused of having too much of, soon got the better of her and some of her apprehension began to subside. The moon peeked out from behind some clouds, making it easier for them to see where they were going.

Joely pushed her glasses up her nose and peered at those inscriptions she could read. There seemed to be no rhyme or reason to the markers. Some looked almost new, the letters and dates carved deeply into stone, while others were so old that reading them even in the full light of day would have been impossible.

Rachel remained at the head of the group. Every once in a while she would stop and, like a tour guide, point out a marker. In a hushed, respectful voice, she told the other girls the histories of those she knew.

"That one used to be the mayor of Cielo," she whispered, pointing to a squat gray headstone. "I recognize the name. He died a couple of years ago of a heart attack, and I heard my aunt and my mom talking about it—he was with a woman who wasn't his wife when he died."

"So what?" Alice asked innocently.

Rachel gave her a look of scorn. "When I say he was *with* a woman who wasn't his wife, I don't mean they were baking cookies. They were in the bedroom."

"Oh," Alice said in a small voice.

They walked deeper into the cemetery, guided only by the fleeting moonlight. Alice and Maria still stayed close to each other, but Joely had gained enough confidence to wander a little bit on her own.

"Hey, check this one," Rachel said. She looked back, but when she saw that Joely was several feet away from the other girls she frowned. "Don't get lost," she called out. "You might disappear for good."

Joely caught up with them.

Rachel pointed importantly to a marker that was nearly six feet tall, and as wide as a car. "This is where my grandfather is buried," she told them. "He's been dead since I was five. I don't remember much about him. Right next to him is a place saved for my grandmother. She's in a nursing home, but she'll be buried there when she dies."

"Doesn't she hate that?" Maria asked, speaking for the first time since they'd come through the gate.

"Why should she?"

"Well . . . knowing that there's a place just waiting for her. It would make me feel like people couldn't wait for me to die."

"It doesn't work that way. My mom told me a lot of married couples do that. That way they know for sure they'll be buried together, and not on opposite ends of the graveyard."

"But what if your grandmother marries someone else?" Maria asked. "When she dies, her new husband wouldn't like it that she's buried next to her first husband. It could cause problems."

"She's eighty years old. She's not going to get married again," Rachel said. She turned her attention to Joely. "What d'ya think, Gregory? Have you peed in your pants yet?"

"It's not so bad here," Joely told her. "Not like I thought it'd be."

Rachel's gaze went to the other two, and she nodded her head. "Okay, since you're so brave . . . go read the inscription on that headstone over there. The pinkish one. It's the grave of Cielo's only convicted ax murderer."

Some of the tension Joely had been feeling earlier returned, but she squared her shoulders bravely and walked toward the headstone Rachel had indicated. This was the test she'd known would be coming. She would face it without complaint, and none of them would ever laugh at her again.

Libby sat bolt upright in bed, her nightgown tangled around her legs, a feeling of panic in her chest. Something had awakened her, but in the disorientation that came in the moments after sleep was cast off, she was without focus.

She listened to night sounds, her thoughts going to the girls. She might have had a dream, one that she didn't remember now but had frightened her awake nonetheless. With all the changes that had been taking place in their lives during this past year, nightmares were probably the least she could expect.

There were no sounds to alarm her. Only insects outside, and a car honking in the distance. She could even hear steady, peaceful breathing coming from the other bedroom a few feet away.

Libby slowly eased herself onto her back, letting relief flow over her. There was nothing to worry about. The night was as it was supposed to be. Her eyes closed.

Then they flew open again, and she was on her feet this time, heading for the bedroom door.

She'd heard the breathing of only one sleeping child from the next room.

Rachel snarled, "Let's go!"

She began to run back the way they'd come, slowing down only long enough to make sure Alice and Maria were following. They were, both too afraid to stay behind.

Joely had been leaning close to the headstone of the ax murderer, obeying Rachel's order, when she realized what was happening. They were leaving her, leaving her alone in a cemetery in the middle of the night. The idea was so horrifying that she froze for a moment, unable to move as the running figures of Rachel, Alice and Maria were swallowed up by the night. Even the moon betrayed her, choosing that moment to hide completely behind a cloud, and Joely had to put her hands out in front of her like a blind person until she found something solid to hang onto.

"Wait! Don't leave me!" she cried. Blindly she groped her way in the direction she'd last seen them running.

Rachel had already reached the iron gate when the moon vanished, but the row of lights several yards away offered enough illumination to give her the advantage. Alice caught up first, her blond hair loose around her shoulders. She'd lost her headband somewhere. Then came Maria, her face pale and her lashes matted with tears of fright.

Rachel was panting. She clung to the gate as though it was the only thing holding her up. "How far back is she?" she asked.

"I don't know," Maria said. They all looked back into the cemetery, and realized they could see only a few feet in. "I heard her calling us. She sounded really scared. Let's wait here for her."

"No, we're going home now! That was the whole point, remember?"

"But it's so dark . . . she won't be able to find her way out."

Rachel gave Maria's arm a yank. Somewhere far off, among the dead, they heard Joely screaming for them, her voice raw.

"See, she's coming—she'll find her way out."

"Oh, God . . ." Maria had the stricken look of a deer trapped in approaching headlights.

It didn't take much more persuasion on Rachel's part. The other girls were too terrified themselves to stay any longer, and the three of them ran toward the streetlights, grateful when they left the gravel and felt solid blacktop beneath their feet.

After a few more blocks they had to separate, each going in the direction of her own home, but before they did, Rachel had one more word of warning.

"Remember, none of us knows anything about this. Get back into your houses without anyone seeing you—"

"Oh, God . . ." Maria moaned.

"—and go to sleep like nothing's happened."

"I won't be able to sleep. She'll tell, she'll tell and we'll all be in trouble . . ."

The three small figures branched out, each eager to get to her own bed and to unquestioned safety.

None of them was able to forget the sound of Joely's screams.

Five

Joely knew she was alone, knew the other girls were so far away now that whatever happened to her here would go unwitnessed. She had to get out. A freight train of panic was rumbling through her, threatening to knock her to the ground in a helpless, whimpering mass of flesh.

All caution left Joely when she thought of where she was, and she no longer cared that she couldn't see where she was going. She ran without seeing, in the general direction of the gate, still screaming for the others even though she knew they were long gone. "Please! Don't leave me alone in here!"

Something loomed before her, and for half a second Joely thought she'd found the way out. Then a sense almost like radar warned her, but it was too late and Joely smashed into the tombstone, her forehead connecting with a bone-crushing impact.

Joely was knocked unconscious immediately;

her body was limp and boneless as she tumbled to the soft earth. The moon came out then, but she lay still and couldn't see that she was less than ten yards from the iron fence that marked the edge of the property.

Libby saw immediately that Joely's bed was empty, that the solitary breathing she'd heard belonged to Tess. She checked the bathroom even though she knew she wasn't going to find her younger daughter there, then the kitchen and the living room with the same growing sense of hopelessness. The feeling in the house was too incomplete, but she had to go through the motions anyway.

It didn't take long—the house was so small— but still she felt precious minutes slipping away. When she went back to the bedroom and shook Tess awake, Libby regretted not doing so immediately, and wondered if she had made an error in judgment.

"Wha . . . ?" Tess sat up in bed and looked at her mother from beneath heavy lids.

"Tess, get up. I can't find Joely."

"What time is it? What do you mean you can't find her? She probably went to the bathroom."

"No, she's not there, I looked. I'm going to call the police, but I want you to stand on the front porch and call her name, in case she's just gone outside for something . . . I don't know, maybe she's sleepwalking."

Tess's feet hit the floor and she was pulling her quilted robe on over her nightshirt even as her mother turned and headed for the phone in the kitchen. She looked over at her sister's unmade bed, then followed Libby. "Mom, wait—"

Libby lifted the receiver and tried to dial, but her hands were shaking and the phone fell with a clatter to the floor. She brought both hands up to her face, as though feeling her cheeks for a fever.

Tess picked up the telephone. "Let me look around a little outside first," she said. "Her pajamas are on her bed, Mom, that means she got dressed."

"What if someone came into the house while we were sleeping and took her?" Libby said, her words stumbling over each other. "I've heard about that, they take kids and . . ." She stopped and stared at the door that opened from the kitchen into the backyard.

Tess looked, and saw that the inside door wasn't closed all the way. She went to it, knowing that this was the way her sister had gone out. "Mom, did you hear me? Joely got dressed. The clothes she wore today are gone, they were on the floor next to her bed when I fell asleep. I'll look in the backyard, you check the front."

But Libby was already out the back door, her face so full of panic that Tess had no choice but to follow her. The backyard was empty. Deep shadows from the bordering trees created many hiding places, but both knew immediately that

Joely wasn't anywhere near. Libby, still wearing only her nightgown, crossed the yard and then stopped, listening to the sounds of the night, her every sense sharpened to locate her missing child.

The first thing Joely noticed when she opened her eyes was that the moon had come back out. She was staring straight up at it, but even though she knew what it was, the moon seemed strangely ill-defined, like a blob of paint dropped on a black canvas.

She realized she'd lost her glasses, and that's why the moon looked the way it did. Rolling onto her side, Joely felt around on the ground with one hand until she found them less than an arm's length away. One of the lenses was cracked, but she put them on gratefully anyway. It was better than nothing.

It took Joely a moment to work her way into a sitting position. Her body felt heavily unresponsive, and was slow to obey the commands of her brain. Her head, which throbbed horribly, seemed too large.

Dazed as she was, Joely remembered clearly what Rachel, Alice and Maria had done, how they'd lured her here, undoubtedly intending to run out on her all along. Ha-ha, very funny. Joely couldn't wait to see them again, so she could tell them how hysterical their little joke had been. Hey, she might even have been killed when she'd smashed her head open on that tombstone—now that *really* would've been something to laugh about.

Still sitting, she took a moment to rest. She seemed to tire easily, and any sudden movement brought on a wave of vertigo. Gingerly she felt her forehead, fingers exploring the lump there, testing it. It hurt, and touching it make her eyes feel like they did when she read for too long with a flashlight under her covers. But the skin didn't seem to be broken, and she felt no blood.

At first Joely thought the white shape a few feet in front of her was the outline of one of the taller markers. But had it been there a minute ago? She closed her eyes and thought about that word her mother used whenever Joely was caught climbing too high or behaving recklessly: concussion. It meant your skull had been cracked, and it could kill you. One of the symptoms, she knew, was double vision, because when she'd fallen off her bike three years before and had hit the sidewalk hard, it was one of the things the doctor had told her mother to be on the watch for.

She hadn't had a concussion then. She'd recovered and was riding her bike again the next day, but Joely knew she'd hit much harder this time. This time she'd actually been knocked out, and that had never happened to her before.

She opened her eyes again, and wasn't completely surprised to see that the white form in front of her wasn't a tombstone at all. It was too narrow, and even as Joely watched, it shifted and changed, struggling to become something. The air around her felt unnaturally cold, then all the oxygen seemed to be sucked away and Joely felt as though she'd been thrust into a dark, airless cave. Her ears even popped, but none of this stopped her from watching the vague shape with interest. She felt no fear. The last of her fear had been knocked out of her.

It became a little boy. Pale and transparent, his face came into focus last, but when it did he was looking directly at her.

The air returned to normal and Joely was able to breathe fully again, though her head was spinning as though she'd just surfaced after being underwater too long. She put her hands flat on the ground to steady herself.

Joely knew the boy standing in front of her was a ghost. There simply was no other explanation, because she could see right through him and had the feeling that if she were to reach out to touch him her hand would go through. But she still wasn't afraid of him. This *was* in a cemetery. There were ghosts all over in a place like this—the only amazing thing was that this one was showing himself to her.

Her neck was getting stiff from the odd angle at which she was sitting, so Joely pushed herself carefully to her feet, testing her legs for strength and hoping they wouldn't give out. They didn't. She was as wobbly as a newborn foal, but she managed to stay upright. The little boy was watching her intently.

"I'm okay," Joely said. Her voice sounded too loud in the quiet cemetery. Even the bugs had fallen silent. "I have to get home. I don't know how long I was there on the ground. I don't suppose you have a watch? Forget it . . . stupid question."

She giggled a little, and wondered if the bump on her head had done more damage than she'd thought. Maybe this whole thing was one big hallucination, and she wasn't really seeing a ghost at all.

Joely looked sharply at the boy.

"Are you really there, or are you in my head?"

He only looked at her with eyes that were round and intelligent. He was wearing jeans and a striped T-shirt, and had sneakers on his feet. Joely felt no danger from him, only a sense of deep sadness and longing.

He began to fade, slowly at first, but then more quickly, as though he'd worn himself out.

"No—wait!" Joely called out.

She took a step forward, one hand out instinctively, and for a space of time more fleeting than a heartbeat they connected. She never touched anything solid, but Joely's hand was plunged into an icy cold so complete that it was immediately numbing to her wrist. She jerked back, holding her hand protectively to her chest, and shivered at the unpleasantness of the experience. She rubbed

73

at her hand until slowly the circulation began to return to normal.

But still Joely wasn't afraid. Earlier she'd thought the last of her fear had been knocked out of her, but now she believed she'd faced her fears and neutralized them. She'd been abandoned at night in a cemetery. What could be worse than that? She'd survived it, hadn't lost her mind or dropped dead from a heart attack. She'd even had a one-sided conversation with a ghost. There didn't seem to be much else that could happen to a person in one night.

Stumbling, Joely found the edge of the property. Moonlight guided her as she pushed through the gate, and she could make out the welcome outlines of the houses a few yards away. At least the people there were alive.

She walked in the direction of her house, staying on the gravel road, still unsteady but determined to get home.

Tess had persuaded Libby to put on a robe and slippers, and together they searched the grounds around the little house. For the past five minutes they'd been looking for Joely, calling out her name. A light came on in the house next door, but no one came outside to investigate.

"I guess maybe you better call the police," Tess finally said. "It doesn't look like we're going to find her on our own."

Some of Libby's panic had subsided as they'd searched in vain for Joely. Like Tess, she no longer believed Joely had been kidnapped, but there was no end to the danger she could face on her own at night. Libby nodded and turned back toward the house.

"Wait." Tess grabbed the sleeve of her mother's robe. "What's that?"

They were standing on the gravel road that passed behind their house. Tess pointed out something in the distance. It was a small figure, about five houses down, walking slowly toward them.

"It's Joely!" Libby cried, and broke into a run.

They reached Joely in moments, and Libby saw immediately that the little girl was dazed and injured. The bump on Joely's forehead was as large as an egg, and her chin was scraped. Even her glasses were broken.

"I'm okay," Joely mumbled. "Are you mad at me?"

Libby put her arm around Joely's shoulders, and together she and Tess walked her back to the house. "Sh-h-h-h—don't try to talk," Libby said.

"No, really . . . I feel fine," Joely sighed. But her eyelids were drooping and she was leaning heavily on her mother. "I saw a ghost at the cemetery. He was a little boy, and he didn't talk to me but I knew he was okay. Can ghosts talk? I had the feeling he wanted to, but he couldn't."

Libby and Tess exchanged worried looks over Joely's head.

They reached the back door of the house. Tess opened the door for them.

"When people die, aren't they buried in their best clothes?" Joely asked as her mother helped her into the kitchen. "Like suits and dresses? That's what I always thought, but this ghost was wearing play clothes . . . just jeans and stuff. Maybe when you die you get to wear the clothes you liked the most while you were alive. It would be awful to be dead and be stuck forever in some awful stiff outfit you always hated, wouldn't it?"

Libby guided Joely into her bedroom, and eased the little girl down onto her bed. Tess stood in the doorway looking helpless until Libby gave her some quick instructions, then she turned and headed for the kitchen.

Joely lay back with her head on her pillow. "Do you believe in ghosts, Mom?"

Libby pulled Joely's shoes off her feet. "I believe in angels," she said. "And I believe one brought you home safe to us tonight."

Dr. Kyle sat on the edge of Joely's bed, his face close to hers as he shone a penlight into her eyes. When he clicked the light out and sat back, he looked satisfied.

"Well, I think she's going to have a headache

tomorrow, but other than that she's fine," he said.

Libby, standing at the foot of the bed, sighed with relief. The clock on Tess's desk told them it was almost one-thirty.

"I told you I was okay," Joely said in a weak voice. More than anything she wanted to get some sleep, but everyone seemed intent on keeping her up all night. She closed her eyes, grateful that the poking and prodding were finally over.

"Thank you for coming out in the middle of the night like this, Dr. Kyle," Libby said.

"Glad to help out." Dr. Kyle put the penlight away in the black bag he'd brought with him, and got up from Joely's bed.

"Should she be sleeping?" Libby asked nervously. Joely was clearly out now, her mouth open, one arm hanging over the edge of the bed. "I thought that was one of the rules with a head injury, that you were supposed to keep them from falling asleep."

Dr. Kyle put a hand on Libby's elbow and guided her gently from the bedroom. "Sleep's the best thing for her right now. She's exhausted. I don't see signs of a concussion, just that bump that looks worse than it is. Don't worry about coming to work in the morning. Stay home with her, and if you have any questions or worries, call me at the office."

"Thank you."

Tess was in the living room. She jumped up

from the sofa as soon as she saw them, her expression questioning. Libby told her that all was well with Joely, then convinced Tess to go to bed and try to get some sleep herself.

"I don't know if I'll be able to sleep, after all that talk about ghosts," she said, but headed for her bedroom anyway.

Libby pulled the belt on her robe tight, then ran her fingers through her hair. She had no idea what she looked like, but she was sure she wouldn't win any contests. She stood in the middle of the room, unable to think of anything other than what her life would be like if she were to lose one of her children.

"Would you like me to stay the night?" Dr. Kyle asked softly.

Libby looked up at him. She'd been bunching and unbunching the front of her robe, unable to keep her hands from their restless activity. She smoothed the fabric down. "I couldn't ask you to do that . . ."

"It's no problem, really. I can stretch out on the couch and get a few hours sleep there, and that way I'll be here if I'm needed."

"Do you think you will be?"

He smiled at her. "Not for Joely, no—but for *your* peace of mind."

Libby was able to return his smile. Just knowing a doctor was going to be in the house was like having a weight lifted from her shoulders. It was an imposition on him, she knew, but she was thankful that he'd made the offer.

After checking one last time on the girls—and finding them both sound asleep—Libby brought a pillow, sheet and blanket to the living room and made a makeshift bed on the sofa for Dr. Kyle. He declined her offer of a cup of hot chocolate, but did say that he wouldn't mind some company for a few more minutes.

"Unless you're anxious to get to bed yourself," he added.

Libby assured him she wasn't, then sat on the recliner and pulled her feet up beneath her. It was strange, being alone with a man again after all these months, even if it was under the most innocent of circumstances. She felt awkward, and nervous about her appearance, vanity returning now as her fear for Joely receded.

"Did you ever find out what she was doing outside in the middle of the night?" Dr. Kyle asked.

Libby closed her eyes momentarily. After calling the doctor and asking him to come over, she had questioned Joely closely; she'd ignored the story of a ghost, more concerned with what Joely'd been doing in the first place.

"She was dared to go to the cemetery at midnight by some other girls in town, so of course she had to do it," Libby explained. "Kids! You get one ready to call the others chicken, and they'll all put their lives on the line for the sake of fitting in."

"Peer pressure."

"She wouldn't give me names. I let it drop

for tonight, but you can bet I'm going to find out who else was involved in this. I'll talk to their parents, make sure they all get their bottoms paddled—"

"Maybe you shouldn't," he said softly.

Libby took a deep breath, and realized she was close to tears. She never wanted to go through a night like this again, but it felt good to have the doctor here, to have a man to talk to. It eased her burden slightly, though she knew when morning came she'd once again be fully in charge and would have to put on her brave face.

Well, she'd *wanted* to be the boss—hadn't she?

Dr. Kyle talked in a calm, rational voice, and Libby liked listening to him. It made sense when he said she might make it worse for Joely if she dragged the other children's parents into it, and as long as no serious damage had been done it might be best to forget the whole thing. Libby let his words soothe her, and somewhere in the middle of one of his sentences she fell asleep, cheek propped on one fist, both feet tucked beneath her. She shifted position once, and was dimly aware of someone putting a blanket over her.

Six

Dr. Kyle was gone when Libby woke up hours later, the only indication that he'd been there being the neatly folded sheet and blanket she'd left on the sofa.

She did stay home that day, and didn't feel at all guilty for doing so.

Working in the kitchen, making eggs and toast for the girls, Libby moved on light feet, humming to herself. In the hours before sunup, when she and Dr. Kyle had been talking, she'd been aware of the house and knew it wasn't much to look at. Her furniture was good but certainly not new, and the carpet in the living room was a green shag straight out of the seventies. At first she'd been embarrassed to have the doctor see the place, but before long she'd noticed that, though he did look around and seemed to take everything in, his expression was one of approval. He was a man who could look past the rather worn exterior of other people's lives and see the more important details, that everything was spotlessly clean, even with two children in the house, that the walls were freshly painted and almost bare because Libby preferred an uncluttered look.

Uncluttered, like her life. She'd divorced her unfaithful husband, left him far behind because she hadn't been able to live with him after finding out what he'd been up to. The affair with a co-worker, besides being a cliché, hadn't been a brief fling, but a real relationship that he'd managed to keep hidden for almost a year before Libby had discovered the truth and confronted him with it.

Libby shook her head. She was letting unhappy thoughts intrude, and with an air of determination she pushed them away. This was not a morning to dwell on the roving eye of one Brandon Gregory. She called out, "Tess, Joely—breakfast is ready. Come and get it."

Tess shuffled into the kitchen first. "God! And Mrs. Coddington wants me at the house an hour early today, because she has so much for me to do and she has places to go. I'm really looking forward to another afternoon in boot camp."

Libby put a plate on the table in front of Tess, bending down to kiss the girl's cheek in the process.

This brought a suspicious look from Tess. "I thought you'd be ready to kill this morning," she said.

"Why? Everything turned out all right. Joely's bruises will heal, and she's learned a lesson. I'm not even as angry with the other girls involved as I was a few hours ago."

"Where is the little creature?" Tess asked, reaching for a piece of toast. "She's not in her bed."

"She's soaking in the bathtub. I took a good look at her when she woke up and it's not as bad as I expected. The bump has gone down some already. Her chin is scraped and she's a little stiff and sore. That's why I suggested the soak . . . the hot water will help."

"Has she talked? Did you get names?"

"No, but I didn't push it," Libby said. She went to the bathroom door and knocked, making sure Joely had heard the call to breakfast, then she came back and sat across from Tess. She cut into the eggs on her own plate.

Tess put down her fork. "If I did something like that you'd be all over me for a week. Why should she get special treatment?"

"I was all for having it out with the other girls and their parents, but Dr. Kyle convinced me that wouldn't be the best way to handle the situation."

"Dr. Kyle? Who's *he* to be telling us how to run our family?" Tess pushed away from the table.

Libby watched her go. The bedroom door slammed just as Joely came out of the bathroom, wrapped in her robe, hair dripping on her shoulders.

Joely sat down and looked at her plate. Although it was true the bump had gone down, she looked unnaturally pale and diminished. She sipped at her orange juice, then put the glass down. "I don't think I can eat anything," she said in a weary voice.

Libby sighed and picked up all their plates. "It doesn't matter," she said. "I don't think anyone's very hungry anymore."

Joely went into the living room to watch TV alone.

She realized she'd gotten off light under the circumstances, but still she felt that she had unfinished business to take care of. All that day she had no choice but to lay low because her mother stayed home from work to be with her, but as Joely rested she thought about what she was going to do next.

On the following day, Saturday, her chance arrived.

"I'm going in to the office for a couple of hours," Libby told her after they'd done a couple of loads of laundry together. "I want to make sure the paperwork doesn't pile up too badly, and there are some bills that should have been mailed out yesterday that I'll take care of. Will you be okay on your own?"

"Sure," Joely said carefully, hiding her eagerness to see her mother leave the house. She'd just folded a pile of Tess's blouses, an act that qualified her for sainthood as far as she was concerned. Tess had been pretty nasty to her lately. "I'll probably watch TV. Or I might sit on the porch and read a book."

"If you need me, you can call me at the office."

"Okay."

"Or maybe you'd like to come with me? You can sit in the waiting room and read while I work."

"No, I'd rather stay here," Joely said, looking like it really didn't matter to her either way.

"Well . . . all right," Libby said. Joely was looking much better only a day after her ordeal. The color was back in her cheeks, and though she had a bruise on her forehead it was almost hidden by her bangs. She was wearing an old pair of glasses in place of the pair that had been broken. These glasses were wire-rimmed and almost round, which she didn't like much, but she could see and that was the important thing.

Joely felt stronger, too. The day before she hadn't done much more than lie on the sofa, wrapped in a blanket, and watch TV and doze. She'd eaten very little but had drunk what seemed like gallons of ice water. Then, just when Libby had begun to get worried again, Dr. Kyle had stopped by and he'd pronounced Joely recovering nicely.

Now Joely waited patiently as her mother left, carefully hiding the fact that she was nearly jumping out of her skin in anticipation. Tess left soon after, mumbling something about school supplies as she slammed out the front door, which cleared the way for Joely to carry through her plan.

Just to be safe, she waited fifteen minutes after they'd gone before springing into action. First she called Rachel's house, and was told by Mrs. Fletcher that Rachel wasn't home. This was exactly what Joely had expected. It wasn't likely that Rachel or any of the others would be inside on a morning like this, but she'd wanted to be sure.

"Do you know where she's at?" Joely asked sweetly.

"No, dear, I don't. She's in town somewhere, but I won't see her until lunchtime."

"Thank you."

Calls to Maria and Alice's house revealed much the same thing, so Joely squared her shoulders and left the house, ready for a confrontation.

Libby found, after letting herself in the clinic's front door, that Dr. Kyle had stacked her work neatly on her desk, and had even thrown out the junk mail so she wouldn't have to sort through it before getting to those things that needed her attention. She had just begun her paperwork when Dr. Kyle showed up.

"I saw your car parked in the lot," he explained. "You didn't have to do this, there's nothing here that couldn't have waited until Monday."

"I know, but it would have been on my mind

all weekend if I'd left it. Thank you for keeping things so tidy."

He pulled a chair over to her desk, turned it around backwards and straddled it. Dressed casually in a plain striped shirt and slacks, he seemed like a different person. Even his attitude was more relaxed. "Helen deserves the credit," he said. "She pulled double duty yesterday."

Libby almost laughed, but managed to keep it in. She could just imagine how well that had gone over with Helen.

"How's our patient this morning?" he asked.

"You wouldn't believe how well she's doing. She ate a huge breakfast and helped me with laundry."

"Kids are resilient," he agreed. "What's she doing today?"

"Staying home. She said she'll either watch TV or read."

He nodded. "That's good. I'm sure she's fine, but it wouldn't hurt her to take it easy for the rest of the weekend."

Joely wasn't taking it easy. She left the house at a dead run, slowing down only when she developed a stitch in her side. She didn't find Rachel, Alice or Maria anywhere downtown, even though she checked all the places they were most likely to be hanging out. She even went as far as the river on the north end of town, thinking they might be there, but with no luck.

Finally, when she was beginning to worry that she might have to head for home and look for them another time, she spotted all three of them walking along a side street a couple of blocks from Alice's house. They were headed in that direction, and Alice was holding a square plastic case in one hand. Another rented movie.

She tried to sneak up on them, but Rachel looked over her shoulder and spotted Joely when she was still half a block away. Rachel's eyes immediately grew huge, and she shouted something to the other girls and took off running. The others ran too, splitting up as each dashed in the direction of her own home.

But Maria stopped before she'd gone more than a few yards. Standing in the middle of the sidewalk, she waited for Joely to reach her, her eyes down, hands limp and defenseless at her sides.

"What's up?" Joely asked. Before leaving the house she'd removed her spare glasses and deliberately worn the broken ones. She'd also brushed her bangs to the side and pinned them with a barrette, so the bruise was clearly visible.

Maria looked at her and winced.

"Where's everybody off to?" Joely wasn't going to make this easy for her.

"I guess they can't face you," Maria said in a small voice. Then she frowned and made herself look Joely in the eye. "I'm sorry for what we did. It stunk. And we didn't mean for you to get hurt."

"I got knocked out. The doctor had to come to our house in the middle of the night. My mom says I'm lucky my glasses didn't shatter and the glass get driven right into my *eye*."

"I know. Everyone in town was talking about it yesterday, about how you were wandering around outside when your mom and sister found you, and that you were all cut up and bleeding." She looked Joely up and down. "You don't look *that* bad."

Joely sat down on the curb; after a brief hesitation, Maria joined her.

"How did everyone know about it so fast?" Joely asked.

"Are you kidding? It was the most excitement we've had around here in weeks, my mom said. Your next door neighbor, old lady Tyree, heard them calling for you that night and was watching from her window when they found you. Rachel is really scared. Everyone thinks you went out alone, and Rachel is so sure you're going to tell on her . . . on us." Maria's worried expression returned. "Are you?"

"I thought about it. I haven't said anything yet."

"How come?"

Joely smiled a little. "Will Rachel be in big trouble if I tell?"

"Oh, huge! Her parents are really strict. She likes to say they aren't, but they are."

"That's what I thought. So, if I tell she'll be in trouble."

Maria nodded.

"But, if I don't tell, I'll have something to hold over her head."

Maria looked at her with a new respect that Joely liked.

Then Maria asked, "What about me and Alice?"

Joely lifted one shoulder in a shrug. "Hey, don't worry about it, I'm not going to tell anyone anything. But I don't want Rachel to know that—I want her to sweat for a while."

They sat quietly for a minute, but this time it was a comfortable silence. Joely knew that Maria meant it when she said she was sorry for what'd happened, just as she knew Rachel was the one who'd put the other two up to it. That was just the sort of thing Rachel would do, and Maria and Alice never did have the guts to stand up to her.

Just as she herself hadn't been able to stand up to Rachel, Joely had to admit. This knowledge made her less willing to condemn Maria for her cowardice, because she'd been just as guilty.

But she was no longer thinking about *how* she'd ended up alone at the cemetery. Now Joely's thoughts were on a subject that had never been far from her consciousness in the past day and a half.

She'd seen a ghost there. Even the passage of time hadn't diminished this belief in the slightest, but she hadn't said anything more about it to her mother or Tess. They hadn't believed her,

90

and she doubted there was anything she could say that would convince them.

Maria, on the other hand, might believe, and Joely wanted to talk about it. Something like this didn't happen every day, and it irritated her that her story had been met with such total disbelief by her family.

And Maria was a captive audience.

They were sitting side by side, but Joely leaned closer to her anyway, looking around to make sure no one was within hearing distance. Maria caught this furtive gesture, and leaned in to listen.

"I'm going to tell you something, but I don't want you to tell anyone else," Joely said.

Maria swore that her lips were sealed, her dark eyes wide and serious. Satisfied that she meant it, Joely told her everything she could remember about her brief encounter with the supernatural. Speaking in a low, solemn voice, she talked about waking up to see the ethereal figure of a little boy, and even described the clothing he'd worn and the look of longing on his face. Talking about it brought the memory back into sharp focus for Joely. The words tumbled out of her, hesitant at first but gathering momentum with each passing minute.

". . . and when I almost touched him my hand froze up," she said, flexing her fingers as though they might bear some physical signs of their brief paralysis.

Maria stared at Joely's hand, lips parted in awe. "Then what happened?" she whispered.

Satisfied, Joely continued with the rest of it. When she was finished, she let her shoulders sag, as though telling it had taken something out of her.

Maria was enormously impressed, and Joely was glad to see that at last someone was taking her seriously.

"W-what are you going to do?" Maria breathed.

Joely already knew the answer to this. She'd given it a great deal of thought, mostly yesterday when she'd been lying around and had had plenty of time to think. "I'm going to go back to the cemetery tonight to see if he'll show up again," she said.

Seven

Libby put a stamp on the last envelope and sat back with a sense of completion. She'd gotten it all done, and now wouldn't have to think about paperwork again until Monday morning, and that was a good feeling.

A noise from the back room reminded her that Dr. Kyle was still in his own office, as he had been for the past two hours. She'd been surprised when he'd shown up, and more surprised when he'd stayed. No doubt he had plenty of his own work to do, but she knew he didn't usually do it on the weekends.

Now, as she stacked the pile of outgoing mail on the corner of her desk so she wouldn't forget to take it with her, Libby wondered if there was some reason other than work for him to be hanging around.

On more than one occasion lately Libby had looked up from whatever she'd been doing to find him watching her, and now she wondered about the expression on his face during those unguarded moments. Had it been interest? Possibly. Or perhaps just curiosity. He knew her ex-husband was from Cielo originally, and, in fact, Dr. Kyle had grown up here as well, and had spent many years away before finding his way back to his roots. As far as she knew he'd never been married. Helen Crandall, in those early days when she'd been friendly and talkative, had filled Libby in on many of these details, yet Libby didn't kid herself that she knew the inner man. That was something only he could reveal.

"I'm leaving now, Dr. Kyle," Libby called out. It seemed too rude to just leave without letting him know.

He appeared almost immediately. "Already?" he said. "You're a fast worker."

"I try."

"Well, as it so happens, I was just about finished here myself. Give me a second and I'll walk you to your car."

"All right . . ." But he was already gone, back into his office.

A minute later he was locking the front door behind them, and they headed for the parking lot.

"Now that you have the rest of the weekend to yourself, what are your plans?" he asked in that deep, serious voice of his.

"Nothing special," she told him. "Housework. Laundry is an endless task. My girls—Tess especially—think they should change clothes twice a day, and once they take something off it goes straight into the hamper. That's pure laziness, I think. It's easier to make Mom wash, dry and fold something than to set it aside to be worn again later. And tomorrow I'm going to mow the lawn and pull the weeds out of those flowers I planted by the front porch."

They'd reached their cars. He had again parked right next to her, but he hadn't yet taken his keys from his pocket.

"What I really meant," he said, "is do you ever go out? Get away from the work and do something just for yourself?"

"Rarely," Libby admitted. "I've been too busy settling in and learning my new job to even think of a social life."

Where was he headed with this?

Libby soon found out.

Dr. Kyle cleared his throat, looked down at his feet for a moment, then finally came out with it.

"There's a good restaurant here in town," he said. "Would you care to have supper with me this evening, Libby?"

She wasn't surprised, but neither did Libby quite know how to answer. He was her employer, and she wasn't sure this was a good idea. If they went out together tonight, what would be the next step? He might ask again, and that could put a strain on their working relationship. Or, if he *didn't* ask again, it might cause friction between them even though Libby liked to think she was mature enough not to feel rejected if that happened to be the case.

His simple question had thrown her into a state of indecision, and Dr. Kyle saw this.

"Don't do anything that makes you feel uncomfortable, Libby," he said. "It's just that I tend to center my life around my work, and when the weekend comes around I stay home because that seems easier than going out somewhere alone. I thought perhaps you tend to be the same way, and since everyone needs to break away from the routine once in a while this would be a chance for us both to remember there is a world out there and it can be an interesting place. No pressure, Libby. Just think of it as getting an old doctor away from a solitary meal in front of the TV on a Saturday night."

She couldn't help laughing, partly because this was just about the longest speech she'd ever heard him give.

"You're not old, Dr. Kyle," she said.

"I'm forty-three, and I feel every year of it."

"That's not old," she repeated. She made her decision. "All right—yes, I'd like that very much. What time?"

"I imagine you'd like to feed your daughters and get them settled in before going out," he said. "Is eight too late?"

"Eight will be fine." Libby was touched by his thoughtfulness.

As she drove away from the parking lot a minute later, Libby hoped she hadn't made a mistake.

Joely and Maria walked out of the drugstore, licking ice-cream cones that were quickly melting in the heat. The drugstore had an old-fashioned ice-cream fountain in one corner, and the girls had pooled their money to buy the cones. Chocolate for Joely, vanilla with sprinkles for Maria.

"My mom doesn't like me to eat ice cream very much," Maria said when they stopped in front of a store window to look at a display of swimsuits. "She's always trying to give me apple slices and raisins, stuff like that."

"Yeah, mine, too," Joely said.

"My grandfather will give me treats when I see him, but he lives up north and we only get to visit every couple of months or so." Maria took a lick at the bottom of her cone, where it was dripping dangerously close to her hand. "What about your grandparents? Where are they?"

"I have a grandmother right here in town," Joely told her. "But we don't see her much. Her house is over on the other side of the mall."

"How come you don't see her?"

Joely wasn't sure how to explain this. "My mom's never gotten along with her very much, I guess," she said. "It almost kept her from wanting to move here to Cielo . . . but then she

97

said she'd live here if she wanted to and no old lady will scare her off."

"Wow. But what about you—don't you like her? She's your grandma." To Maria, whose only living grandparent was the giver of gifts and forbidden sweets, this was almost impossible to comprehend.

"I don't know her that much," Joely admitted. "I've only been around her a few times, and she wasn't very friendly. I don't know why. Mom says that's just the way she is, and I shouldn't take it personally. I haven't seen her once since we moved back, and she knows we're here so I guess if she wanted to call us she could, but she hasn't."

"Wow," Maria said again. She gave up on her cone and dropped what was left of it into a garbage can. Her hand was sticky, so she wiped it on her shorts.

Joely finished hers as they continued walking. The day was getting hotter, the air stifling with no breeze to offer relief. They reached the library, and Joely said, "I want to go in here. I might be able to find some information."

Maria followed. At least the library was air-conditioned.

At the front desk Joely asked the librarian about books on ghosts. After giving her cracked glasses and bruised forehead a curious look, the librarian pointed the girls in the right direction.

Joely found a small section on the occult, and selected two books that had the word "ghosts" in their titles. The girls planted themselves at a large rectangular table, but it didn't take long for Joely to realize that these books weren't going to be of much use.

"These aren't any good," she said, closing the book she'd been scanning and pushing it away. "I wanted to find something about mysterious events here in Cielo . . . but there's nothing."

"Maybe you should look in the section on the town history," Maria suggested. Then she wished she hadn't said anything at all, because most of all she wanted Joely to forget the whole thing.

"Yeah, or the old town newspapers," Joely said, thinking out loud. "Would they have those here?"

"I don't know." Maria leaned across the table and spoke in a loud whisper. "You aren't really going to *do* that, are you? Go back to the cemetery tonight?"

"Sh-h-h-h!" Joely looked around to make sure no one had overheard, but the library was almost deserted. Besides themselves, there was only the librarian and a young woman with two toddlers in the magazine section. One child was asleep in a stroller and the other, about three years old, sat cross-legged at his mother's feet, thumb in his mouth and a picture book open on his lap.

"I don't think you should do it," Maria said, keeping her voice lower this time. "You'll get in trouble if you get caught."

"You weren't so worried about if I was going

99

to get caught the other night," Joely pointed out.

Maria flushed, and her eyes shifted away from Joely's. "I told you . . ."

"I know—Rachel put you up to it, and you didn't mean for anything bad to happen to me."

"That's right."

"I believe you. But this time it's *my* idea. I'm not asking you to come along—"

Maria flinched.

"—just don't tell on me and spoil everything. The only reason I'm even telling you is because if something happens and I don't come back—"

Maria's dark eyes grew huge.

"—I want someone to know where I went."

"W-what do you mean, if you don't come back?" Maria stammered. "You *have* to come back!"

"I will," Joely said confidently. "I'm saying just in case. Nothing's going to happen, except I might faint or something if I really do see what I saw the other night. At the time I wasn't one bit scared because he was just a little boy and he looked sad, not mean or like he wanted to hurt me. But I have to admit I'm sort of nervous about seeing him again. Just thinking about—"

"Girls."

Joely and Maria looked up into the face of the librarian. Without realizing it, their voices had again risen in volume.

"You'll have to keep it down, girls," she told

them. "The other people who come here count on this being a quiet place to read or study."

Joely looked around and realized that there were more people now than there had been a few minutes earlier. An old man was in a chair by the window, reading a newspaper; two women were sitting at a round table a few feet away with a stack of books between them, and several people were scanning the rows of shelved books.

"Sorry," Joely whispered.

The librarian wasn't angry. She was a kind woman who liked children and especially approved of Joely Gregory because she was a frequent visitor to the library. She smiled at the girls to let them know there were no hard feelings, and went back to her position behind the front desk.

Since they hadn't found anything useful, Joely and Maria decided it was time to leave anyway. Once outside the protective cocoon of the air-conditioned building, the shimmering heat hit them full blast, rising up from the sidewalk in almost visible waves. Joely could feel it penetrating the soles of her tennis shoes. Beads of sweat popped out on her forehead, and her cotton shirt stuck unpleasantly to her skin.

"But what if it isn't *him* you see tonight?" Maria asked.

Joely stopped walking. "What do you mean?"

"What if some other . . . well, dead person shows up instead? Like that ax murderer Rachel said was there?"

Joely sneered to show her contempt for Rachel, but at the same time she suddenly felt the heat fade as goose bumps popped up on her arms.

"I don't believe there really is any ax murderer," she said. "That was just Rachel talking to scare us."

"It still seems a big chance to take." Maria held on to the faint hope that she could talk Joely out of this foolish scheme.

But Joely was determined. "I'm going to do it. I'll call you first thing in the morning to let you know how it went."

"I hope you *do* call. I'm going to be a nervous wreck until I hear from you and know you're okay."

Eight

Having not been out with any man other than her ex-husband in over seventeen years, Libby enlisted the aid of her friend Francine in preparing for her evening out. Francine threw herself into the task with enthusiasm, criticizing Libby's wardrobe, helping her apply her makeup, and basically making Libby feel as though she'd made a mistake in agreeing to have supper with Dr. Kyle.

"Jeez, where'd you get that dress? Throw it out, it's hopeless." Francine grabbed the pale blue dress Libby'd been holding up and tossed it on the bed.

Libby looked at the discarded dress with a feeling of despair. "What's wrong with it?" she asked. "That's always been one of my favorites."

"The key word here being *always*," Francine sneered. "That thing is so out of style you could send it out on a date with a pair of bell-bottoms." She went to Libby's closet, yanked open

103

the doors and began pushing her way through the clothes there.

Libby sat on the edge of her bed and watched, afraid of what Francine was going to find for her to wear and almost sorry she'd invited the other woman over.

Francine, a couple of years older than Libby and single now after being divorced for the third time, had taste that Libby charitably called flamboyant. Her red hair was teased into a frightened beehive, and Francine favored bright colors and exaggerated prints in clothes that clung to her figure.

"You shouldn't wear blue," Francine said, her voice muffled because she was half inside the closet. "You're too fair, you need bright colors or you'll fade into the background. Don't you have anything red?"

"I've never worn much red," Libby told her.

"You should, it's a great color and men like it."

"*I* don't like it," Libby said stubbornly.

Francine emerged from the closet, a dress in each hand. "These aren't too bad."

"Not those, Dr. Kyle will get the wrong idea. That black one's too formal for tonight, and the dark green one—well, Brandon bought that for me and I've never liked it." Libby lowered her voice. "It's very low-cut."

"It's perfect." Francine handed the dress to Libby. "Put it on, then we'll figure out what to do with your hair."

They argued for the next hour, but finally ended up in a compromise in which Libby wore the green dress but with a silk scarf that draped over the front and one shoulder so that she didn't feel exposed.

Tess and Joely stared at their mother when she emerged from the bedroom; Francine beamed with pride, taking full credit for this lovely creation.

Libby's hair hung loose to her shoulders, but it was moussed and fluffed into a soft, curly cloud. Francine had coached her in the application of her makeup, and the mascara that Libby had applied made her eyes look large and luminous.

"You look pretty, Mom," Joely said.

"She looks great," Francine corrected. "Libby, you're gonna knock that man on his ass. He's going to wonder why he didn't ask you out on a date weeks ago."

"This isn't really a date," Libby said, looking at the girls. "It's just a friendly dinner."

Then the doorbell rang, and Joely said, "Your date's here, Mom," as she jumped up to open the door.

"It's not a date," Libby mumbled, but she could see that no one believed her.

A few minutes later Libby was sitting at a table for two in Cielo's best restaurant, listening as Dr. Kyle—Tim, as he'd insisted she call him—answered her questions about his childhood. It was all she'd been able to think to ask him without feeling like she was being too personal.

"I grew up in Cielo," he told her. "My father was an insurance salesman until he died when I was in my early teens, and my mother was a homemaker. They both worked hard; I think that made me ambitious."

Libby nodded. It explained why he hadn't been turned off by the humble conditions of her own home.

"I knew early that I wanted to be a doctor," he continued. "For an insurance man my father had been careless about his own coverage, so college was something of a struggle financially. It didn't matter . . . you can do anything if you want it badly enough."

"Your family must be very proud of you," Libby offered.

A waitress appeared with their meals. Libby had ordered shrimp, a favorite of hers, and Dr. Kyle—Tim—was having steak. Men, she'd noticed, seemed partial to red meat.

Since it was Saturday night, the restaurant was nearly full, and Libby kept nervously touching her scarf to make sure it hadn't slipped out of place. Tim had complimented her several times on how nice she looked. It didn't take long for Libby to warm to his praise and to the way he'd touched her arm when they'd walked from the parking lot to the restaurant. It felt good to have a man pay attention to her again; it gave her ego a much-needed boost.

Tim cut into his steak. "My family," he said thoughtfully. "To tell you the truth, we're so spread out now that we rarely get together any-more. I have some cousins throughout California and Arizona, and aunts and uncles that I haven't seen in years. My father, as I told you, has been dead for a long time. I have no brothers or sisters."

"And your mother?" Libby asked.

"She died a year ago, and I was left the house I grew up in . . . such as it is."

"Is that the house you live in now?"

He nodded. He cut his steak into very tiny pieces as he ate it. The baked potato received the same meticulous attention, so that Libby was nearly finished with her meal before he'd gotten halfway through his. She made an effort to slow down; she didn't want to come off looking like this was the first meal she'd had in a week.

"My intention at first was to clean the house out and sell it," he told her. "But at about the same time old Dr. Ives announced that he was going to retire and wanted to sell his practice. So there I was . . . with a house and job if I wanted it. It seemed logical to come back here to where I'd started. I'd been in practice in the San Francisco area for a few years, but I was only one of several doctors at that clinic, and didn't have the feeling of being needed that I knew I'd find here." He smiled at her and set his fork down. "Never thought I'd end up coming back, but now that I'm here I have the feeling it's to stay. Cielo is the Spanish word for 'heaven,' did you know that?"

"Yes, though you couldn't convince my girls of that right now," Libby laughed. "They think I've moved them to the sticks, where there's no major shopping complex and they have to either walk or ride their bikes to get around. I never thought I'd end up here, either—but I'm glad I did it. I wanted to get away from the city. I worried so much about the girls there."

"You feel safer here."

"Much," Libby agreed, and nibbled on the last of her shrimp. She was feeling more comfortable, and was beginning to think she might even be able to call him Tim without stumbling over the informality. Tim was very good-looking, perhaps more so to her now that she was beginning to see him as a person and not just her employer. His rare smile especially transformed his face, and Libby found herself wanting to see more of that smile. His teeth were white and straight, his chin strong. He looked like he'd shaved only moments ago, the skin was so smooth.

Tim was saying something about the work that needed to be done on his house, but as he talked Libby was wondering what it would be like to kiss him—if he would be forceful, or as gentle as he was with his patients . . .

Libby coughed and forced her mind away from such thoughts. She was getting ahead of herself, and anticipating something that might never happen.

"What were you thinking?" Tim asked unexpectedly.

"H-m-m-m?" Libby feigned innocence, but could feel a blush creeping into her cheeks. "Oh, nothing in particular. Just enjoying this wonderful meal."

Tim smiled, his eyes crinkling at the corners. "If I've ever seen anyone look like the Mona Lisa, you were it just a moment ago," he said. "Do you keep secrets, Libby? I find it hard to believe some fish and a few vegetables could make a woman look so dreamy and contemplative."

"They're very good vegetables," Libby murmured.

"Then I wouldn't mind being a piece of broccoli right now."

She choked briefly, then burst out laughing. Tim joined her, and for a moment they enjoyed a sense of intimacy that was almost sexual. The room seemed too warm, and as Tim finished his steak Libby took that opportunity to fan herself with her cloth napkin.

After that their conversation stayed on neutral territory. Libby talked more about her divorce, and Tim confirmed her belief that he'd never been married. They talked about movies they'd seen, books they'd read, and their favorite vacations—Mexico for Libby, Reno for Tim, who confessed to a fondness for blackjack.

They grew relaxed with each other, and the evening went too quickly. They were both sorry when it had to come to an end.

Tim paid their bill and they left the restaurant. "I promised to take you home early, didn't I?" he said as they walked to his car. "Are you going to hold me to that?"

"I did tell the girls I wouldn't be late," Libby said, truly regretful. "I'm not even sure now why I did that. They're not babies anymore, they don't need a sitter and they're not afraid of being in the house alone. Francine might be right when she says I worry too much. I could call Tess and Joely, and tell them I'm going to be later . . ."

Tim touched her shoulder. "Don't do that," he said. "They're probably anxious for you to get home so they can pump you for information."

"How did you know?"

"An educated guess, based on my knowledge of the innate snoopiness of children—especially where their parents are concerned."

They were at his car, but stepped aside and waited as two couples walked past, laughing loudly and sounding as though they'd had a few drinks. One of the men gave Libby an openly appreciative look as they went by—so open that his date stopped laughing and glared at him.

Libby waited as Tim unlocked the car door. Her scarf had slipped a little, and she moved it back into place. "You talk like a man who knows children," she observed.

"I should," he said as he opened the door and held it for her. "I've had hundreds of them in my care over the years, some briefly and some for extended periods of time. I've inoculated them, cleaned off their scraped knees, and inspected them for possible abuse or neglect."

Libby got in the car and Tim went around and got in the other side. He slid in close to her, his arm across the back of the seat.

"Don't disappoint your daughters," he said. "We'll have other opportunities to be together."

He kissed her, and all the anticipation Libby had felt about this moment, all the wondering whether she'd welcome—or even allow—this to happen, culminated in the meeting of their lips. His were gentle, and he brought one hand up and put his fingertips lightly on her jaw as he kissed her, the gesture so tender that Libby ached for more.

Then they moved apart, and while Libby sat back and felt her pulse fluttering in her throat, Tim started the car and drove out of the parking lot.

He said good-night to her at her front door, making no attempt to kiss her again, or touch her in any way. Libby was faintly disappointed. A peck on the cheek might have been nice, but Tim only told her how much he'd enjoyed her company, and waited politely while she opened the front door.

The girls looked up at her as she dropped her purse on the recliner by the door. Libby heard Tim's car drive away outside.

"How'd it go?" Tess asked.

Libby stepped out of her shoes and told them it had gone just fine.

"Is that all? Which restaurant did you go to? What did you eat?"

"Do you like Dr. Kyle?" Joely asked.

"He has a nice car," Tess said. "Doctors make a lot of money, don't they?"

"Are you going to go out with him again?"

Libby sat on the sofa beside Joely and answered all their questions to the best of her ability. She tried to keep it light, sensing an underlying anxiety in both girls as they tried to gauge the extent of their mother's interest in this new man.

Finally the girls seemed satisfied, and the three of them watched TV together until bedtime a short while later.

Tess and Joely watched TV. Libby stared at the screen, but her thoughts kept returning to Tim Kyle and the hunger she'd seen in his eyes immediately after his lips had left hers.

Nine

Tucked safely in her bed, Joely lay awake and listened to the house settle down around her. Tess was the first to fall asleep, after fiddling with her stereo for a while and then giving up on finding anything to listen to. Her mother was in her own room, but the light was still on so Joely had no choice but to wait patiently. She was well prepared; she'd taken a nap that afternoon to make it easier to stay awake tonight.

The nap hadn't been enough. Joely found herself fighting sleep, willing her eyes to stay open, but feeling them grow heavier with every passing minute.

Finally, at five minutes before midnight, the light in Libby's bedroom went out. Joely waited.

Tess snored softly from the bed a few feet from hers, but Joely didn't let that lull her into a false sense of security. Mothers slept much lighter than sisters, probably because sisters didn't really care much if you sneaked out in the middle of the night.

At twelve-thirty Joely couldn't wait any longer. She had to take her chance, because she was getting sleepy again and knew she couldn't fight it much longer. She had to get up, had to get moving around to shake off the heaviness that weighted her arms and legs.

She tiptoed out of her bedroom and to the back door. Although every step she took seemed, to her own ears, to echo throughout the silent house, no one came to investigate.

Then Joely was out of the house and trotting down the gravel road toward the cemetery.

No one had believed her about the ghost. They all thought that what she'd seen had been caused by a bump on the head. They'd tried to humor her, especially her mother, but Joely had heard them talking about it in the next room, talking as though she'd suddenly gone deaf or something. She suspected that even Maria didn't completely believe, but had only been caught up in the intrigue, and willing to be attentive out of her own feelings of guilt.

Joely *knew* what she'd seen, and she wanted to see him again. That little boy had been there for a reason; she'd figured that much out in the past couple of days. He hadn't appeared when Rachel and the others had been in the cemetery with her, but had waited until Joely was alone.

She didn't know why, but Joely had the feeling it had something to do with her having been hurt that night. She'd been knocked unconscious, and had come to sometime later to find the figure of the boy forming and then looking at her with compassion, as though he knew what it meant to be hurt and he'd wanted to let her know that someone cared. So maybe she owed Rachel something for that. An act of maliciousness had resulted in the biggest adventure of Joely's life.

Now she wanted to see if he would come back if she *wasn't* hurt—that was going to be the real test.

Still, Joely almost lost her nerve halfway to the cemetery. All the hours of planning, the excitement of doing something forbidden, hadn't prepared Joely for the fear that suddenly gripped her when she lost sight of her house and knew she was approaching a point where there would be no turning back. She actually stopped in the middle of the road and thought about what she was doing. This could be dangerous. She might not be as recovered from her injury as she'd thought, and could pass out again . . . or get caught. *That* was a frightening thought. Joely knew her mother to be a fairly patient person, but she also knew that if she got caught out at night again that patience would be stretched to the breaking point.

What got her feet moving again was the memory of that little boy in the striped T-shirt and blue jeans. She had to see him again. If he wasn't there tonight, she'd try to forget about him, but if she didn't make this effort the memory of him would begin to fade, until eventually even she would doubt that he'd been real.

Joely didn't want that to happen.

She pushed herself forward, ignoring the little inner voice that kept trying to intrude and tell her this was foolish.

It was darker tonight than it had been on her previous trip, and Joely felt her heart beating in rhythm with her footsteps. It was just ahead, she could see the outline of the iron gate.

Then she was through the gate. Joely stopped, straining her eyes to see past the hazy outlines of the headstones. Did she really want to go deeper into this forbidden territory? No—she wanted to stay put and hope he'd come to her, but somehow Joely understood that she had to prove herself, that she had to do the thing she feared most if she were going to be granted the privilege of seeing him again.

She tiptoed past the headstones, ignoring the inscriptions, watching where she stepped so that she didn't meet with another accident. The problem was, she couldn't remember exactly where she'd been knocked out the other night. That part of the experience was too vague, cloaked in the terror she'd felt at the time. All she could do was guess at the location, and hope she could at least get close.

Joely saw him.

He was a few feet in front of her, and at first she thought it was just late-night mist gathering. But the mist seemed to take on a specific shape as Joely stopped in her tracks, holding her breath for fear she'd do something wrong and blow it. As had happened the other night, the air temperature around her seemed to drop several degrees, and Joely felt a strange buzzing in her head that reminded her of the sound she sometimes heard coming from power cables. For a moment it was such an unpleasant experience that she wanted to turn around and leave the grounds, to free herself from this suffocating sense of invasion. Joely gasped, clutching the collar of her shirt with both hands. She was choking . . . the oxygen was being forced out of her lungs . . .

As suddenly as it had started, it was over. Joely felt weak with something like shock, but this was nothing compared to what she'd just been through, and it was a lot easier to take.

"What was *that*?" she croaked.

The boy was fully recognizable now, and Joely saw that he was smiling as though happy to see her. Some of her strength returned. The creeping shadows around the tombstones offered no threat; time stood still as they faced each other.

"Who are you?" Joely asked. She took one careful step forward, then stopped. "What's your name? Can you talk to me?"

He didn't answer, and she had the feeling he couldn't.

"Now what are we going to do?" she wondered out loud.

She'd been counting on asking him a few important questions. What was it like where he was at? Did he hang around the cemetery all the time, or did he go someplace else and only come here when he wanted to? There were many questions, but mostly Joely's thoughts were a disorganized jumble. She hadn't given the idea of life and death enough consideration in her eleven years to fully comprehend the enormity of what she was experiencing, but she did sense that she should find out all she could now, because later, when she was older, it might all make more sense.

The boy was still translucent, and he seemed to fade in and out, like a radio signal on a distant station. He also appeared to be thinking about their situation. As Joely watched, the boy lifted one hand and crooked a finger at her.

"What?" she asked. "You want me to come closer?"

The boy smiled.

"Well . . . I guess I could do that, but not much, okay? I remember what happened last time." She flexed the hand that had been numbed the other night, and took one baby step forward. Despite knowing that she was in no real danger from the boy himself, Joely remained cautious.

She needn't have worried. At the same time she stepped forward, the boy moved back, so they were no closer than they had been. He then crooked his finger again, and she allowed him to lead her deeper into the cemetery, curious now as to what it was he was trying to tell her. The headstones around them were silent witnesses to Joely's progress. She adjusted her glasses and twisted the hem of her shirt, distracting herself from too many thoughts. Sometimes it was best just to coast along and not try to analyze things too much.

The boy stopped, and so did Joely. She didn't recognize this part of the property, but she could hear distant traffic sounds far off behind her, and that gave her some indication of her location.

"What?" she asked.

He was pointing at a marker. It was almost directly in front of Joely, a small concrete cross that barely reached her chest. She had to lean forward to read the inscription.

"Martin Philip Stano . . ." She stumbled over the long last name, "Stanovich." Joely inhaled softly through her teeth and looked up at the shape standing beside the marker. "Was that you? Are you telling me your name?"

Although he didn't answer, the look of peace that came over the boy's face told her enough.

"Martin Stanovich," she whispered, getting used to the sound of it. "I don't remember hearing that name in town yet, but I guess there're a lot of people I don't know."

There was more than just the boy's name engraved on the surface of the marker, and Joely returned her attention to it. The smaller inscription below his name was a date, with another below that. She knew what this meant. It indi-

119

cated the date of his birth . . . and his death. A quick mental calculation told her that Martin Stanovich had died twenty-five years ago, a number that meant very little to Joely because it was too far in the past. But there was something that touched Joely deeply—Martin had been only nine years old when he'd died. That was younger than she was now, and the unfairness of it brought tears of sympathy to her eyes.

It also frightened her as perhaps nothing else could have, because it brought to her the possibility of her own mortality. She'd never known anyone young who'd died before. Her great-grandmother on her mother's side had died two years before, but she'd been over eighty years old and had been in a nursing home for as far back as Joely could remember. There'd been nothing shocking or unexpected about that death.

Young people weren't supposed to die. Joely knew this wasn't really true, that children and even babies died all the time. She knew this intellectually, but emotionally she'd remained distant from these facts. Now she was being forced to face something that she might have preferred to avoid for a while longer.

"What happened to you?" she asked, brushing away a tear with the back of her hand. "Were you sick?"

Though she'd been hoping Martin would find another way to communicate with her, Joely found instead that the boy actually seemed to be growing dimmer, as though even this much contact had taken something out of him. At first he became hazy around the edges, and by the time she realized what was happening he'd become so indistinct that Joely could no longer make out the expression on his face.

"Wait!" she cried.

He was gone, and the slight illumination he'd brought with him also vanished, leaving it so dark that she could see barely five feet in front of her.

Joely turned and walked carefully in the direction from which she'd come, relying on instinct to lead her back to the front gate. She stumbled once, but was able to catch herself before she fell, and twice she almost walked into a headstone but managed to swerve off to the side at the last moment.

By the time she reached the gate Joely's eyes had almost adjusted to the gloom.

"Okay, that wasn't so bad," she whispered as she followed the gravel path home. "Next time I'll just know to bring a flashlight."

She reached the edge of her own backyard. The house was dark, which meant her absence hadn't been noticed.

And she *did* intend to go back as soon as possible to see Martin Philip Stanovich.

He had something to tell her.

Ten

He watched what was going on around him. He was feeling small again, but he waited, wondering if the feeling would leave him like it sometimes did, or if he would become helpless in its grasp, forced to take action to dispel the rage that rose up in his throat to choke him.

The rage was always there. It grew as he became smaller. Sometimes he could conquer it, send it back to the dark basement of his soul, lock it away with sheer willpower. Sometimes. He struggled against it because he knew it would make him do something dangerous to himself. It could drive him out into the night to search for release.

The smaller he got, the more the memories filled his head, torturing him, tormenting his soul. The memories were the worst part, because they were food for the rage. She'd slapped at him with her hands. She always slapped first. After a while the fingers would close into fists, sometimes the fists holding a broom handle or heavy silver spoon.

He tried to cover his ears, knowing that if she slapped them hard enough his head would ring for hours afterwards. She struck, missing his ear but catching him just below the eye. In his memory he couldn't hear words. He knew they were there because her mouth moved, twisted with her fury as she beat him, but it was a silent picture that swirled and danced hatefully in his head.

She grabbed a handful of his hair and shook him, then dragged him toward the cellar door.

He tried to fight her, tried to call out for help even though he knew there was no one to help him. He dug his heels into the floor, trying to pull himself free but knowing he was no match for her. Her face was a red, blood-filled balloon above him.

She had the cellar door open, still holding his hair with one hand so he couldn't get away, and she began to push him toward the dark pit. He begged for forgiveness, even though he didn't know what it was he'd done wrong this time.

He found himself being thrown forward, floating for a moment on air until he hit the hard wood steps about halfway down. He tumbled the rest of the way until he finally landed on the dirt floor, bruised and dazed but with nothing seriously damaged. He'd learned, over the years, how to tuck in and roll, protecting himself as best he could.

As much as the cellar terrified him, as much as he fought being sent here, it was in some ways a relief because she never followed him down here. The cellar always remained dark during his stay. There was a light with a chain somewhere overhead, but the bulb had long ago burned out. The cellar was mostly unused, even his mother didn't like to come down here. Her washing machine and dryer were in a room just inside the back door, and she kept her canning supplies in the kitchen.

No, the cellar was his place, where he knew he'd end up when he failed somehow to meet his mother's demands, demands that were inclined to change from one day to the next, so that he always felt like he was walking on the unsteady deck of a ship at sea.

He curled up on his side and tried not to think about the spiders that he knew were down here. He'd seen plenty of them in the days before the bulb had burned out. They were in every corner, crawling over surfaces, trying to get at him. He shut his eyes tightly, trying to force these thoughts from his mind. If he didn't, he'd start imagining that he felt them, and that was as bad as the real thing. When you couldn't see the intruder, it didn't matter if it was real or in your head, the terror was the same.

When the first spider crawled over him he bit down on his lip and brushed it away. One wasn't so bad. He could handle that.

But, of course, there were more. They sensed

his fear, he was sure of it, and when he could no longer control himself and he had to scream, the bubble of resentment in him grew until his only comfort had been to imagine that it was *her* down here, and the spiders were making a meal of her.

He shrieked until his throat was raw and his voice had taken on a foghorn quality. He pulled at his clothes, ripping his shirt from his back and digging his nails into his skin, feeling the hundreds of legs on him . . .

The cellar, his prison, became a place of torture from which his only means of survival was to let his mind float away from his body, until he was looking down at the shirtless boy below. He felt sorry for the boy, but mostly he felt anger.

He was small, and that made him weak.

The spiders were gone, the cellar no longer threatened. But the prison remained. It festered in him, and when it boiled to the surface he had no choice but to go out and prowl.

Eleven

Brandon kept the car parked well away from the house so that he wouldn't be easily spotted, but still close enough to watch the front door.

So far there'd been no activity. Not too surprising, in that it was only a little after six on a Sunday morning, and Libby was notorious for liking to sleep in on Sunday mornings. Even back in the days when they'd made an effort to go to church together as a family, they'd always had to go to whichever church featured a 10 A.M.— or better yet, noon—service, because otherwise she wouldn't make it.

The town was waking up. He watched as a papergirl made her way down the street. She looked only twelve or thirteen, but she was pulling an impressive load of newspapers behind her in a red wagon, delivering the plastic-wrapped bundles to the front porches of most of the houses. He watched her progress with interest. She kept the wagon on one side of the street,

126

taking six or seven newspapers in her arms and zigzagging across the street to deliver them, then returning to her wagon to pull it along and get a new load.

An ambitious girl. He admired the fact that she was doing the job herself, and not riding comfortably in the front seat of the family car as a sleepy parent drove her along the route.

Not until she'd almost reached his parked car did Brandon realize she was going to see him. He'd been so interested in what she was doing that it hadn't occurred to him until too late that he was going to present a suspicious figure. He tried to slump down in the seat, but, as he'd feared, she looked over at his car just as she was passing and spotted him.

The girl jumped, letting out a little squeak of surprise, then she tightened her grip on the handle of her wagon and hurried past him, looking back over her shoulder several times as she delivered the last of her papers on this block. At the next corner she turned left and disappeared from sight.

Brandon returned his attention to Libby's house almost two blocks away. This might've been a mistake. He probably should have called first, but he'd had such a strong urge to see the girls that he'd impulsively decided to surprise them. And he wanted to see Libby, too—he had to admit that, even if only to himself. It had been over three months since he'd seen her, the longest period of time they'd been apart in the past seventeen years. Even though they'd been separated for some time before the divorce had actually been final, they'd at least been living in the same city and he'd gone to the house to pick up the girls and do something with them almost every weekend. He'd seen Libby those times, too, because she'd always come to the door to tell him what time he had to have them back, peeking over his shoulder to see if Greta was waiting in his car. She had been only once, and the hurt that had filled Libby's eyes at the sight of her had been enough to prevent Brandon from making that mistake again. Maybe if Libby had said something, had lit into him and really given him hell for having the nerve to bring along the woman who'd played a part in breaking up their marriage, he might have been able to go on the offensive and give some of it back to her. But Libby hadn't said a word then or later. She'd only looked away quickly, called to the girls to hurry up, then excused herself and gone back into the house, leaving him to wait on the porch.

Leaning back against the seat, Brandon ran a hand over the stubble on his chin. He should have shaved, but, once again, he hadn't been thinking ahead.

Suddenly there was a loud rapping on the glass next to his left ear, and Brandon shot straight up, almost high enough to bump the top of his head on the ceiling of the car.

There was a man standing beside the car, looking in at Brandon. It had been his knuckles knocking on the window that had so abruptly pulled Brandon from his thoughts.

"Can I have a word with you?" the man called, his voice muffled through the glass.

Brandon rolled the window down halfway. The man was in his late forties or early fifties, dressed in polyester pants and a shirt that was only half tucked in. His hair was uncombed. He looked like someone who'd been recently awakened and dressed hastily.

"What are you doing out here this time of the morning?" the man asked bluntly. He frowned, taking in Brandon's shaggy hair and two-day stubble.

Brandon attempted to smooth down his hair with both hands. "Doing? Nothing, just . . . uh, waiting."

"Waiting for what?"

Then Brandon understood what had prompted this visit. He'd frightened the papergirl, and she'd probably stopped at the first familiar house she'd come to around the corner and reported a lurking pervert in the neighborhood. He could almost smile at that, except that he had the feeling this guy wasn't going to see anything humorous in the situation.

"Hey, I didn't mean to make anyone nervous," Brandon said. "My ex-wife and my daughters live just up the street. I'm here to see my girls, but it's kind of early so I was waiting a while so I wouldn't wake them up before knocking on the door."

The man didn't look convinced. The window was still only halfway down, and he eyed the button on the inside of the door, noting that it was down. The door was locked, undoubtedly thwarting his plan to yank it open and drag Brandon out.

"They live down the street? Then why aren't you *parked* down the street? Do you have some identification on you?"

Now it was Brandon's turn to get angry. Okay, he did look suspicious, he was willing to concede that point. But he hadn't actually done anything to justify this third degree. He hadn't tried to talk to the papergirl, or anyone else. Last he'd checked, there were no laws against sitting in your own car on a public street.

And who did this guy think he was, asking him for identification?

"Yeah, I do," Brandon said. "But that's not really any of your business, is it?"

"Okay, better get on out here." The man pulled on the door handle. It didn't budge, but he wasn't giving up. "Come on out now, before someone ends up calling the police. We can do it that way if you want."

Brandon might have turned the key in the ignition and gotten the hell out of there, but he noticed now that four or five other men had come out of their houses and were watching with interest. Two of them approached the car; one even stood directly in front of it.

The situation was quickly going from bad to worse.

Brandon opened the door and got out. Keeping his cool, he repeated what he'd told the first man, and found himself being escorted toward Libby's house. No one touched him, but the men discreetly surrounded him, one walking ahead, one behind, and two on either side. He felt like a condemned man being led to the firing squad. Just his luck that not one of these men looked familiar to him. He still knew plenty of people in town, but these were all strangers to him.

Then, of course, he had to point out Libby's house, and knock on her door to prove himself innocent of evil intentions. He couldn't have made a worse impression on Libby and the girls if he'd been brought to the house in the backseat of a police car.

"What's going on?" Libby peered out at them, pulling her robe closed in front and looked understandably confused. "Brandon? What are you doing here?"

The rumpled man—the one who'd first approached Brandon's car—stepped forward. "Mrs. Gregory, do you know this fella? He claims to be your ex-husband, but he was sitting all slumped down in his car a couple of blocks up, looking like he was up to no good."

Libby squinted. "Mr. Andronetti, is that you? Who are all these people?"

Brandon sighed. "Libby . . ."

Some of Libby's confusion disappeared and she glared at Brandon. "Oh, yes, he is my ex-husband. For heaven's sake, Brandon, we aren't even awake yet and you've managed to get into trouble? What were you doing?"

"Like I tried to explain to the lynch mob here, I came to town to see the girls, but it was still kind of early so I was waiting a while before coming to the house. I *thought* I was being considerate."

"Meghan Donnelly, the little girl who delivers the Sunday papers, says he was staring at her in a real strange way," Mr. Andronetti told Libby.

Libby was shaking her head, and she took Brandon's arm and pulled him into the house. "There's nothing to worry about, Mr. Andronetti," she assured him. "He's something of a jerk, I'll admit, but basically harmless."

"You're sure?"

But the small group was already breaking up, losing interest, and Libby had them convinced that they could release Brandon to her custody.

"Christ, can you believe that?" Brandon huffed as soon as the front door was closed. "And why did you call me a jerk? Weren't things bad enough without you—"

"Daddy!"

"Dad, is that you?"

Joely and Tess burst into the small living room,

132

still in their pajamas, and threw themselves at their father. Brandon stooped to pick Joely up and, with his free arm, pulled Tess to him. Libby retreated to the sidelines and watched. After a few minutes of this she went into the kitchen to make coffee.

"Hey, need any help?" Brandon asked, following her.

She shook her head, wishing he'd stayed in the living room. The girls were still clinging to him, Joely acting like she was four years old again and not an eleven-year-old who was too big to be picked up.

"Hey, what happened to you?" Brandon asked, pushing Joely's bangs aside to examine the purple bruise on her forehead.

"I fell down, it wasn't a big deal," Joely said.

Libby set about making the coffee resentfully. Even though he was forty years old, Brandon looked closer to her age, maybe even a little younger, and that really pissed Libby off. He'd always worn his brown hair long, but instead of looking ridiculous as he got older, it seemed to suit him. It was also impossibly thick, and not one strand of gray had yet made an appearance. He was muscular and totally masculine in his jeans and plaid work shirt, and Libby almost hated him for looking so good when she felt tired and haggard in her bathrobe and floppy slippers.

"Why didn't you call and let us know you were coming?" Tess asked, staying so close to her father's side that he couldn't take a seat at one of the kitchen chairs. "Mom, did you know he was coming?"

"I didn't know a thing about it." Libby measured coffee grounds and put them in a paper liner.

"I wanted to surprise you," Brandon said.

"I heard your voice, I thought I was dreaming," Joely told him, her arms around his neck.

"Maybe you were," he said. "Maybe you're still dreaming!" He tipped her backward and rubbed her neck with his scratchy jaw. Joely screamed with delight.

"Please," Libby said. She poured water into the top of the coffee maker. "It's a little early for this much noise."

"Sorry, Mom," Joely said, still giggling.

"Sorry, Mom," Brandon echoed.

Libby turned away from him so the girls wouldn't see the expression on her face. She knew what he'd meant by that: It was his way of subtly putting her down, letting her know that she was always the one to ruin their fun.

But they did settle down somewhat, and the girls even backed off enough so that he could sit at the table. They pulled their chairs close to his, while Libby stayed standing beside the sink.

"How long are you staying?" Tess asked. "Can we do something together today?"

"Of course we can do something, that's my

whole reason for coming. And I'm going to stay for about a week."

The girls squealed. Libby looked up sharply, suddenly afraid that he expected to stay with *them*.

Brandon grinned at her for a moment, then let her off the hook. "I'm staying with my mom," he explained. "That way I'll be close enough to see you all as much as I can. I'm taking some vacation time to be here."

"Better get dressed, girls," Libby instructed.

"But, Mom—"

"Now. Your dad's not going anywhere."

"What's the big hurry?"

"Tess, go get dressed like your mother wants," Brandon said smoothly.

Both girls grumbled briefly, but did finally leave the kitchen.

As soon as they were out of the room, Libby turned to him. "What's going on?"

Brandon lifted his eyebrows. "What do you mean? I wanted to see my girls. I miss them a lot, Libby . . . more than I ever expected to."

"You could've fooled me. You don't call, you—"

"What good's a phone call when it only reminds us that we're not together? I figured it was best to wait until I could get here in person. And don't forget that I've taken several days off from work so that I can have some quality time with them before school starts."

"Quality time?" Libby crossed her arms and glared at him. "You've been reading pop psychology articles again, haven't you? Where's Gretel—outside waiting in the car?"

"Greta didn't come with me. I didn't want her to. Why are you making this so tough? The girls are glad to see me."

"Of course they are. You're going to shower them with presents and fun times, and when you're gone I'll be the villain because I'll have to make them clean their room and help out around here. I don't trust you, Brandon. You're up to something." Libby turned away from him and faced the sink, keeping the anger and hurt to herself. With the girls in the next room, this wasn't the time to argue.

Brandon got up from the table and walked toward her. Dammit, why couldn't they have a conversation without it turning into full-scale war? He'd promised himself this wouldn't happen, but of course it did anyway. They were like water and gasoline—they'd never mix, and one stray spark could cause both to burst into flames.

He had more he wanted to say to her—about how he hadn't been one hundred percent responsible for the direction their marriage had taken, but that he was willing to accept the blame because he should have been stronger and shouldn't have been so easily led astray. There was still so much unfinished business between them, and Brandon had hoped that the passage of time would've numbed some of the pain, or at least made it possible for them to spend five minutes together without lashing out.

Before he could voice any of this, the girls came back into the kitchen, dressed for the day and with eager expressions on their faces.

They placed themselves between Brandon and Libby.

"What are we going to do?" Joely asked, standing close to her father but not attaching herself to him. Tess had talked to her about that in the bedroom.

"That's mostly up to you two," Brandon said in a cheery voice. "I know there's not a lot in town, but we should be able to amuse ourselves. Then, after lunch, I'll take you over to see your grandma . . ."

Tess rolled her eyes and Joely looked pained.

"She says you haven't been to see her once since you moved to town." Brandon looked across the kitchen. "Libby, do you want to join us?"

"No. Thanks anyway."

"Come on, Mom," Joely began, then stopped when Tess gave her an evil look.

Libby saw this, but it didn't matter. She pulled the belt of her robe tighter, so tight that it felt like it was going to cut her in half. "No," she repeated, looking only at the girls. "This is your day with your dad, to tell him all about what you've been up to these past couple of months. There's a lot for you to catch up on—after all, he hasn't seen you in a while."

Because it was still too early for them to go anywhere, Libby had no choice but to invite

Brandon to stay for breakfast. He accepted the offer, and while he and the girls ate, Libby excused herself and kept busy in other parts of the house. She made her bed, washed and got dressed, even went to the basement and threw a load of wash into the machine, all in an effort to avoid having to look at Brandon. Nothing she did, however, could prevent her from hearing the laughter that floated easily throughout the house, and resentment grew heavy in her chest until it was at last time for them to go.

Brandon herded the girls toward the front door. "I won't keep them out late," he promised.

"Don't worry about it. I'm sure you'll all have a good time."

"You could still come with . . ."

"Don't let Joely load up too much on sweets," Libby said quickly. They were almost out the door and she was anxious to close it behind them. "She breaks out if she has too much sugar."

"Aw, Mom—don't tell him that."

"I'll keep an eye on her," Brandon said.

Libby closed the door, then she leaned her back against it, wondering why her legs felt so weak that they were barely able to support her.

All because Brandon Gregory had walked through her front door and shown her that the space of a hundred miles and a few weeks wasn't enough to erase the power he had to jumble her emotions and fill her head with memories both sweet and painful.

"Damn him," Libby muttered, wiping the tears from her cheeks with the back of her hand.

As happy as Joely was to be with her father, she was unable to give him her full attention. The family didn't seem complete, and she wished now she'd made more of an effort to get her mother to come along. Tess disagreed.

"I can't believe you really wanted Mom to come with us," Tess scolded when they'd gone into the ladies' room in what passed for a mall in Cielo.

"I didn't want to leave her behind," Joely tried to explain. "She looked so sad . . ."

"Yeah, and she would have looked a lot sadder if she'd come. All they do is fight, haven't you figured that out yet?"

Joely raised her chin stubbornly. "Not all the time. They didn't used to. We used to do stuff together and it was fun."

"Not recently." Tess sniffed and checked her reflection in the mirror above the sink. "Oh, maybe a long time ago it was okay, but for the past couple of years they only pretended around us. Then they didn't even bother to pretend anymore."

Before Joely could respond to this the bathroom door opened and two women entered the room; one was middle-aged, the other elderly. They were loaded down with packages, and barely glanced at the girls.

Joely stalked out of the bathroom without waiting to see if Tess was going to follow. What did Tess know, anyway? All she ever did was look for something to complain about, and she didn't give Joely any credit for having a brain. But Joely knew things that her sister had never even imagined—like that a person could communicate from beyond the grave.

Even in all the excitement of her father's arrival, the boy named Martin Philip Stanovich was never far from Joely's mind. She'd managed to find a couple of minutes to herself that morning, while her father and Tess were in the living room talking and her mother in the bathroom doing something, to call Maria and let her know she was all right. This had been risky because there'd been the danger of someone in the house overhearing what she was saying, but she knew that if she didn't call Maria the other girl would worry so much that she might do something crazy—like tell her parents. So she'd called Maria to assure her she was all right, but hadn't had the time or the privacy to go into any details.

She longed to share this with her father, but Joely knew she had to stifle the impulse. She'd keep Martin to herself for awhile longer.

Brandon was waiting outside the movie-theater entrance, looking at the posters of coming attractions, when the girls returned from their trip to the bathroom.

"Hey, I was starting to get worried," he said

when first Joely, then Tess reached his side. "The movie starts in five minutes and we still have to buy our popcorn."

The theater had three screens. Brandon bought their tickets, and together they walked into the lobby. "How come we're seeing this movie?" Tess asked, looking at the title on the ticket stub he'd handed her. "I thought the other two looked better."

"This is the only one I'd dare take you girls to," Brandon explained. "The others are too adult."

"But this is a love story."

"Don't knock it." Brandon requested an extra large popcorn and three colas from the teenager at the concession stand. He laughed at the girls' expressions. "Hey—give it a chance. Your mother always loved a good old romance. We should've gotten her to come along, this would've been just the thing to put her in a good mood."

As they followed their father through the nearly empty lobby, Tess and Joely exchanged looks behind his back.

Joely's face said, *See, I told you so.* And Tess's replied, *Oh, shut up.*

"Come on in." Francine held open the front door for Libby. "The coffee's on, I've unplugged the phone, and if you want to cry I have a fresh box of tissues ready. No one's ever accused me of being unprepared."

Libby entered Francine's untidy house, and felt that it was exactly what she needed. She felt untidy herself. After Brandon had left with Joely and Tess, Libby had sat around in ratty jeans and a loose shirt for a couple of hours before calling Francine and telling her what had happened. Francine had ordered her to come over immediately, and Libby had brushed her hair and her teeth, but hadn't bothered with makeup or much of anything else.

"I didn't know if I should call you," Libby said as Francine sat her down at the kitchen table, pushed a stack of papers aside and placed a mug of coffee in front of her. "If you have plans I'll understand. You probably have better things to do than listen to me complain about—"

"Oh, stop it," Francine scolded. After pushing several books to the floor, she sat across from Libby and rested her elbows on the table. "I want details. Did he really just show up on your doorstep without any notice? None of my ex-husbands would dare try something like that. But then I was married to wimps."

Libby held the coffee mug but didn't drink from it yet. She let its warmth flow into her palms. "The girls were so happy to see him," she said miserably.

"What did you expect?"

"I don't know . . . but not that. I felt completely shoved aside, like they'd been waiting for him to show up and whisk them away from this horrible life I've forced on them. One word from

142

him and I think they'd both pack their bags and go back with him today. Especially Tess. We haven't been getting along that well lately."

"Do you think it'll come to that?" Francine asked.

Libby thought about it. "No," she said after a moment, her relief great at this realization. "Brandon wouldn't want the responsibility of having them full time."

"Then don't worry about it. Worry'll just give you gray hairs and you'll forget the good stuff going on in your life right now."

Libby snorted. "Like what?"

"Like how did the date with the doctor go last night? I've been waiting to hear about that—what is Tim Kyle *really* like when you strip away all those layers of conservatism and professional attitude? I'll bet he's an animal when he lets go. Come on, I have no sex life of my own right now, so I'll have to live vicariously through you."

Libby wasn't going to be so easily distracted. "I forgot all about Tim," she admitted. "Since Brandon showed up I can't think of anything else. Why couldn't he stay away and let me get on with my life?"

"Because that wouldn't be any fun," Francine answered. "Like all men, he likes to shake things up, especially if he thinks you might be getting used to not having him around. Probably last night, while you were out with Tim, a hundred miles away this little light turned on in Brandon's head and warned him that you were with

143

another man. I don't know how they do it—but he didn't waste any time getting here, did he?"

Libby sipped the coffee. Most of what Francine said was nonsense, but her voice was familiar and soothing, and at least she was sympathetic.

The two women spent the day together, trashing men in general and ex-husbands specifically. After lunch Francine brought out several bottles of liqueur, and they began to experiment with drinks involving fresh fruit and a blender.

Libby giggled after the first frothy concoction, cried when she thought about Brandon being in town for a whole week, then laughed again when Francine forgot to put the lid on the blender before hitting the start button for the second round of drinks. They grew bleary-eyed and told each other about their first sexual experience— Libby admitting for the first time that hers hadn't been with Brandon.

"I'm shocked," Francine said, and burped. "But also proud of you."

"Me, too," Libby slurred. "Who does he think he is, anyway?"

"That's the attitude."

"To hell with him."

"Absolutely."

When Libby went home some hours later she was groggy and immediately sprawled across her bed to take a nap. The afternoon had done her some good, even if the therapeutic qualities of alcohol were only temporary.

Twelve

Even though Andrea Polzer knew she was going to be late getting home, she made no effort to hurry. Her mother had been mean to her this morning before she'd gone out to play, so now Andrea was going to take her time and let her parents wonder where she was.

It wasn't dark yet, but the sun was getting low on the horizon, making the shadows that walked ahead of Andrea look long and absurdly thin. She was supposed to be home for supper by six, and it was already almost eight. She stopped walking and waved her arms in the air, watching as her shadow-figure did the same with arms that seemed five feet long. Giggling, Andrea started walking again—slowly.

She hadn't intended to be *this* late, but she'd been playing at the park on the east edge of town when some of her classmates from fifth grade the year before showed up. They got to playing and the time had slipped away. Andrea and her friends had been especially involved in discussing what differences they'd find when they all started sixth grade in the fall. It was going to be their last year of grade school, which would make them the grade that all the younger kids looked up to. Andrea remembered how, when she was in second or third grade, she'd watched the sixth graders and thought they looked almost like grown-ups.

"I'm going to get a new ten-speed to ride to school this year," Andrea had bragged to her friends Suzie Barnard and Nicole LaGrande.

"What's wrong with your old bike?" Nicole had asked. "You've only had it since your last birthday."

"That's a kid's bike," Andrea'd sniffed. "I'm too old now for that kind with the big handle bars and the banana seat."

Nicole had looked over at her own bike parked a few feet away. It was exactly the type of bike Andrea had just described.

Then Andrea had made the mistake of telling them both exactly which ten-speed she was going to get, and how much it was going to cost. After that it hadn't been as much fun, because the others had accused her of showing off, of bragging about her rich parents. The three girls had gotten into a shouting match, which ended when Andrea got up and stalked away.

Her family wasn't really rich, but Andrea was an only child, whose parents could spend more money on her than those with three or four kids

146

could. Andrea knew this because she'd once overheard her mother and father talking about it, but now she began to feel bad about the way she'd talked to Suzie and Nicole. It wasn't Suzie's fault that she was the youngest of several kids, or Nicole's that her father had hurt his back and hadn't worked in almost a year.

Andrea promised herself that the next time she saw them she'd be especially nice, and would try to remember not to say anything about getting a new bike.

Her house was almost in sight when the voice came from the shadows. It was nearly dark now and she was getting nervous, but Andrea couldn't help stopping when she saw the figure that stepped out from beside a clump of thick bushes. The man held a small, fluffy kitten in his arms—one of her favorite things in the world. Besides, she knew who he was. It wasn't like this was a stranger.

"It's almost dark, how come you're still out?" His voice was calm and had a comforting quality to it. He stroked the kitten's fur.

"I guess I forgot what time it was," she said, and moved closer to get a look. "Mom's going to be mad."

"Just give her one of those pretty smiles of yours, and she'll forget all about the time. Hey, do you like cats? I think this one is lost."

"You mean it isn't yours?" Andrea tried to look at the kitten, but it seemed that he had stepped back, closer to the thick growth of bushes.

It was shadowy here, and she looked round to see if there was anyone else in sight. There wasn't.

"No, I just found it," he said. "And there's another one over here, too. Come on and have a look."

This was too much for the little girl to resist, and she approached the row of bushes. It wasn't until a hand clamped hard over her mouth and she was pulled down and out of sight of the road that panic filled her. Andrea fought and struggled, her eyes wide with disbelief, but she couldn't break free. She was distantly aware that the kitten had been dropped and scrambled for freedom.

A scream was trapped in her throat, imprisoned by the large hand that blocked off her intake of oxygen. Bushes scratched her bare legs and caught in her hair as she was dragged out of sight. When her vision began to dim and she felt her arms and legs growing heavy and slow, Andrea thought about all the times her parents had told her to trust no one. She hadn't listened to their warnings, but she promised she would if she could just have another chance.

It wasn't fair that this was happening to her—she was supposed to get a new bike.

Word of the little girl's disappearance spread quickly once her parents became concerned enough to call the police. They didn't do that until almost ten o'clock, because while there was still some daylight left they assumed that Andrea was just out playing and would be home soon. When it had grown dark, Hal Polzer had gotten into his car to look for Andrea, while Gena stayed home in case their daughter showed up on her own in the meantime. Gena Polzer had used that time to call Andrea's friends, but by then no one had seen her for at least a couple of hours.

Gena maintained her composure until Hal came home alone, told her he'd had no luck finding Andrea, and suggested they call the police. That's when Gena got hysterical.

The police force in Cielo contained less than three-dozen men, many of them part-timers, but the chief recognized a touchy situation when he saw one and he called the county office thirty miles away for additional manpower. A missing child case was never taken lightly, even though ninety percent of the kids ended up being quickly located. Usually they were at a friend's house and had forgotten to call anxious parents, though there was the occasional teenage runaway. Chief Watts knew that probably wasn't the case in this situation, because the missing girl was only ten years old and from an outwardly stable home.

By midnight private citizens joined in the search for the girl. Many of those were parents of her classmates.

Libby didn't hear about it until the next morning when she went to work, and by then the search had been going on all night without positive results. People were getting scared, and hope diminished with every hour that passed.

Helen Crandall had managed to put aside her animosity long enough to greet Libby with the news as soon as she walked in the front door.

"Don't you listen to the radio?" the nurse asked, eyes bright as she saw the effect her words had on Libby. "It's all that's on—TV, too, but not as much. I heard they had specially trained dogs out searching the wooded areas outside of town."

A chill of fear passed through Libby. She went to her desk and called home to talk to the girls.

They were both still there. Joely answered.

"Don't go out today," Libby ordered. "Stay in and watch TV or read."

Joely grew immediately alert. "But why?" she cried. "I wanted to do some things today. It's boring being home alone."

"You won't be alone. Tess will be there with you."

"No, she won't. She has to work this afternoon."

"Oh, God, that's right." Libby rubbed her eyes, aware that Helen was making no secret of listening to her side of the conversation, and she almost hated the woman. "Put Tess on. She'll have to stay home today."

"But, Mom . . ."

"Do it!"

Tess came on the line, but she also protested.

"Mrs. Coddington is expecting me," she said. "This is Monday, her bridge day, she'll be furious if I cancel. She might fire me. I need this job . . . I'm saving my money for school clothes."

Libby listened for as long as she could, then cut in to tell Tess about the missing child, hoping this would make the girls see the importance of staying in. Tess wasn't impressed.

"Nothing's going to happen to me and Joely in the middle of the day. And that little girl will probably turn up any minute and it'll be that she was lost or something—just like with Joely the other night. We were scared, but everything turned out to be okay. This will be something just like that."

"Maybe, but if I can't be home then I want you both to stay in."

"For how long—the rest of our lives?"

"Until this girl is found I don't want either of you wandering around."

Tess was silent for a minute, then she said, "How about this—I'll take Joely with me. That way she'll be with me all the time, and no one's going to bother us if we're together. And don't forget, Dad's going to pick us up later, so we'll be perfectly safe."

Several people had come into the office and were standing on the other side of the sliding glass door, waiting for Libby's attention. Helen tried to say something about it, and Libby brushed her off with a wave of her hand. But she knew she couldn't stay on the phone much longer.

People were getting impatient, and the way they hovered made it impossible for Libby to think.

She gave in because she simply couldn't argue with Tess any longer.

"Okay—take Joely with you. But you absolutely must stay together all day."

Libby hung up. She took a few seconds to close her eyes, shutting out everything but her own thoughts. She probably *was* being overly nervous, but years of living in the city had settled a permanent layer of dread over her heart. Even in a town like Cielo, where the crimes were usually minor and quickly solved, bad things could happen.

"Miss?" The voice cut into her thoughts. "If you're through figuring out your grocery list, or whatever it is you're doing, I'd like to know when the doctor will be able to see me. I took time off from work to be here."

Helen snickered.

Libby stood, hands out in a peace-making gesture. "I'm sorry for the delay," she said to the man standing there. She opened her appointment book to see who this first patient was. "Mr. Gable, please go with the nurse, she'll take you to the examining room." Libby pulled Mr. Gable's file and handed it to Helen. "Mrs. Beck, you're next. Have a seat and I'll make sure you don't have to wait long. Mrs. Niccolo, let me get you some coffee . . . I know just how you like it."

Libby kicked into high gear and had things

under control again within minutes. She spent the rest of the day fielding calls and trying to do her job. People were on edge, and the main buzz in the waiting area was about the Polzers, and how the search for Andrea had been widened to beyond the river.

Even Tim felt the tension in the air, and he snapped out orders in a way completely unlike him. Once, after he'd been particularly abrupt, he came back and stood beside Libby's desk.

"I owe you an apology," he said. He ran a hand through his hair. "The filing system here is a mess—we need to modernize, put everything on the computer. I shouldn't blame you because something can't be found. You haven't been here long enough to be responsible for a misplaced file."

"It's all right," Libby said. By then it was late afternoon, and she felt drained.

"It's just that Andrea Polzer was in my office only last month, for a bee sting. Nice little girl."

"Yes, I remember," Libby said.

Tim cleared his throat and looked in the direction of the waiting room. "How're we doing here. Who's left?"

"Two patients—a baby to be inoculated and a worker from the construction site with a splinter."

"We'll get them through as quickly as we can. I'm sure you're anxious to get home to your daughters."

Libby thanked him and agreed that she was.

Even at the busiest times that day, they had never been completely out of her thoughts.

The latest news on the radio was that the search had turned up nothing.

Thirteen

Brandon picked up both girls in front of their house at four-thirty, as planned, and, like everyone else in town, he also knew what was going on. For most of the day it had been all he'd heard about. His mother had become so anxious that by the time the afternoon rolled around Brandon couldn't wait to get away from the house. He'd left her sitting in front of the TV, watching the local channel for the latest developments.

As soon as Tess and Joely were in his car they began complaining about having to spend the day together.

Brandon listened to them as he drove, but soon grew impatient. "Your mother did the smart thing," he said when they paused for breath.

Joely, who'd been expecting sympathy from her father, sulked. It had been a terrible day. She'd been forced to go to the Coddingtons' with Tess, when she'd really wanted to get back to the cemetery to see if Martin would show up again. She'd even tried to sneak out once, but Tess had caught her and then hadn't let her out of her sight for the rest of the afternoon. Tess had put her to work, making her sweep the kitchen floor and vacuum the den, and Joely was pretty sure she wasn't going to get paid for any of this.

Because of his own mother's state of mind, Brandon had changed his plans for supper with the girls. He knew how his mother could be when she was anxious about something—she'd get on a subject and never let it go until she'd driven everyone around her crazy. Before leaving the house Brandon had told her he wouldn't be back with the girls after all, and had then left quickly before she could start in on him. She'd have plenty to say to him about it later, he was sure, but in the meantime he wasn't going to spoil the evening with Tess and Joely by subjecting them to their grandmother's hysteria.

He drove them instead to a pizza place in town, and that's where they heard that the mutilated body of ten-year-old Andrea Polzer had been found less than two miles outside of town. A waitress told them as she brought their pizza to the table, and the news spread through the room like wildfire.

"Poor little thing. I heard she was a mess—cut up and stuffed in a garbage bag," they overheard from the next table.

156

The pizza sat before them, but neither Brandon nor the girls could think of eating it.

Joely pulled her knees up and wrapped her arms around them. She looked at her father with enormous eyes. Tess was chewing on her thumbnail.

"I hope they find the bastard and hang him in the middle of the town square for everyone to see. That's what needs to be done. There's too much getting away with that sort of thing." This came from a booth behind them.

"There are no town squares anymore."

"You know what I mean—make an example."

"Sounds like you're talking about a lynch mob."

"Why not? The justice system obviously doesn't work anymore."

Joely began trembling. "Dad . . ."

Brandon got up from the table. "Let's get out of here," he said.

The girls followed him to the car. Once inside, he locked the doors and sat staring straight ahead, hands gripping the steering wheel.

Tess spoke first. "Maybe we should get home. Mom will hear about this and she'll be a wreck."

He didn't answer her immediately. Finally, he asked, "Did either of you know that girl?"

"I saw her around a couple of times," Joely whispered. "That's all."

"Me too," Tess said.

Brandon released the steering wheel and turned the key in the ignition. He had to get the girls

157

back to their mother. Libby was better for them at a time like this. He wanted to comfort them, but didn't know how. He wanted to tell them that none of this had anything to do with them, that they were safe—but the words wouldn't come.

Brandon wasn't sure if he believed it himself.

Libby was putting the last file away when Francine burst into the clinic and told her that the child's body had been found.

"I can't believe something like this could happen again," Francine fretted. "Is there no place that's safe anymore? What are we supposed to do—barricade ourselves in our homes and never come out? It's getting so decent, law-abiding citizens aren't safe anywhere. I'm going to buy a gun."

Libby, who'd had to sit down before her legs gave out, looked up at her friend with a blankness that bordered on shock.

"What do you mean?" she asked, "about something like this happening again?"

"You know about what went on before . . . oh, that's right—you didn't live here then."

"When, Francine?"

"It was about twenty-five years ago. I was just a kid myself at the time, but I'll never forget what it was like to know that there was a nut on the loose and the police didn't seem to be able to do anything about it." Francine wa standing beside Libby's desk, but she nervously rearranged little items—a pencil holder, the stapler, a box of tissues—until she caught Libby's expression. "I thought you would've at least heard about it. Four children were murdered. Didn't Brandon ever mention it?"

"Here in Cielo?" Libby was barely able to get the words out.

"No—only the first two were local kids. A girl and then a boy, both strangled. The next one was from a nearby town, but close enough that people couldn't believe the incidents weren't related. Then the last one . . . let's see . . . oh, yeah, she was just passing through the area, on vacation with her parents, poor thing, when she was found dead. Those last two were cut up so badly that dental records were needed to identify them."

Libby winced.

"All of this happened within about a thirty-mile radius of Cielo."

Libby had to ask. "No one was ever caught?"

"No, never. But then the killings stopped and people began to say that it had been some hippie who finally moved on. This was back before that Charles Manson group, but there were still a lot of that type around, especially here in California where every nut in the country seemed to come."

Libby wished she hadn't been told this. But twenty-five years ago—that was such a long time it couldn't possible have anything to do with what was happening now.

"Where's the doc?" Francine asked. She cranked her neck to look into the back rooms, but couldn't see anything.

"He left a few minutes ago," Libby told her. "I was on my way out, too, but then I remembered these files I'd left out and I came back to put them away." She lowered her head to her hands. "I can't believe it, but I'm actually glad Brandon is in town. He was going to pick the girls up and take them out for pizza—I don't know what I'd do if I thought they were alone right now."

Francine wanted to talk some more, but Libby cut her off, promising she'd call her later, and locked up the office. She drove home, and was just rolling into the driveway when Brandon and the girls also reached the house. One look at their collective faces told her that they'd also heard the news.

"We thought it would be best to come home," Brandon explained, following Libby into the house.

No one ate supper, though Libby did halfheartedly try to convince the girls that they needed something. Brandon kept pulling the curtain aside to look out the front window, until Libby finally asked him to stop.

The hours dragged relentlessly, until Tess and Joely excused themselves to their bedroom. Brandon stayed on, and he and Libby talked quietly

160

in the living room, the lines of battle abandoned for the time being.

"Now that I think back, I seem to remember hearing something about some killings a long time ago," Libby whispered. She held a glass of iced tea in her hands and every few minutes would press it to her cheek as though to cool her skin. Sitting curled up on one corner of the sofa, her bare feet were tucked beneath her. Brandon, who'd wanted something stronger than tea, was working on his second whiskey and water. He was on the sofa also, but on the other side, so a distance of about three feet separated them.

"Maybe it was your mother who told me," she continued. "Shouldn't you be with her? She might be afraid, now that that child's body has been found."

Brandon drained the last of his drink and wondered if he dared ask Libby for another. Two might be the limit to Libby's hospitality. "No one's going to bother that mean old lady," he said, his words running together a little bit. "Hell, any psycho killer who showed up on *her* doorstep would find himself running for his life within five minutes."

"How old were you when it was going on?"

"What? Oh . . . those dead kids years ago? I would've been in my teens at the time. Yeah, high school. To tell you the truth, that was right in the middle of my worst adolescent phase, and even something like that didn't touch me much.

I was busy thinking the world revolved around me."

"But surely you—"

Libby stopped when the phone rang. She jumped up to get it before it could ring a second time. A few minutes before, she'd peeked in on Tess and Joely and had been glad to see that they'd finally fallen asleep. She didn't want anything to awaken them now.

It was Tim Kyle calling. As Libby spoke to him she was aware that Brandon was being very quiet in the other room.

"I wanted to see how you were doing," Tim said. "I've been watching the news all night. This is a terrible thing. So senseless."

"I know," Libby said. "The girls haven't said much. I almost wish they would ask me questions, but if they do, what can I possibly say?"

"I'll understand if you want to stay home with them tomorrow," Tim said.

"Thank you, but that's not necessary. My ex-husband is in town for a few days. He'll stay with Tess and Joely tomorrow."

The silence on the line was as sudden and complete as that from the living room. Libby thought they'd been disconnected.

"Tim?"

A pause of two more heartbeats, then, "Yes, I'm here."

In the other room, Brandon said, "Tim?"

Libby turned her back to him and spoke softly into the phone. "I'll be at the office tomorrow,

Tim. I can't miss work every time something happens in town."

After she hung up, Libby leaned toward her reflection in the window above the sink to check her appearance. It wasn't good. She looked haggard, and knew she couldn't blame the poor quality of the reflection on that. Events of the past weeks, even months, were catching up with her—and now this.

Brandon got up from the sofa and started toward her. She saw him approaching out of the corner of her eye, his empty glass in hand. Before she could ask him if he wanted another drink, the phone rang again.

"You're very popular," Brandon said from the doorway.

Libby ignored him and picked up the receiver. The voice that assaulted her brought back a flood of memories, very few of which were pleasant, and Libby struggled to keep her dislike from showing itself on her face.

"Is my son there?" Dorothea Gregory demanded. "I called your place a few minutes ago. The line was busy—who were you talking to for so long?"

"I was on the phone for only a few minutes," Libby responded before she could begin to wonder why she should attempt to justify her actions to this woman.

"I asked you a question." The shrill voice drove out all chance for thought. "Is Brandon there? Don't lie to me. He told me this afternoon he was going to see my granddaughters."

"He's right here," Libby said. "I'll put him on right—"

"What's he doing there so late? He should be here with me, especially with all that's going on in this town. It's the growing decay of society, the loss of morals. I'm all alone in this house."

Libby saw that Brandon had come into the kitchen and stood within touching distance of her. "I'll let you talk to him about that."

Libby handed the phone to Brandon and walked away, her arms crossed and hands on her shoulders, creating a shield against the poison that came from the mouth of her ex-mother-in-law.

When she was able to look up again she saw that Brandon wasn't having much more luck than she'd had.

"I didn't want to leave Libby and the girls alone right now," he was saying. His expression was pained, but he showed no signs of backing down. "You're safe enough, just bolt the front door and don't open it until I get there. . . . No, I don't know when that'll be." His eyes met Libby's and he rolled them in exasperation. "Yes, but . . . no, she's *not* plotting anything. I know, but . . . I'll get there when I get there. You can't blame . . ."

For Libby, the situation suddenly changed from distressful to ludicrous, and she had to put both hands over her mouth before Brandon saw that she was laughing. Dorothea Gregory was an old biddy who'd told Libby at her engagement party almost seventeen years ago that she wasn't good enough for her son. At the time Libby had been shocked, but youthfully determined to prove Brandon's mother wrong. It didn't take long—a couple of years at most—for her to realize that nothing ever changed Dorothea's mind about anything once it was made up, and Libby'd stopped trying. The fact that her mother-in-law despised her was something Libby had learned to live with. She'd even managed to stop caring. Only for Tess and Joely's sakes had she ever wished things could have been different, but even the arrival of those sweet babies hadn't been enough to thaw the ice on an old woman's heart.

Brandon was still struggling. "Tess was not rude. She never has liked cookies and all she did was say no thanks . . . Libby has done nothing wrong in the raising of—"

Libby left the kitchen, nearly doubled over now with laughter. Let him deal with it. She waited in the living room for him to finish. At least the girls were asleep and didn't have to hear this.

Fourteen

Joely lay awake in her bed, though earlier she'd closed her eyes and pretended to be asleep when her mother had opened the door and looked in. The phone had rung twice; she hadn't been able to determine who the first caller was, but had figured out that the second was Grandma Gregory. She could tell by the frustrated, stilted tone to her father's voice. It was very much the same way he'd sounded on Sunday afternoon, when he'd taken her and Tess over to their grandmother's house for a belated visit.

What a disaster *that* had been. Rather than being happy to see them, their grandmother had acted as though the visit was a major imposition, and only after they'd been there for almost an hour had she dragged out some packaged cookies and reluctantly offered them some. Joely had taken one just to be polite, but Tess had declined and their grandmother had looked at her

166

like she was something that'd recently crawled out from under a rock.

Turning over on her side, Joely pulled the sheet up over her shoulders and shut out the sounds from the other room. There were more important things for her to be thinking about at the moment.

She hadn't known Andrea Polzer well, but Joely had seen her around town, and the idea that Andrea was now dead was a frightening thought. The mental picture Joely got of Andrea was of a chubby girl with long hair worn in braided pigtails and a space between her two front teeth.

How had she died? All Joely'd heard so far was that her body had been found. Whenever she tried to pick up more information than that, the adults around her fell silent and exchanged meaningful glances. Joely deeply resented the fact that even her own parents didn't seem to think she deserved to know what was going on.

"You aren't asleep, are you?" Tess whispered from the other bed.

Joely thought about pretending again, then decided not to bother. "No," she answered.

"Dad's staying pretty late . . . and they haven't even been fighting."

Joely thought about this. "Do you think they're going to get back together?"

"Stop thinking like that. It's not going to happen because he's still seeing that Greta. The one they used to fight about all the time."

"How do you know?"

"He called her from Grandma's house when we were out on the porch and he said he was going inside for a drink of water—except I went in a minute later to use the bathroom and I heard him on the phone with her."

Joely propped herself up on one elbow. "How did he sound?" she asked.

"Not like I expected him to. I got the feeling she was unhappy that he'd come here, because he was explaining how he wanted to spend his vacation time with us, and how he hadn't seen much of us lately."

"Well, that's good . . . isn't it?"

"I guess. Unless he plans to drag us over to Grandma's house all the time—I don't think I could stand much more of that."

"Me either," Joely agreed.

Tess fell silent for a moment, and both girls heard the soft murmur of their parents' voices from the direction of the living room.

Then Tess said, "You know what freaks me out most about that kid getting killed? She lived just a couple of blocks down from Mrs. Coddington's. I saw her once going past, and she waved to me."

"Really?"

"So now you know why we were so worried that night you went out. There's all kinds of crazies in the world. Something could have happened to *you*, just like it happened to Andrea."

Joely had no answer for this. The truth was,

she'd given the matter some thought herself. So far she'd spent two separate occasions in the company of a boy who could only be described as a ghost, yet he was less of a threat to her than the real people who walked around.

Martin Stanovich wouldn't hurt her. Joely knew this as surely as she knew there would be no more opportunities for her to sneak out at night, but neither did she *want* to go to the cemetery after dark again. That meant she'd just have to go see Martin during the day. He might not make an appearance in the full glare of sunlight, but Joely intended to find out as soon as possible.

Tess seemed about to say something more, when both girls detected a shadow crossing the strip of light where the bedroom door was cracked open about an inch.

They remained silent, their breathing shallow and steady, perfected by many years of feigning sleep.

Libby pulled the door shut until the latch clicked. Back in the living room, she said, "I thought the girls were awake, but I guess not. Tomorrow Tess will go to Mrs. Coddington's again, but Joely shouldn't be underfoot there all the time. Could you keep her tomorrow? I'll feel so much better about being at work if I know she's with you."

"I was planning on it," Brandon said. "I'll call her in the morning and let her know exactly what time I'll be here. I have a few things to do, but I'll try to get here before Tess has to leave."

Libby nodded, and sat perched on the arm of the sofa. After getting off the phone Brandon had asked her for another drink, and she'd fixed it for him with the feeling that his request had come as an act of defiance against his mother. Dorothea Gregory had all but ordered him home—"home" being her place—and he was now taking his time, determined to prove he was his own man and had no curfew.

If only he'd shown some similar backbone when they'd been married, Libby thought. It was ironic that when the ties of their marriage had been cut he'd also snipped those apron strings. She'd also often wondered if his infidelity had been linked to his desire to rebel against the women in his life. Libby'd never thought of herself as particularly dominating, but perhaps Brandon had.

"So, tell me about Tim," he said, his voice smooth and careful.

"Tim Kyle, the doctor I work for," Libby explained. "He's a local originally. Maybe you knew him in school, you're close to the same age."

"The name sounds familiar, but we probably moved in different circles."

"Ah, yes . . . you were a member of the jockstrap club, weren't you?" Libby said.

Brandon grinned, then he set his drink down on the end table, scooted over and pulled Libby

170

down from the arm of the sofa. Before she realized what was happening she fell back almost into the crook of his arm, and although she immediately straightened up they were still sitting very close to each other.

"Cut it out," she said, and poked his ribs with her elbow.

"I was an athlete," Brandon admitted, oblivious to her discomfort. His breath ruffled her hair. "You should have seen me back then in my football uniform—I had those little cheerleaders swooning at the sight of me."

"I'm glad I *didn't* see you then," Libby said. "I'm sure you were insufferable."

"I was irresistible."

"And so modest."

"Modesty is wasted on the humble."

Libby edged away from him. She had a long and convoluted history with this man, and despite the pain of recent months it was too easy to remember that there had been some good times—years when they'd been unable to keep their hands off each other, when their passion had remained even after the girls had been born and the responsibilities of parenthood had become too real.

When had it started to go wrong? Aware that she could smell his aftershave, tempered by his own masculine scent, Libby had to hold her hands tightly together on her lap to keep from fidgeting nervously.

He was distracting her from the horrors of this

long day, but the direction in which their conversation was headed seemed not much better.

"It's getting late," she said, "and I have work in the morning."

Brandon seemed about to say something more, but then he shrugged and got to his feet. "Okay," he said. "Don't worry about Joely tomorrow, I'll be close by all the time."

"I have to worry." She followed him to the door. It was easier talking to him now that they were no longer sitting together on the sofa. "Give your mother my love."

He stopped halfway out the door. "Funny," he said.

Libby smiled sweetly. "I'm quite serious."

"Right. That'd drive her nuts—she's convinced all you do down at that office is sit around bad-mouthing her to anyone who'll listen."

"That doesn't surprise me."

"If I tell her you send your love it'll infuriate her."

"I know." Libby pushed the door shut on him before he could say anything else. All right, it'd been a cheap shot—but it had felt good.

The house was silent when Libby climbed into bed more than an hour later; even the ticking of the clock on the wall in the kitchen seemed muted by the heavy night air.

Outside, an unnatural hush had fallen over the town. Doors were double-locked, windows checked, extra patrol cars cruised empty streets. There was an air of anticipation, and frightened

172

parents whispered to each other, sharing their hope that the perpetrator of this horrible crime would quickly be identified, and their fear that this was only the beginning of a nightmare.

Maria Rafael slept in her room with the overhead light on. After hearing about the death of Andrea—whom she'd once gotten into a quarrel with at a pool party—she'd become so nervous that she couldn't stand to be in a room by herself, even in her own home. It had taken her parents over an hour to convince her that she could safely sleep in her own bedroom, but even then she'd insisted on having the light on.

Her dreams were uneasy, filled with images of looming tombstones that popped up out of the ground to block her escape from a seemingly endless cemetery. She could hear Rachel Fletcher laughing, but then Rachel's laughter turned to screams in the distance.

Maria moaned and twisted her fingers in sheets that were damp with her sweat. Her eyes were squeezed tightly shut, her face a knot of fear.

She couldn't find her way out . . . they'd left *her* behind with Joely this time, but even Joely wouldn't help her because she was busy looking for a little boy she said lived there. It wasn't Rachel who was screaming, Maria realized as she stumbled about in the mist-shrouded cemetery.

The awful sound was coming from her own throat.

Then Maria's parents were in the bedroom with her, and they tried to comfort the frightened child as sobs ripped through her.

"Oh, honey . . . we're right here," Monica Rafael said, trying to calm her daughter. "It's okay now. It was just a bad dream. Nothing can happen to you with us here."

Maria gasped and clung to her mother.

Lou Rafael hovered nearby. He patted his daughter's small shoulder, not knowing what else he could do for her.

"I didn't mean to leave her there," Maria cried. She was aware now that she was safely in her own bedroom, but the panic from the dream was not so easily shaken off.

"Who?" Monica asked. She looked up at her husband, but he just shrugged.

"Joely . . ." Maria whispered. The words were almost lost in the soft fabric of her mother's robe.

"Maria, honey, it was a dream. Try to forget about it; I'll stay here with you."

Maria eventually fell into a fitful sleep, but, true to her word, Monica stayed with her daughter for the rest of the night. She did this for Maria, but also for herself. The world was not a safe place, as they'd all so recently been reminded. All she could do was stand guard over her own home, and try to protect that which was most precious to her.

Fifteen

Joely left the house through the back door and headed down the gravel road. She didn't have much time, and she hurried along as best she could without actually breaking into a run that might attract attention to her. Even though it was almost noon, she had the feeling any kid spotted alone was going to be noticed, and she was anxious to reach her destination before that could happen.

Luck had gotten Joely out of the house in the first place. She'd been wondering all morning how she was going to manage it, when her father had called to tell her he'd be by to pick her up shortly after lunch.

"I'm sorry I can't get there sooner," he'd said, "but your grandmother has a list of things she wants me to do here. I'll work fast—I think she's been saving up some of these chores for months, waiting for me to get here." He'd then lowered his voice and added, "She's an old lady alone,

Joely . . . it means a lot to her when I'm here, and even though some of this stuff could wait I'm going to try to get it done for her. You understand?"

As Joely assured him she did understand, her spirits had been soaring. This was the opportunity she'd been hoping for.

The next obstacle had been Tess, but she'd been easily manipulated. Tess had, when she'd found out Brandon was going to be late, offered to stay with Joely until he arrived. This was the last thing Joely wanted, but instead of saying so she'd simply become obnoxious, whiny, and in general so loathsome that she'd driven her sister crazy. She'd fiddled with Tess's stereo, talked back when told to get dressed and brush her hair, and spilled a glass of milk on the kitchen floor.

Finally, Tess had thrown up her hands in surrender.

"Okay—I don't *care* if you look like a wreck when Dad gets here," she'd yelled. "You do what you want. I'm going to my job. *Some* of us around here have more important things to do than clean up after some spoiled little creep!"

With that, Tess had slammed out the front door, and Joely'd run to her room to get dressed.

The sun was shining brightly, but the town had a deserted feel to it. No faces peeked out from behind curtains to watch as she went past. The cemetery, when she reached it, almost seemed an island of safety compared to the rest of Cielo.

In the heart of the property there were full-grown trees, and the sunlight that came through the branches overhead, was filtered and weak. Martin was there as soon as Joely was deep enough into the cemetery to be within sight of his headstone. He seemed almost to be waiting for her, as though he'd known she would come. It was strange to see him in the daylight, shadowed though it was. He was more transparent, and Joely had the feeling it was a great effort for the boy to show himself this time.

"I didn't know if I'd see you today," she said softly, stopping a few feet away from him. "There's a lot going on in town. I won't be able to get away at night again—my mom's really nervous, and she hears everything that goes on in the house now. Did you know I was coming? Can you . . ."

Martin raised a hand and Joely fell silent. She could feel his frustration. It came off him in waves, reaching her as an almost palpable force, and infecting her with similar feelings. How could they go on like this? Their communication was painfully stunted, and for a moment all they could do was stare helplessly at each other.

Martin wanted to talk to her, but the barrier that kept him from making himself heard was still up—maybe forever.

"I wish we could work something out," Joely sighed.

Martin faded, so gradually at first that Joely didn't realize it was happening until he was almost gone. The last she saw of him was his hand still in the air, beckoning. Then he was gone.

"Hey!" she cried, and moved to where he had been, despite her earlier unpleasant experience with such action.

It didn't matter this time. He really was gone, and Joely was left with only an empty space where he'd been.

"Hey . . ." she repeated helplessly. "I didn't come here today for you to take off so fast. What's going on? Martin—don't go!"

She turned around, arms outstretched, unwilling to believe that she'd gone to all this trouble for nothing.

She saw him.

Martin was several yards away, standing serenely beside the trunk of a young maple tree, waiting to be noticed. He smiled when her eyes finally landed on him.

Joely's relief was so great that she hurried toward him, ready to forgive.

And it happened again. She'd almost reached him when she realized he was no longer there, but this time Joely was only bewildered. What was going on?

Each blade of grass on the ground was sharply etched, the headstones were dotted with tiny imperfections, the older ones more pockmarked than the recent arrivals. The leaves in the trees rustled with deep green movement, giving the air a cool underwater effect.

The fine details of her surroundings were not lost to Joely, but they seemed to mock her with their solid reality. She wanted to see Martin's cloudy, indistinct shape—to her, he had become the reality.

She didn't panic this time, but instead waited until he again made himself known, farther away than before and waiting for her to catch on.

"Okay, I get it," Joely said, walking with determination toward him. "You're taking me somewhere—right?"

Joely's bewilderment vanished. She'd been so worried about how they were going to communicate, but Martin had found a way. He wanted to show her something, obviously, and since he didn't have the words to tell her to follow him he was simply luring her in the right direction. Now that she understood this, Joely followed along eagerly. Only when she reached the front gate did she stop and again wonder what was going on. Where could he take her from here?

Somewhere off in the distance a car horn sounded three times and then fell silent. A plane flew high overhead in a cloudless sky. A breeze lifted the ends of Joely's hair and brought the aroma of cooking meat to her nose; probably someone in one of the nearby houses was fixing lunch and had left the kitchen window open.

It didn't seem possible that Martin had brought her here, to the very edge of the cemetery, where one world collided with the other. Martin belonged in the place that was identified by deep shadows and the smell of damp earth.

She squinted in the sunlight and wondered about the time. She didn't own a watch, but wished now she'd borrowed one of Tess's.

Then time was forgotten, as was Tess, her father and anything else other than the pale figure of a little boy in jeans and a striped T-shirt . . . standing across the gravel road and several houses down, waiting for Joely to notice this latest, incredible accomplishment.

Martin had left the cemetery. In broad daylight he had ventured out and still obviously wanted Joely to follow his lead. She had assumed he was bound to the hallowed grounds of the burying place, had believed this for no other reason than that it seemed logical. Yet Martin had just stepped out into *her* place, and in doing so had shattered the last, long-held myth.

"Holy shit," Joely whispered.

She looked around to see if anyone else was observing this phenomenon, but now, as earlier, the backs of the houses along this way had a closed-up look. There was no other person in sight.

Martin waited patiently for Joely to get over her shock. Out here, without the protective umbrella of old trees, Martin was paled almost to invisibility. It had to be difficult for him to make himself seen under such conditions. His edges had no distinct outline, and the expression on his face was harder to read. Joely saw that he was standing in front of a tire swing on a rope, and she could see the tire easily through the stripes of his shirt. Although he'd always been wispy and without substance, out here he seemed to be not much more than a puff of smoke.

This lent a sense of urgency to their situation. Martin led her down the gravel road, away from the line of houses, and as they walked along the outer edge of the town Joely kept an eye out for anyone who might witness this strange ritual.

She saw no one, though Joely did begin to wonder if a casual observer would see Martin at all. Perhaps he was only visible to her. That one time she'd reached out to touch him, and had been momentarily swept into a cold, dreamlike place that didn't welcome living flesh, she'd had the impression that their minds were linked somehow. Even though she was careful to keep a distance between them now, Joely still felt that Martin was as much in her head as he was standing before her.

No longer on the gravel road, Joely was now walking through tall weeds, pushing aside bushes that snagged her shorts. "Where are we going?" she panted. "Really, Martin . . . this is rough going. Can you give me a hint? Oh, no . . . don't disappear on me again. I don't know how much more of this I can take!"

It was no use, he was gone, and for once Joely was tempted to put an end to this and just go home. This was the longest length of time they'd been together, and it was almost getting to be too much for her. Her bare legs were scratched and bleeding in several places, her shoes had taken in some sand and small pebbles that made walking torture, and her whole body ached with thirst and exhaustion. Even her glasses kept sliding down her sweaty nose.

There was an old building up ahead. Squat and ugly, it was long abandoned and nearly hidden by an overgrowth of wild bushes and crooked trees. Even the road in front of it was no longer used, the asphalt cracked by the relentless pressure of nature uncontrolled.

The building rested at the base of a hill. Joely'd seen it before, from a distance when Libby had taken a wrong turn once, and had used this road to turn around and get back on the right track. Tess had asked then about the obviously deserted building, thinking it was an old factory or something.

"No, I think it used to be a school," Libby had explained to them at the time. "It was built in the early part of the century, but Cielo grew south, instead of north as people had expected, and after a while this school was inconveniently located and outdated. As new schools were built, this one was finally shut down."

"Jeez, it couldn't get much uglier," Tess had observed, looking out the side window as Libby turned the car around.

"It probably wasn't that bad while it was in

use, but a place falls apart fast once it's been abandoned."

Joely'd had no particular feeling about the empty structure at the time, but looking at it now she sensed an underlying rot that seemed deeper than mere neglect. This building had gone bad long before the students had moved on to a better location.

And there was Martin—standing near a side door, waiting for her to catch up.

Joely didn't like this. Fighting her way through the weeds, she approached the area reluctantly. Martin didn't fade away this time when she got close, but waited for her until she reached the doorway, then smiled his encouragement.

"This was your school, I guess," Joely said, her nose wrinkled in distaste. It even smelled bad here, the air sour with something she didn't want to think too much about. "You would have been in about fourth grade, right? I remember when I was in fourth grade my teacher was Miss Sinclair. She left after Valentine's day when she got married, and we had a substitute for a couple of weeks while she went on her honeymoon. When she came back she was Mrs. Lazaro."

The door in front of her was ajar, falling part way off its hinges and hanging at an angle. Inside, Joely saw only darkness.

"When she came back she had pictures of her new husband and told us where they went on their honeymoon. I don't remember now where it was they went."

Joely was chattering nervously, but while she talked her mind was trying to decipher this puzzle. Martin didn't want her to go *inside* did he? She could stand just about anything but that—but there he was nearly in the opening now, daring her to come a little farther.

"I don't think I can go in there," Joely protested. "It's too creepy . . . and my mom would kill me if she ever found out."

But that argument didn't hold water, Joely knew, because she'd been doing a lot of things lately her mother wouldn't have approved of.

Martin was gone. He was inside, and she understood that he expected her to go in also.

Taking a deep breath, Joely pushed at the leaning door with both hands, then gasped when it collapsed with a terrible crash that sent years-old dust up into her nose. Joely covered her mouth with both hands and stood wide-eyed for long minutes, until the dust settled and her heart no longer felt like it was going to burst through her ribs.

It took a while, but finally she gathered her courage and stepped over the fallen door and into the school.

She found herself in a hallway. It stretched in both directions, and Joely could vaguely see a cracked tile floor and open doors that probably led to the classrooms. Off to her left, light struggled to come through the dirt on a pair of glass doors. Probably that was the way the students had gone to reach their playground. To the right the hallway extended until it turned a corner, going to the larger, main part of the building.

Martin stood down on that end, and Joely groaned in despair. Of course he wouldn't make this easy for her. He was going to take her to the one place where she most definitely didn't want to go—into the belly of the beast.

Sixteen

Tess sat on a chair in front of the bathroom mirror and tried to concentrate on what she was doing. It wasn't easy, because Joely stood in the doorway and just wouldn't go away. Joely had a wild story to tell, and she was going to tell it whether Tess wanted to listen or not.

"Give me a break," Tess moaned. She adjusted the towel around her neck and gave her sister a dirty look. "I'm trying to do something here, and if I don't pay attention I'll end up looking like something from the circus."

"I don't know why you want to bleach your hair anyway," Joely said.

"It's not bleach, it's a summer rinse. It helps the sun lighten my hair just enough to give it some highlights. Now, go away."

"But you have to listen to this," Joely insisted. "This boy, Martin—"

"The ghost," Tess sighed.

"Yeah, the ghost. He took me to the old

school building and I went inside to see what it was he wanted to show me."

"If Mom knew you'd gone in there she'd have a fit." Tess separated her hair carefully with a comb and pointed the tip of the squeeze bottle into the part.

"He took me to the furnace room. I couldn't see anything at first, but I found some old rags and cleaned the dirt off the window and then it wasn't so bad. There's no electricity in the building, so it's pretty hard to see inside. Anyway, once he got me there he looked so sad I wanted to cry for him. You should have seen his face, Tess—he looked just miserable."

"He's a ghost. What would he have to be happy about?"

Joely ignored this. "Then he faded away, like he'd used up all his energy, only this time he didn't come back. I looked around the furnace room some more, but I didn't see much of anything. Animals had been in there, it smelled really bad. There *is* something he wants to show me—I just can't figure out what it is."

Tess set down the squeeze bottle and carefully wiped some dripping liquid from her forehead. She looked at Joely.

"Okay, what is this," she said. "A delayed stress syndrome from the divorce? Is Mom going to have to take you to a psychiatrist? You know I don't believe a word of what you're saying."

"I didn't think you would. That's why I want you to come to the school with me. Maybe Martin will be there again—but even if he isn't you might see something in the room that I missed . . . oh, I don't know. I just want you to see it."

"Are you nuts?" Tess stared at her sister. "You expect *me* to go into that building with you? First of all, I'm too busy to humor you and your little fantasies. Second, you said it was dark, so it's probably dangerous."

"We can take a flashlight," Joely said. She stepped around Tess's chair and sat on the edge of the bathtub.

When she'd gone to the old school building with Martin the day before, Joely'd lost all track of time and had been later getting home than she'd planned. As it had turned out, though, her father had been running late, too, and she'd reached the house only moments before he'd arrived. Out of breath and sweating, she'd barely had time to pull herself together before he was at the front door.

"Let's go get some ice cream or something," Brandon had suggested when they'd run out of small talk. "It's too hot to stay in all day. Too bad Tess has to work."

"She doesn't work tomorrow," Joely told him as they walked to his car.

"Good." He opened the door for her and Joely got in.

All afternoon Brandon tried to keep up a cheerful front for Joely, but they both were still very aware of the heavy cloud of tension that had descended upon the town. Everywhere they went they were reminded that a child had recently died, and that alone was enough to convince Joely that she couldn't tell her father about Martin, or her trip to the old school. She'd wanted to tell him, had almost blurted the whole story out more than once, but common sense had prevailed and she'd kept her mouth shut.

There was no way her father would understand any of what she was going through, and he'd probably tell her mother about it. If *they* became united against her, Joely knew she'd never have the chance to get out of the house again.

It was okay to tell Tess, though. Tess might not believe the story at first, but she wouldn't snitch on Joely for leaving the house.

"Forget about it, I'm not going," Tess said.

"Please," Joely begged. "Just this once, and then I promise I'll never bother you about it again."

"It's time for me to rinse out my hair." Tess stood and turned on the water in the sink, tested it with her fingertips until it was the right temperature, then stuck her head under the spray of water. She rinsed thoroughly, then wrapped the towel around her head and began to rub her hair dry. "Mom said we weren't to leave the house," she said, her voice muffled.

"We won't tell her."

"Forget it." Tess left the bathroom.

Joely was like a small terrier that had gotten

its teeth into something and wasn't going to let go. "We can take our bikes and be there at the school in a few minutes. We'll be back before Dad gets here at eleven. I know the way into the building now, and with a flashlight it won't be bad at all."

"Leave me alone."

"Martin might even be there. You're passing up the opportunity of a lifetime."

"I don't believe in ghosts."

"Neither did I. Please, Tess . . . *please.*"

"Oh, God, don't whine." Tess put her hands over her ears. When Joely did that it was just like someone dragging their fingernails down a chalkboard. It drove her nuts.

Joely sensed weakness, and she continued her relentless attack. "I promise . . . just this once and I'll never ask you again. I'll leave you alone forever. *Please,* Tess."

Tess was no match for such an assault. Glaring at her sister, she crumbled under the pressure. "All right! You win! Let's get it over with, and when we get back home I don't want to hear your voice again for another twenty-four hours."

"You won't, I swear." Joely ran to the kitchen and came back with the flashlight Libby kept under the sink. Tess grumbled about having to amuse a psychotic sister and complained that her hair was still wet, but she went to the garage with Joely to get their bikes, and within minutes they were pedaling down the back road in the direction of the old school.

"I'll be glad when I can get my driver's license," Tess said, legs pumping as she struggled to keep up with Joely.

Joely looked back over her shoulder. She wanted to surge ahead, but forced herself to slow down and wait for Tess. Neither of them used their bikes much anymore, Joely because hers was a couple of years old and was getting too small for her, Tess because her ten-speed had a faulty chain that slipped off easily. Ordinarily they preferred to walk, but on this morning they both understood the necessity for speed.

"Why did I let you talk me into this?" Tess griped.

"There it is! There's the old school," Joely called out triumphantly.

Libby sat in the sweet-smelling café and sipped at the coffee the waitress had brought. Francine sat across from her.

Libby was on her morning break. Usually she stayed at the office during her breaks and just sipped coffee at her desk, but this time Francine had shown up and talked her into getting away for a few minutes. Libby had tried to refuse, but Tim had overheard them talking and urged her to go.

"There's not that much going on here this morning," he'd said. "It's a slow day anyway—you might as well take advantage of it."

So Libby found herself in the café, playing

with a coffee she didn't really want and feeling guilty about having left her post.

"The doctor seems very concerned about your well-being," Francine said with a sly smirk. She looked over her mug with arched eyebrows. "Most bosses resent every minute their employees spend on breaks. Yours practically pushes you out the door."

"He's always thoughtful," Libby murmured. "And he was right, it's a slow day. There have been some cancellations."

"Thoughtful *and* good-looking," Francine said, the smirk becoming more pronounced. "That can be a lethal combination. Has he tried to corner you at the filing cabinets yet?"

"Francine, it's a working relationship. He's my boss."

"Was he your boss the night he took you out?"

"That was—yes, he was my boss then, too," Libby stammered. She tried to speak softly so that the people at the surrounding tables didn't get an earful, but Francine had a dismayingly loud voice and made no effort to tone it down.

Francine looked doubtful. "What do you call him?" she asked.

"What?"

"When you went out with him—what did you call him then?"

"Tim," Libby admitted.

"Ah-ha."

"He insisted."

"I see."

192

"Francine, stop it. You're trying to blow this whole thing out of proportion."

"Maybe. But I find it interesting that for someone who claims to have no interest in romance, you have Dr. Kyle—I mean *Tim*—in one corner, and good old Brandon in the other. What must your dreams be like?"

Libby set down her coffee cup. Some spilled on the table, so she took a paper napkin and blotted up the liquid.

"At the moment," she said, "my dreams are mostly of a little girl who didn't make it home. Until they find the person who murdered her, I won't feel safe."

Francine immediately stopped her teasing. "Yeah, I know what you mean. I've been watching the TV news, but there hasn't been anything new about it on. I'm thinking of getting a dog. A big one, with sharp teeth."

"Do you really want to do that?" Libby asked.

"Just something for protection. Hey, it's either a dog or a man, and I figure a pit bull would be a lot easier to get along with."

Libby smiled. "You may have a point. For now I'm just glad that Brandon is nearby in case I need him, and the girls are together, safe at home."

Tess was startled at how dark it was once they got inside the building. Even the flashlight did little to break through the gloom.

Joely led the way, stepping carefully over fallen boards and discarded newspapers. Tess brought up the rear and tried not to let herself get too far behind. The place was creepy, but she couldn't turn back without admitting that she was afraid.

"Slow down," she said, and bumped her knee on an overturned chair. "Ow!"

"Watch it," Joely cautioned.

"Now you tell me. If you're going to carry the flashlight, the least you can do is wait for me."

"Sorry." Joely stopped. She looked around, a puzzled expression on her face. "That's funny . . ."

"Nothing about this place is funny," Tess said when she caught up.

"I thought I remembered the way to the furnace room, but this doesn't look right. I hope we didn't take a wrong turn." Joely pointed the flashlight to her right. "Maybe it's through there."

Tess brushed at something that stuck to her hair. The hallway was coated with cobwebs, and probably crawling with every type of bug imaginable. She was going to give this little expedition about thirty more seconds, and then she was going to take Joely home even if it meant dragging her.

"All right, we've gone far enough—" she began.

"There it is!" Joely cried, and disappeared into the dark mouth of a doorway.

"Come back here!" Tess called. Left without the flashlight, she was suddenly stranded. She held her hand out and tried to feel for the wall she knew was somewhere in front of her.

Joely came back, shining the light in Tess's eyes. "I found the furnace room," she said. "Stop messing around out here, will you? I want to show you this place. I think it's important."

Tess grabbed her sister's shirt. "Don't you go off and leave me like that again, or I'll take the flashlight and see how *you* like it."

Joely just pulled Tess in the direction from which she'd come, keeping the beam of the flashlight low so that they wouldn't stumble along the way. Tess went, still complaining and ready to look for the nearest exit, until she found herself in the middle of a large, concrete-floored room. Here, at least, there was some weak light trying to get in through the dirty window, and when her eyes adjusted to the gloom she saw the ghostly outline of a huge square furnace, its metal sides dulled by years of disuse.

"Now what?" Tess whispered.

Despite herself, she was awed by their surroundings. The rest of the building had been treacherous, and heavy with a sense of decay. This room, though, seemed to almost crawl with the whisperings of evil. Stone-cold and silent, Tess could believe in ghosts while in this place.

"We'll wait here a while," Joely said softly. She leaned against a desk that was covered with dust so thick it obscured the grain of the wood. Its drawers had been pulled all the way out, leaving empty spaces like missing teeth.

"Martin showed me where this was in the first place. He'll come back now . . . he'll come back to let me know *why*."

Tess looked at her sister in a way she never had before. "You're crazy," she said.

"Sh-h-h," Joely hissed.

Tess was wearing a watch, and by bringing it close to her face she could keep track of the time. The minutes crawled by so slowly that twice she pressed it to her ear to reassure herself it was still running.

A half hour passed before Tess couldn't take it any longer. She wrenched the flashlight out of Joely's hands and took the girl firmly by the shoulder.

"That's it," she said in a strong voice. "I've played this game, but it's over. We're going home now, and you're not going to say anything to anyone about this place."

"Just a little longer," Joely protested. She tried to hang back, but Tess was furious and not allowing it.

"And you're not coming here again either, do you understand that?"

They made their way back into the hallway, and Tess kicked aside everything in her way in her haste to get them out of there.

"You're just being chicken," Joely cried.

"I'm being smart, which is what you'd better be from now on if you don't want me to tell Mom what you've been up to."

"You won't tell on me."

"Think again. You've gone too far this time. Where's that door?"

Tess was forced to stop for a moment to get her bearings. A sweep of the flashlight finally brought the way out into focus, and she sighed with relief.

They had almost reached the door—Joely still dragging her feet—when something caught the corner of Tess's eye. She turned her head sharply, but saw only stacks of unused lumber and a broken coatrack leaning against a grimy wall.

Joely, caught off guard by the suddenness with which Tess stopped, bumped into her sister.

"Hey—"

"I saw something," Tess whispered.

"Where?"

"Over there. A person . . ." Tess shook her head, and glared at Joely. "Now you've got me doing it."

Then they were outside, the daylight so bright that they had to squint against the glare. But behind them was gloom and dark memories best left unexplored, and Tess hurried to put as much space between it and them as she could.

Even Joely no longer complained, though she was bitterly disappointed that Martin hadn't appeared. She needed proof, that was the only way anyone was ever going to believe her. As she threw her leg over her bike and obediently followed Tess, she made up her mind. She'd just have to try again.

Seventeen

For Deana Overby, walking into a bar was like coming home. She strutted into Goldy's, confident and ready for fun. The bar was small and dark, but almost half full. This was a good sign for a week night. It meant people were getting out, not waiting for the weekend to have a good time.

Deana knew Goldy's well, and her favorite table on the far side of the room was empty. Sitting, she signaled to the bartender, and within moments a scotch and water had been placed before her. She sipped it, scanning the place. A few familiar faces were out. A married couple she saw around town were at the table next to hers, and Deana let her eyes slide by casually. She'd had a brief fling with the husband a couple of years earlier, but as far as she knew the wife had never found out about it. Deana didn't usually have anything to do with married men, but she'd been caught in a weak moment at the time and preferred now to pretend it'd never happened.

Most of the single men in Goldy's were sitting at the bar. That was something she'd noticed. Women would sit at tables either alone or in groups, but men, unless they were with a date, preferred to perch on the tall stools at the bar. That way they could pretend they'd just stopped in for one cold beer and weren't really out looking to pick up women. Then, if they did happen to leave the bar alone later, they could maintain the illusion that this had been their intention all along. The male ego.

Women had no such hang-ups. Deana didn't mind sitting at a table alone, because that implied an invitation she definitely wished to extend.

It didn't take long. She wasn't halfway through her drink when the waitress brought another. "From the guy at the bar," she said.

"Which one?" Deana asked.

"White shirt and tie, glasses. I don't know him."

The waitress left. The man at the bar turned and looked at Deana. She smiled her thanks and, predictably, he got down from the stool and came over to the table. She thanked him verbally this time and invited him to sit "for a minute."

Deana sneaked a peek at her watch. Only nine-thirty. She was doing good. She'd only had to buy one drink for herself, and that was important because money could sometimes be a problem. Not tonight, though. She was set for the evening, and William was safely at home in bed and was probably asleep by now. She had nothing to think about other than the man sitting across from her.

"My name's Deana," she said sweetly, dipping a fingertip into her drink.

William Overby wasn't asleep. His mother had tucked him into bed before leaving the house at nine o'clock with the usual empty promise that she'd be home early, then she'd gone out the front door and he knew he wouldn't see her again until morning. Sometimes not even then, and he would have to get himself dressed for the day, being careful to choose clothes that matched because if he didn't she'd scold him later.

Maybe she really would be home early this time. William clung to that hope, his eyes wide as he looked around his bedroom, searching the corners, his breath catching in his throat as he thought about things hiding under his bed.

He was only eight and didn't like being left home alone, but his mom had been doing it almost for as long as he could remember. She said he was big enough to go to sleep on his own, and she didn't see any point in paying a sitter to watch TV and eat all the food in the refrigerator. He should have been used to it, but he wasn't. There was a nightlight in his room, but it didn't help. The overhead light would be much better for chasing away shadows, but William didn't dare turn it on because if he fell asleep and if his mother did happen to come home early and find it on, she'd be angry.

He tried, but after awhile William knew he wasn't going to sleep. It was almost eleven when he finally got out of bed. He did this sometimes when he was alone. Usually he just watched TV until he felt he was getting sleepy enough to go back to bed, but this time even the TV didn't soothe him.

Whimpering, William sat on the edge of the sofa and tried to convince himself that he didn't hear the sound coming from the back of the house.

It was a sneaky, sort of scratching noise that had originated on the back porch but now seemed to be coming from inside, and William found it impossible to ignore. It wasn't constant. There would be silence for long minutes, then just when he'd begun to think it was gone, he'd hear it again and his heart would begin pounding. He kept the volume on the TV turned down low. If there really was something working its way toward him, William wanted to be able to hear it. It wasn't going to sneak up on *him*.

The little boy brushed thick brown hair away from his forehead and pulled his knees up to his chest. He knew where his mother was. She'd told him she was going to Goldy's, her favorite bar. She'd even taken him there a few times on

Saturday afternoons, when it was okay for kids to be in there and they served sandwiches. William had thought it was an ugly place, with dark wood paneling on the walls and carpet that was dotted with cigarette burns, but when he'd told his mother this she'd laughed and said those things didn't matter much at night.

He tried to picture his mother at Goldy's, hoping to find comfort in a mental picture of her. This didn't work because it only reminded him that she wasn't here with him.

And he was hearing that sound again. It was closer this time, like something that was hoping he'd fall asleep on the couch and wouldn't see it coming.

Fat chance.

William slipped his thumb into his mouth, something he hadn't done since he was four.

Deana was in heaven. The man with her was an attorney from a neighboring town who'd stopped in for one beer on his way home, and he liked talking about himself. He'd told her he wasn't married, and as there was no pale circle around his ring finger she tended to believe him. Deana was going to take this slow and careful. There might be something more for her here than just a one-night stand to chase away the loneliness, and she'd dated a lawyer once before, a couple of years ago, so she knew how to talk to this man about his work and sound intelligent and informed. That made him happy, and he ordered more drinks while he looked at Deana with naked longing. She was pretty and still young; he was mousy-looking, going bald, and she wondered how he'd had the nerve to send a drink over to her in the first place. Probably he'd had more than the one beer before she'd walked in, and that had fueled his courage.

After midnight he made a show of looking at his watch. "Boy, I never meant to stay this late," he said. "I shouldn't drive home after drinking so much."

Deana nodded her understanding, but didn't say anything. If he was hinting for an invitation to her place, he could forget that idea. William was there and she hadn't even gotten around to telling him yet that she had a child. She'd work *that* little revelation in at a later date. She wasn't going to be too easy with this one. Like an expert fisherman, she knew how to give a little slack on the line before reeling a catch in, and this was one fish she wasn't going to let get away.

"No, I definitely wouldn't want to get picked up for drunk driving," he said, chuckling nervously.

Deana smiled at him.

He cleared his throat. "Is there a decent hotel in this town?"

Deana put a hand over his. "I think that would be a good idea. I'd hate to see anything happen to you."

* * *

William stood it for as long as he could, but finally he reached the point where he had to find his mother, no matter what the consequences. Because he didn't dare go into his bedroom for his clothes, he took some things from the hamper in the closet and put them on quickly, hands shaking as he pulled socks onto his feet.

When he left the house, William nearly burst through the front door to freedom. Outside was better, even though it was after midnight now and very dark. At least he was doing something other than just sitting and being afraid. He was going to go to the bar where he knew his mother was, and she'd come home with him when he told her about the noises in the house. He knew she would. She might be a little mad at him at first, but she'd get over it.

She had to.

William didn't have to walk far before he began to understand that it was going to take longer to reach Goldy's than he'd thought. The bar was on the other side of town from their house, and as he made his way through the dark streets this started to seem like a pretty bad idea after all. He also began to rethink his mother reaction to the sight of him. He started walking slower, unsure now as to what he should do.

When the car pulled up alongside him, William looked at the friendly face at the open window. The driver scolded him in a way that didn't place blame.

"Son, what are you doing outside at this hour?"

The fear he'd experienced in the house was too distant now to be real. William shrugged until his shoulders nearly reached his ears. "My mom's at Goldy's. That's where I was going, but I think I changed my mind. I'm gonna be in trouble."

"No, you're not. Hop in and I'll take you home. No one has to know a thing."

Gratefully, William ran around to the other side of the car and got in. "Really, you won't tell?"

"Not a word. I promise."

Eighteen

"Lunch is ready, Coach," Tess called in an over-bright voice. She carried the tray into the bedroom and set it down on the portable table beside the bed.

Coach Coddington was in his wheelchair by the window, exactly where Tess had left him a few minutes earlier when she'd gone to the kitchen to prepare his tray. He was looking out the window, but she had the feeling he wasn't as indifferent to her as he pretended. She'd stopped bringing a purse with her when she came here because, although she'd never been able to catch him in the act, she knew he'd been in it more than once. He was sly, and sometimes he almost seemed to be mocking her.

"Your mother made noodle soup for you," she told him. "It smells real good. She said you didn't eat much breakfast this morning, so you should be pretty hungry by now."

Tess walked to the wheelchair and stood beside it for a minute. This was Coach's view most of the day, this window that faced the street in front of the house. A car went by, and Tess quickly looked at the man.

His eyes followed the car as it zipped past.

For the next half hour Tess fed Coach his soup. It was a slow process, and while she fed him, Tess talked. It made the time go faster, for herself and, she hoped, for him. She experimented by changing the subject often, and soon realized that when she talked about herself or her family, Coach seemed to lean forward in his chair.

"And I know Dad is trying to make up," Tess said, working some of the wide, flat noodles onto the spoon. "But he was mean to Mom that last year or so, and I can't help but think about that sometimes. I even saw him with his girlfriend once. No one knows this, but it was about three months before Mom told Joely and me that she and Dad were splitting up. It was a Saturday, and I'd taken the bus to the mall with a couple of friends. We hung around the mall most of the day, and ran into some boys we knew. One of them had a car and he told us he'd give us a ride home, so we went out to the parking lot, and that's when I saw Dad . . . he was sitting in the front seat of a car I didn't know, practically necking with some blonde. Greta. I didn't know who she was at the time, but I found out later." Tess sighed, her expression distant. "He didn't see me, and I never said anything to anyone about it, but I didn't talk to him for about a week. He knew something was wrong. Oh yeah, he a tried a couple of times to ask me, but finally he stopped trying and sort of avoided me for a while. Maybe he figured out that he was better off not pressing me."

Pausing for a moment, Tess looked out the window. "I should probably stop thinking about that time," she said. "It's in the past, and it's not like I don't have plenty of new stuff to worry about. My sister, Joely, is an example that springs to mind. There's something going on in her head lately, but I don't know if it's just normal kid stuff that she'll work through on her own if she's left alone—or if it really is serious and I should tell someone about it before she gets herself hurt." She picked up the spoon and continued feeding Coach. "One thing I know—I shouldn't have let her talk me into going to that old school building with her. That only encourages her fantasies."

Tess looked down and saw that the bowl was nearly empty.

"Hey, you did really good," she said. She picked the cloth napkin up from the tray and gently wiped Coach's chin. "I'm going to go throw a load of laundry in the washer. Do you want to listen to some music while I'm gone?"

There was a decent stereo system in the bedroom, and Tess wheeled Coach over to it and selected a cassette tape of classical music for him. She didn't know if he really liked classica music, but since he had a large selection of the stuff she figured it was a safe bet he did. When the music started she wheeled him back to his window and said, "Mozart will keep you company till I get back. I won't be long."

But, because the laundry hadn't been presorted this time, the job took longer than usual, and Tess didn't get back to the bedroom as quickly as she'd expected. An apology was on her lips as she walked through the doorway, but the words died before they'd been fully formed. Tess stopped to stare into the room.

The music playing on the stereo was not that which she'd put in. The Mozart tape had been removed, and Handel's *Water Music* now flowed from the twin speakers. Coach, in his wheelchair, was beside the stereo. He'd moved himself from the window, around his bed, and to the far side of the big bedroom. And he must've changed the tape himself because Mrs. Coddington was not in the house.

"Guess the other tape ran out while I was gone," Tess said, forcing down the hint of unease that tickled her stomach.

He didn't answer, but a small smile played at the corners of his lips. It was that smile more than anything that bothered her. That and the gleam in his eyes. She kept well out of his reach as she moved about the room. Tess soon found an excuse to leave the bedroom again, and didn't return until she began to feel guilty. She'd never seen Coach move by himself in all the weeks she'd been caring for him, but obviously he was more mobile than he liked to let on. Why keep it a secret? The idea that he wasn't entirely helpless unnerved her, but she didn't entirely understand why it should bother her so much. She'd certainly never wish paralysis on anyone.

She just didn't like this feeling that she was being toyed with.

Looking for something to distract herself from such thoughts, Tess took the tape out of the stereo and turned on the radio. The afternoon news was being broadcast, and that was when Tess learned that a little boy was missing.

Nineteen

Libby was at the office when she heard the same news. Another child was gone. A mere two hours later, word arrived that the battered body of little William Overby had been found, and the town went crazy.

Libby left her desk and walked back to Tim's office, where she pushed open the door without knocking. Helen Crandall was standing in the middle of the room, a crumpled handkerchief pressed to her face. Tim stood beside her; he was patting her shoulder, and he looked up when Libby came into the room.

Helen glared at Libby, but straightened her spine and stalked out of the room without a word.

"I didn't mean to interrupt," Libby said helplessly.

"Don't worry about it," Tim said. He leaned back against his desk and rubbed his hands over his face. He appeared exhausted, and for the first time since Libby'd known him, looked his age. "Helen takes things hard, but in this case maybe she's justified. You heard that the little boy was found dead—"

"Just now," Libby said. "I can't believe this is happening, here of all places." She stepped closer to Tim, and he reached out and took her hand.

"This really hit Helen," he explained. "She lives not far from the Overbys, she's watched that child grow up, playing in his yard and riding his bike up and down the street."

"It's awful—but why does she treat *me* like I'm dirt on the bottom of her shoes?" Libby hadn't meant to blurt this out. She'd come into Tim's office seeking comfort against the horror of another death, but Helen had given her a look of such withering hatred that she couldn't help but react to it.

"That's not your fault," Tim said. Still holding Libby's hand, he pulled her closer, so that they were standing only inches apart. "When I took over the practice last year, I think Helen pictured us as becoming a team—you know, the doctor and his wife as nurse, running the office together. She came on strong when I first got here. I tried to be tactful about turning down her invitations and keeping a professional distance. Whenever I had the chance I'd work it into the conversation about how it's a bad idea for colleagues to become personally involved—she got the hint and backed off, but I don't think she'd really given up on the idea. Then you came to work here, and, being an intelligent woman with eyes in her head, she saw how I was beginning to feel about you."

Libby eased her hand free, gently, so as not to hurt his feelings. She couldn't think about this right now. There was too much going on, and she felt pulled in several different directions. "Tim, that's not why I came in here," she said. "I just needed to . . . now that another child has . . ." She looked up at him and felt her control crumbling into so much dust around her feet. "I don't know if I'll be able to stay here in Cielo, not with—"

Then, somehow, she was in his arms, and Tim was holding her to his chest. He stroked her hair and made soothing sounds, letting Libby cry until there was nothing left in her anymore. There was nothing remotely sexual in their contact. Libby clung to him, eyes squeezed tightly shut, grateful for the warmth of his embrace and the calm way he let her ride out the storm.

When she felt herself capable of rational thought again, Libby blew her nose on the clean tissue he'd somehow slipped into her hand, and looked up at him in embarrassment. He was so kind.

"The office—" she said.

"Don't worry about that. I'm sure Helen has everything under control out there, and is probably enjoying every minute of it."

Libby sniffled one last time into the tissue and looked up at him questioningly.

"That way she can prove how valuable she is," he explained with a smile, "and how unnecessary *you* are."

"I feel that way."

He laid his palm lightly against her hair. "Don't even think it. You're worth a dozen Helens to me." He released her and stepped away from the desk. "You stay in here as long as you need to, then wash your face and go home to your daughters. You're a good mother, Libby; I'm sure you want to be with them."

"Yes." She pushed her hair back behind her shoulders, and took a deep breath. She did want to get home, and she regretted now the time she'd wasted on a self-indulgent crying jag.

To her surprise, the outer office was empty. It was already nearly the end of the working day, and apparently Helen had taken it upon herself to send home those few patients who'd been waiting. Libby couldn't find it in herself to be annoyed at this. She was only glad the way had been cleared for her to leave.

Brandon was waiting outside the office door, on the sidewalk, when Libby left the building a few minutes later. Even though Tim was walking beside her when she spotted him, she felt such a sense of relief at the sight of her ex-husband that she forgot everything else and rushed to his side.

"Have you seen the girls?" she asked, her hand

on his arm. "This is so awful. Why did we come here?"

Brandon looked over the top of Libby's head at Tim. The doctor stared back at him.

Libby caught the exchange of looks, and regretted having temporarily forgotten Tim. Stammering and embarrassed, she introduced the two men, noting the stiffness in the way Tim nodded his head.

Then Brandon, speaking to Libby as though the doctor had conveniently vanished, said, "I've been with Joely most of the afternoon, and I picked up Tess at the Coddingtons' about an hour ago. They're both at the house now. If you don't mind, I'll follow you there and stick around for a while."

"Of course you're welcome," Libby said. "Stay for supper." What else could she say? Brandon was being helpful, she wasn't going to turn him away. Her eyes slid sideways to Tim, then she asked Brandon to meet her at the house in a few minutes.

He seemed reluctant to leave, but finally shrugged and said something about picking up milk on the way home—Joely had mentioned being out.

As soon as he was out of sight, Tim said, "Home."

Libby fished for her car keys. "What?"

"He said he'd pick up milk on his way home. Not on his way to your house."

"Did he? I didn't notice."

"He seems to have moved right back in."

"You're making too much out of an innocent remark," Libby said. How could she explain to him that Brandon was like a comfortable pair of old shoes, soothing in their familiarity even after she'd outgrown them? He was here and she was grateful, because in a new town and a new house, with insanity spreading almost daily around them, he was as solid and acceptable as a beacon in the night.

It was too difficult to put into words, but by the time they'd reached the cars Tim had replaced his frown of disapproval with a tender smile. "Call me later if you want," he said as she unlocked her car door. "It doesn't matter how late. I keep odd hours anyway, always up half the night working on that old house."

"Maybe I will," Libby said, relieved that the confrontation she'd dreaded had been avoided.

At the house a few minutes later she found Brandon already there with the girls. Tess had started supper, and Joely sat at the kitchen table drinking from a freshly poured glass of milk.

The TV stayed off because none of them wanted to be reminded of the latest bad news, but a comfortable routine had been established almost while her back had been turned. While Libby changed out of her work clothes, Brandon set the table. The girls helped him like they never willingly helped Libby, and she didn't have the energy to resent it.

After she'd taken a few minutes in the bathroom to wash her face and brush her hair, Libby started making a salad to go with their supper. She grated the carrots, and listened as Tess talked about Coach moving around in his room on his own. Brandon had an apron around his waist and was turning hamburger patties in the frying pan. He looked at Tess every few minutes to convey his interest.

Joely, seeking some attention herself, challenged Tess's story, saying Coach couldn't do anything for himself, but Tess stuck firm to her claim.

Libby was tossing the salad when the phone rang. It was Francine, and she immediately began babbling about the one subject Libby didn't want to hear about just yet.

"I've met that kid's mother a few times, and she's no prize," Francine said, righteous indignation in her voice. "Poor thing, I think he was pretty neglected most of the time. Deana Overby came from money, but her family pretty much gave up on her in the past few years. She never was married. They didn't hold that against her— not many would these days—but she was always hanging out with the wrong type, picking up men and sleeping around in general. I think her parents made a half-hearted effort to get the little boy away from her a few years ago, but gave up when they found out how difficult that sort of thing really is."

"I can't talk about this right now," Libby said, looking across the room to see the girls standing close to their father. "Brandon is here and supper is almost ready."

There was a meaningful pause, then Francine said, "I think you might be making a mistake."

Libby lowered her voice. "He's just as concerned about what's going on as I am, and the girls are delighted he's sticking around."

"Will they be as delighted when he's still there for breakfast?"

"He won't be."

"Maybe not this time, but you're headed in that direction."

"No, I'm not."

"Then I'll bet *he* is. Tell me if I'm right—he's being attentive and considerate, flexing his muscles, making everyone feel warm and safe in his manly presence." Francine couldn't conceal her scorn.

"We'll discuss this another time," Libby said firmly, and hung up the phone.

"Who was that, Mom?" Joely asked.

"Francine."

Brandon cocked an eyebrow.

"Don't start," Libby warned him. There was no love lost between her friend and her ex-husband.

He put his hands up in a gesture of innocence. "I didn't say a thing."

"No, but I can read your mind."

The girls both giggled, and Libby realized that, for the time being, hostilities had been set aside and they were acting very much like a family unit again.

Twenty

With two children murdered in such a short time, Cielo became the focus of wide attention. The local news media descended, as well as state investigators and the FBI. The town was crawling with strangers, and most parents found this not a source of concern, but comforting. Surely no harm could come to any more children with so many extra law enforcement officials on the scene.

Even Libby was gratified to hear that a team of FBI agents had taken up residence at the police station and were using all the sophisticated computer equipment available to them to compare these recent cases with similar child deaths throughout the state and even the country. She found herself scanning the faces of people she passed casually on her way out of the grocery store or while picking up supplies for the office, trying to guess which ones were agents and which were merely reporters covering a hot story.

She wasn't very good at it, she found. When a man politely stopped her as she loaded a bag of groceries into the back of her car and asked if he might ask her a few questions, she looked at his conservative suit and serious expression and assumed he was the law.

"Yes, of course," she said as she closed the car door.

He pulled a notebook from the inside pocket of his suit and flipped it open importantly. He was younger than she would've expected, late twenties at the most, but he seemed to know what he was doing.

"You live here in Cielo?" he asked, pen poised over paper.

Libby told him that she did, then further accommodated him by supplying her name, place of employment, and marital status. He scribbled furiously, taking down everything she told him.

Then he asked, "How do you feel about the safety of your family? Are you doing anything different since this started, to keep your own home from being violated?"

Libby frowned at him. "What kind of question is that?" she asked.

He waited for her answer, his face carefully arranged in an expression of concern; but beneath that, Libby detected sharklike eagerness, and she became suspicious.

"Are you with the FBI or something?" she asked.

Now it was his turn to be surprised. "I never said that."

"You acted like—"

"No, I never said anything about being FBI, lady. I just asked if you'd mind talking to me for a minute."

"You asked if I'd answer some questions."

"Sure, but I never misrepresented myself to you. I'm covering this story and I need as much local opinion as I can get. People want to hear how this has affected someone just like you—a mother who wonders if one of her children could be next—"

"You're a *reporter*?" Libby turned and reached for her door handle. "I don't want to talk to you."

"That's okay, I probably have enough anyway." He closed his notebook and tucked it away.

Libby spun around and took a step toward him. He looked startled, but stood his ground. She raised a finger to him, then lowered it again when she saw that her hand was trembling. "Look," she said. "I didn't know who you were— and you aren't going to use anything I told you in any newspaper."

"What's the problem? I work for a very respectable publication. Everything will be handled tastefully, I assure you."

"No. You won't print my name, or anything about my family. Do you really think I want that information out there, for anyone to read? You could be making us a target."

"That's very unlikely—"

"Probably," she agreed. "But this is not something I'm inclined to take any chances on."

She opened the car door, furious with herself for letting this happen. She didn't even blame the young man who stood so uncertainly behind her. He was trying to do his job. She should have done hers, and found out exactly who he was before she'd opened her big mouth.

He tried to say something more to her, but Libby drove away without listening.

At home later, she told Brandon and the girls about the incident.

"Are we going to be in the papers?" Joely asked.

"We'd better not." Libby opened a cupboard and began to put away cans of soup, cereal, and a box of Brandon's favorite cookies.

"But why not?" Joely asked. She took a gallon of orange juice from the sack and carried it to the refrigerator.

Tess gave her sister a scornful look. "Because, genius, if there's a psycho killer still in town he might come after *us* next, if our address is in the newspaper."

"Don't say that," Libby snapped.

"But it's true."

"Nothing about us is going to be in print. I told him that, as soon as I found out who he was." Libby slammed the cupboard door so hard that both girls jumped.

Brandon came and put his arm around Libby's shoulder. "It wasn't your fault," he said.

Both girls stood absolutely still and watched their parents. Libby made no move away from Brandon. Instead, she rested her head on his shoulder and sighed.

Tess nudged Joely with her elbow.

Joely opened her mouth. "Dad, are you—"

Tess jabbed her sharply in the ribs.

"Ow!" Joely cried, and moved out of her sister's reach. "What'd you do that for?"

Libby lifted her head and looked at them. "Girls, please—I don't have it in me to listen to this tonight."

"It was an accident," Tess said. "Sorry, Joely. Come on into the living room with me, I'll show you the new sales catalogue that came in the mail. We've gotta start looking at school clothes."

"Don't turn the TV on," Libby called out as the girls left the kitchen.

"We won't," Tess promised.

In the other room, Joely put her hands on her hips and confronted her sister. "What was that about?" she demanded. "You just about killed me with your sharp old elbow."

"Because you were going to say something stupid."

"How do you know?"

"Because you *always* say something stupid."

"But didn't you notice the way they were together? It was almost like it used to be, before they started fighting."

223

"Of course I noticed, and I didn't want you to ruin it." Tess pushed Joely toward the sofa and shoved a thick catalogue into her hands. "Here, look at this. That way if they come in here they won't know we were talking about them."

Joely defiantly tossed the catalogue aside. "You're always so bossy," she said. "I'm sorry I even took you with me the other day, to the old school. I should've—"

Tess leaned down so that her face was only inches from her sister's. "Don't you bring that subject up again," she warned, her voice a low hiss. "I should never have let you talk me into going there. It was a dumb mistake on my part. I thought I was humoring you, but I'm tired now of your stories and your fantasies. And *you* won't be going there ever again, either. If I suspect you're even *thinking* about it I'll blow the whistle on you so fast you won't know what happened."

The girls glared at each other.

"You can't stop me from doing what I want," Joely sneered.

"Oh, yes I can."

In the kitchen, Libby was wondering what was happening to her life. Brandon kept his arm around her, and she had no desire to move away from his familiar warmth. She could hear the girls talking in the other room. What did they think of their father's presence in the house? They had to be aware of the shift in her feelings for Brandon—they weren't blind, and the questions would surely soon begin. When they did, Libby wasn't sure how she was going to answer them.

"I missed those girls a lot more than I expected to," Brandon said softly, his breath warm on her hair.

Libby brought her hand up and rested it on his shirt. She played with a button. "They've missed you, too," she admitted. "This whole thing has been hard on them . . . but they're adjusting."

"Are they?"

"Yes. Joely's been making friends. Tess has kept busy with her work for Mrs. Coddington, but I'm sure she'll make friends too, when school starts."

"Do they ever talk about me?" he asked.

"Sometimes."

"Good or bad?"

Libby smiled. "A little of both."

But this wasn't really what she wanted to be talking to Brandon about. The girls were a bond between them that could never be broken, but for the moment Libby was more concerned with her own feelings, and whether Brandon shared her confusion. He didn't seem confused. He was stroking her hair, his hands as gentle as she remembered, and when he put his fingers beneath her chin and lifted her face, she was ready for the kiss she knew was coming. His lips on her were a welcome companion, and she hummed low in her throat with pleasure.

Brandon pulled back and smiled down at her. "I've missed that," he whispered.

"Missed what?"

"That little sound you make when you're feeling good. It's uniquely you, Libby, and I've heard it in my dreams."

"I don't make any sound," she protested.

"Yes, you do."

She pulled back, but not far enough so that she left the circle of his arms, and looked up at him. "What are we doing?" she asked. "Tess and Joely are only a few feet away, if they walked in now they'd get the wrong idea."

"This isn't anything they haven't seen before." He bent down as though to kiss her again.

But this time Libby did pull completely away and stepped back out of his reach. It was happening too fast. Her life was in turmoil, not only because of Brandon, but also because of Tim and the nightmare of what was going on in this little town she'd moved to so recently. She wasn't thinking clearly enough to let herself get caught up in something she might regret later. It would be too easy to get caught up in Brandon's charms again, but if she did that and it fell apart again later, her daughters would be hurt the most by it.

They were all just beginning to heal. Libby couldn't recklessly open those old wounds again.

"What's wrong?" he asked.

"I need to think."

"Why? Don't analyze everything to death, Libby—for once, just go with your feelings."

"Like you do?" she asked.

"Yeah, sometimes."

"Well, that pretty much sums up what brought about the end of our marriage, doesn't it?" Libby ran her hands through her hair and moved farther away from him, but not before she saw the pain her words, however truthful, caused him.

He stood in the middle of the kitchen, hands limp at his sides, and didn't try to defend himself. "Okay," he said simply. "Maybe I should go. I just thought—"

"No, don't go."

Brandon threw his arms out in frustration. "I don't know what it is you want from me, Libby."

She inhaled deeply. "Stay," she said, "because the girls are expecting you to and I don't want to have to tell them you're gone. As for anything else—this isn't the right time."

He nodded, and without another word set about helping her put away the last of the groceries. For the rest of the evening he played quiet card games with the girls, talked about the upcoming school year with Tess, and in general behaved himself to such an extent that Libby had to consider the possibility that he truly regretted the bad blood that had existed between them for the past year.

Late in the evening, when the girls were getting ready for bed, the subject of little William Overby was finally brought up. Tess stepped into this territory cautiously, needing some reassurance from her parents, but unsure as to whether or not anyone was going to be willing to talk about it.

Libby was tempted to put Tess off. It would have been so easy, because she didn't particularly want to think about it, but a look from Brandon silenced her. With Joely curled up on his lap, he invited both girls to ask questions.

Tess wanted to know if the same person who'd killed Andrea Polzer had also murdered William Overby, and if so did this mean there was a serial killer nearby. Joely was more concerned with the dead children's families, and what this would mean to them.

Brandon didn't always have an answer to their questions, but he tried, and Tess and Joely both seemed to accept it when he had to honestly admit that he didn't know something.

At one point Joely said, "Maybe those kids' parents wouldn't feel so bad if they knew for sure that there was a heaven, or at least someplace where people go after they die, where they're still themselves."

"What do you mean?" Brandon asked.

"Well, isn't a ghost just a person's soul? What if—"

Tess cut in. "Nothing's going to make those parents feel better for a long time. I knew a girl in eighth grade who died of leukemia. That was bad, but at least her family had some time to prepare for it."

The conversation went in that direction for a while longer as Libby watched silently from the sidelines. Despite his faults, Brandon always had been good at communicating with his daughters. He didn't avoid unpleasant subjects, as she knew she tended to. Seeing them together like this gave her a renewed sense of family that she was reluctant to shake off.

A part of her, Libby admitted, if only to herself, still felt the old longing.

Twenty-one

He could feel himself losing control. It had never happened this way before, so soon on the heels of the last time, and it worried him to think that this might become a trend, because caution was what kept him safe. He'd always prided himself on being smarter than those who sought to bring him down.

The little girl had released him . . . or so he'd thought. He'd found her, and she'd been perfect, just what he'd needed to remind him of who was in charge.

He'd even enjoyed stepping back and watching the way the ants had begun to scurry around, so brainless in their excitement, bumping into each other in panic. This part had been amusing, like a show put on for his entertainment.

But then, much too soon, the feeling of strength these episodes brought to him began to fade, and he'd been left confused and disappointed.

He hadn't gone out looking for another child, but had come across the little boy walking alone at night almost by accident. That had seemed a sign—it was so perfect, the boy must have been put there especially for him.

And now, incredibly, he was feeling this need again to seek out the weak and the undeserving. Never before had he gone out so often in such a short space of time. There had even been times in the past when he'd gone years without thinking about it. Those had been times of peace, when he'd been able to live his life without the gnawing fear that, sooner or later, he might make a mistake.

There was too much going on in his head.

And his gut.

He was going to have to go out again or he'd become diminished, so small that he would become powerless.

He began to watch, waiting for the right time, the perfect victim . . .

Twenty-two

Tess was forced again to take Joely with her to the Coddingtons'. Their Grandmother Gregory wasn't feeling well and Brandon was going to stay with her for most of the day. He'd called and asked Tess to keep Joely with her, and she'd had no choice but to comply.

Joely had been surprisingly uncomplaining about the arrangement, but Tess still had a few things to say to her.

"Mrs. Coddington is going to be home today," she said as they parked their bikes in front of the house. "So stay close to me all the time because she won't like it if you wander around touching her stuff. She's very picky."

"What if she doesn't want me here at all?" Joely asked hopefully.

"That's not a problem. I called her while you were taking your bath and told her I'd be bringing you. She understands how things are right now. I think she figured out that if I couldn't bring you I'd have to stay home, and she wouldn't want to lose her slave for a day."

Inside the house Mrs. Coddington gave Tess a list of things to do. She was a formidable woman, but when she looked at Joely her features softened a bit and became almost kind.

"Having you young girls here reminds me of how much I miss working," she said. Her eyes behind her glasses grew wistful. "I had your mother's job, you know. I worked for Doctor Ives for many years, until he decided to retire, and then for Dr. Kyle when he took over. The office was always full of children, and I knew every one of them by name."

Tess didn't know how to respond. She'd never known Mrs. Coddington to be so talkative, and to realize she didn't actually dislike kids was almost too surprising to believe.

Mrs. Coddington didn't seem to notice Tess's silence. "And when Coach was healthy and working at the school," she continued, "he was always bringing the kids around for impromptu softball games and get-togethers. There used to be young families with children all up and down this street. It's an older neighborhood now."

"Yes, ma'am," Tess said.

Mrs. Coddington shook herself out of her reverie. "Well, we've wasted enough time for one day," she said briskly. "Tess, I cleaned out some closets last night and have some boxes that will be going to Goodwill. They're in the hallway. They're fairly heavy, and I'd like them moved into the garage for now. Perhaps your sister can help you with that task."

The brief softness was gone. She was all business again, and Tess and Joely hurried to their work, eager to get away.

"Hoo, boy," Joely said as she shifted the boxes to find the lightest one. "Do you have to listen to stuff like that every day? It was kind of spooky, the way she was looking at me."

Tess picked up a box that felt like it was filled with books. With Joely following close behind, she headed for the garage. "That's probably the most I've ever heard her say at one time," she said. "I don't know—maybe she's just lonely and she finally had to get some of it out. I never thought about it before, but it can't be too pleasant living in a house with a son you know will never get better. Can you get that door?"

Joely balanced her box on one hip and opened the door that led from the house into the attached garage. She felt around until she found the light switch on the wall, then flicked it up.

"Hey, there's two cars in here," she said.

"Yeah, I know. Let's put these down against that wall over there."

"Why does she have two cars?"

Tess arranged first her box, then Joely's, beside a metal shelf holding half-used cans of paint. "The blue Cadillac is Mrs. Coddington's," she explained. "It's the one she uses all the time. The tan car used to be Coach's, but he hasn't driven in years so it's just sitting here.

234

She told me once she'll probably sell it someday, but so far she hasn't been able to bring herself to do it."

"It's not even dusty," Joely observed. "Does she clean it off?"

"I suppose she must."

"Maybe she'd sell it to you."

Tess wrinkled her nose. "No, thanks. When I get a car it won't be some ugly old four-door thing."

They went back into the house and got the last of the boxes, then began to prepare Coach's lunch tray. Joely watched carefully, did whatever Tess asked her to, and tried to keep out of the way as much as possible. A couple of times she tried to wander off, but Tess always called her back before she'd gone more than a few feet.

Joely kept her eyes open, waiting for the opportunity she knew would come sooner or later.

Her chance came while Tess was feeding Coach his lunch, a mixture of noodles with vegetables mixed in. Joely didn't watch this part too closely. She found it too sad, to see an adult as helpless as a baby.

Then Tess spilled some of the noodles, and turned to Joely. "I forgot to bring a napkin," she said. "Will you go to the kitchen and get one for me?"

"Sure." Joely jumped up, so eager that she almost forgot to be cautious.

She left the bedroom, forcing herself to walk slowly. She didn't want to arouse Tess's suspicions at this point. Instead of going to the kitchen, she tiptoed through the house to the front door, uncertain as to where Mrs. Coddington was and hoping the old woman wouldn't appear and demand to know what she was doing. It didn't happen. Joely made it to the front door, and was out of the house without anyone noticing. There she hopped on her bike and, her legs pumping as hard as they could, headed in the direction of the old school building.

Tess waited almost five minutes before she called out to Joely to hurry it up with that napkin. When she received no reply, she set the tray aside and got to her feet.

"I'll be right back, Coach," she said.

It took her a few more minutes of searching before it dawned on Tess that Joely was not in the house. Mrs. Coddington was writing letters at her desk in her small library. She looked up with a frown of disapproval when Tess appeared in the doorway, and told her that, no, she had no idea where the child was.

Tess ran to the front door then, and flung it open even though she knew it was too late. Joely was long gone.

"When I get my hands on her she's going to regret this *big* time," Tess said to no one in particular.

Joely reached the school and propped her bike up against the gnarled trunk of a tree, then made her way into the now-familiar building. She wished she'd had a flashlight, but there'd been no way to smuggle one out of the house without Tess catching on to her plan.

This was her third trip into the building, and she had no trouble finding her way to the furnace room this time. Getting back here had become almost an obsession for her since she'd brought Tess. She couldn't shake the feeling that there was something important here, something that she would see if she just looked around long enough.

Nothing had changed since her last visit. The broken desk still stood against the wall. There were some shelves and rusted metal chairs piled in a corner. There were even a few dusty pictures hanging on the walls, some tilted at odd angles, others with their protective glass broken, and Joely wondered why so much stuff had been left behind when the school had been closed.

Martin appeared so suddenly that Joely screamed and jumped nearly a foot in the air. He was just there, standing beside the desk as though waiting for her to notice.

"Jeez," she cried, placing her hand on her chest. "You scared the life out of me. Oh . . . sorry."

She peered at him through the gloom. "I don't know why I keep coming back here," she said. "I'm going to be in deep trouble when I get back to Tess. She might even tell Mom that

I ran off on her. But this place is . . . this is important for some reason, isn't it?"

Martin was looking at the desk. He didn't seem to be paying much attention to Joely, so she stepped closer in the hope that he'd remember she was here. She noticed then that he wasn't really looking at the desk, but instead had his gaze focused on the brick wall behind it. Martin lifted one hand and pointed to a spot about a foot up from the baseboard.

"What is it?" Joely asked. "It's just an old wall."

Trying to pinpoint the exact area that so interested Martin, she crouched down. Her nose was less than two feet from the wall when she realized the mortar around one of the bricks didn't look right. Sticking a finger into a crack between that brick and the one next to it, Joely felt something give.

She worked at it for almost five minutes before she was able to get the brick out of the wall. Finally, though, it came away, and Joely was able to see that there was empty space behind the wall.

She looked up at Martin, who stood helplessly nearby, watching. "I think I know what you want, but I don't like the idea much," she said.

There was something back there. Joely knew there had to be, because why else would he have directed her to the spot? Now she was supposed to put her hand into that black hole and feel around, but all she could think about was spiders and other creepy-crawlies and a scene from a movie she'd seen in the city last summer.

This was no time to chicken out. "Okay," she said, drawing courage from the sound of her own voice more than anything else. "Here goes." Her fingertips made it all the way into the opening before she pulled back. "I can't do it," she apologized.

Not ready yet to give up, Joely looked around on the floor until she found a thin stick about two feet long. Perfect. Using that, she poked around behind the brick wall, then she felt the stick bump something. She nudged the object carefully, feeling it give, gauging its approximate size. Finally, after much experimentation, she was able to snag whatever it was with the end of the stick and pull it closer to the opening. There she saw a piece of dull red cloth so dirty with age that it took her a moment to recognize it as a bandanna.

Joely took a corner of it with her fingers and pulled the bandanna out of the hole. She let it drop to the floor. The ends were tied together in a knot, and something was clearly inside. She poked it with her fingertip a couple of times before getting up the nerve to tug at the knot, but once she got started she worked on it until it loosed and the bandanna fell open.

The items she saw nestled in the folds of the fabric were so ordinary that Joely was caught by surprise. She'd expected something more exotic to be hidden in a secret place behind a wall, but all she saw here was an inexpensive-looking ring with a blue stone in the middle, one large flat button, a St. Christopher medal on a silver chain, and a pink plastic barrette with a few strands of red hair still clinging to it.

"Is this all?" she said, disappointed by these pathetic items.

Martin was right at her shoulder, closer than usual. He pointed to the objects, his expression sorrowful.

Joely picked up the barrette and held it in the palm of her hand. Martin ignored it. He continued to look at the other objects.

Putting the barrette down, Joely picked up the St. Christopher medal. The medal itself was about an inch in diameter, the chain long enough to slip easily over a person's head. As far as Joely knew, people didn't wear St. Christopher much anymore.

Knees aching from being crouched for so long, Joely pushed herself to a standing position. Martin stood with her, and one wavering finger pointed at the medal in Joely's hand.

"This is what you wanted me to find? Okay, but what does it mean? Why is this important to—wait a minute." Joely's breath caught in her throat. "Was this yours?"

Martin was disappearing. Before Joely could beg him to stay a little longer and try to explain this to her, he was gone, and she was left alone again in the room. But she'd seen something new before Martin had disappeared completely—

there'd been a brief glistening of something on his cheek that Joely was almost certain had been tears.

She was anxious now to get out of the building. Without thinking about what she was doing, Joely slipped the silver chain over her head. The medal rested against her heart. Then she picked up the bandanna with its remaining items, folded it back up, and put it in the back pocket of her shorts.

She wanted to show these things to Tess. It had to be Tess, because the few times she'd tried to call Maria lately, Maria had refused to come to the phone. Mrs. Rafael had tried to be kind and said something vague about Maria not feeling well, but Joely knew she'd scared the other girl off.

It didn't matter. At last she had something concrete to back up her story, and Joely couldn't wait to wave this proof in Tess's face.

Twenty-three

Libby still went to work, but she arrived late and was barely able to keep her thoughts on the scheduled appointments. Fortunately, there were few. People were canceling, rescheduling for a later date in the hopes that Cielo would work itself out of the dark night of fear that had taken over it.

Helen tried to act like nothing was out of the ordinary, but even she was having a difficult time ignoring the fact that she and Libby were stuck together in an office where, for long stretches of time, they had only each other for company.

Eventually, they had to start talking.

"People would rather stay home and watch the news than have a wart removed or a case of the sniffles treated," Helen said, pouring herself a cup of coffee. "If it's not absolutely vital, they figure it can wait."

"I don't blame them," Libby said. She was sitting at her desk, having just hung up the phone on yet another cancellation.

Helen was warming to the subject. Her dislike of Libby was not stronger than her desire to gossip. "I've been hearing talk," she said, "that these latest deaths might be related to the several that took place here twenty-five years ago."

"That seems too far-fetched," Libby protested.

"It's just a theory that's being given some consideration."

"But twenty-five years is too long, it can't have anything to do with what's happening now."

Tim appeared in the doorway, and both women stopped talking. He'd stopped at Libby's desk often during the day, but he always had something positive to say, either about one of his patients who was doing well, or the progress he was making in the refurbishing of his house. Libby welcomed these distractions because he seemed to be the only person in town who was capable of talking of something other than death.

But Libby also recognized that there was a situation that was going to have to be faced—Tim was becoming increasingly open in his feelings about her. He often touched her shoulder or her arm when he talked to her. There was nothing overtly sexual in the physical contact, it was merely a light touch during conversation when he was making a point; but that was about all it took, Libby knew, for people to notice a shift in their relationship and to begin talking.

It was almost a relief when he asked her to come into his office. This might be an opportunity for her to remind him of the need to be discreet.

"Did you see Raymon Bergin when he walked out of here today?" Tim asked as soon as they were alone. "He had a bounce in his step like a young man again. Seven months ago he was fifty pounds overweight and couldn't get up the stairs at his home without becoming winded. I told him to stop smoking and put him on a mild exercise program. He complained, but to his credit he's stuck to it and probably added an extra ten years to his life."

"He does look good," Libby agreed. "Of course, I didn't know him seven months ago."

"You wouldn't recognize him as the same man."

Tim stood in the middle of the room as though uncertain of his next move, but he kept talking. Libby nodded as he spoke about his patients, then she took a stool from near his filing cabinets and perched on it. When she sat, the skirt she'd worn rode up on her thighs. She tugged it down over her knees.

Tim glanced at her, then looked away quickly. "And, uh, I've decided to discontinue Karlyn Salo's prescription. I think she's abusing it."

"You may be right," Libby agreed.

Tim stopped and gave her a crooked smile. "You know I didn't invite you in here to talk about my work, don't you?"

"I suspected as much," Libby said. She found his awkwardness touching.

He approached, not stopping until he was standing less than a foot from her. "I didn't realize how out of touch I'd become until recently," Tim said in a low voice. His eyes searched her face. "For the past few years I've been so involved in my work that I didn't take the time for a personal life. Especially when I was in the city. It was a very competitive atmosphere there, I had to keep on my toes all the time to meet the demands made on me. I didn't mind, at the time I thought it was what I wanted. Then I came back here to Cielo, and began to realize what I'd been missing."

Now it was Libby's turn to look away. She'd known Tim was growing more bold in expressing himself, but she wondered if she was ready to hear what he obviously wanted to say. Brandon was too much in her thoughts—it was unfair to Tim to expect him to take a backseat to her ex-husband.

"I know your work is important to you," she said, hoping to keep him on a safer subject.

"That's just it—I'm finding that it *isn't* as all-important as I'd once thought. I'm ready for more."

"Tim—" Libby watched helplessly as he leaned closer to her.

Before she could try to get out of his reach, he took her in his arms and was kissing her with a passion Libby found astonishing. Staid, serious Dr. Kyle was revealing a hidden fire as he bent her back and probed her mouth with his tongue. Libby was limp in his embrace, too stunned to immediately react.

She hadn't been kissed in almost a year, and now suddenly men were coming out of the woodwork, ready to sweep her off her feet. To her surprise Libby's body began to respond despite the feeble attempt of her brain to caution her to slow down. Only when Tim's hand found its way to her thigh, under her skirt, did her sensibilities return. She pushed him away.

"Wait," she gasped. She hopped down from the stool, but then had to grab it because her legs didn't seem capable of supporting her.

Tim looked triumphant. "I knew this was going to be good," he said. "We have something special, Libby."

"This isn't really a good time," she said, still holding the stool.

"Why—you mean because we're here in my office? I know it's not the most romantic atmosphere, but we'll have plenty of time for that later."

"No," Libby said. She was feeling stronger. She straightened her shoulders and smoothed the front of her blouse. "I mean it's not a good time in my life for me to be getting involved. There's so much going on, and the divorce is still so fresh—I can't jump from one long-term relationship right into another."

A cloud passed over Tim's features. "Your ex-husband is in town," he said simply, as though this explained everything.

"That's part of it," Libby admitted. "But not all."

"He's not good for you. He hurt you badly once. People like that don't change, he'll do it again the first chance he gets."

"Tim, whatever happens, I have to keep in mind that Brandon will always be a part of my life because he's the father of my children. The marriage is over, but he's not going to go completely away—and I wouldn't want him to."

The doctor sighed. He put his hands in his pockets and looked down at his feet for a moment. "Yes, I understand that," he said in a very low voice. "Just be careful, Libby, please. You're very important to me, and I believe he's dangerous."

Back at the Coddingtons' house, Joely was faced with the dilemma of how to get inside again. She didn't want to just open the door and walk in, but neither did she want to ring the doorbell and wait for whoever might answer it.

The problem resolved itself when Tess flung open the front door before Joely had even stepped onto the porch.

"Get in here right now," Tess ordered. "You've been gone for almost an hour, and don't try to lie to me about where you went—you were at that old building, weren't you?"

Joely entered the house meekly. She was prepared to accept whatever harsh words Tess wanted to fling at her, because she was going to ask a huge favor as soon as her sister calmed down.

"Yes," Joely admitted. "I went there again, but only because it was important."

Tess had Joely by the arm and she dragged the younger girl down the hallway to the bedrooms. "Mrs. Coddington is still in her library. She doesn't know you ran out on me. You're lucky."

They reached Coach's bedroom. He was in his wheelchair by the window, but facing into the room instead of looking out. His eyes drifted past the girls indifferently.

Tess pushed Joely down into a chair. "Sit there and don't move. I'm supposed to change the sheets on the bed."

"I could help," Joely offered.

"I don't need your help."

Joely sniffed and tried to look pathetic.

"And don't even try that on me," Tess said, pointing a finger, "because it won't work."

She pulled the bedspread off and set it aside, then began to yank on the sheets. Anger made her hands clumsy. Tess struggled with one of the pillows, and when she got it loose from the pillowcase it landed on the floor at the foot of the bed.

Joely got up picked up the pillow for Tess. She held it out to her sister silently, a peace offering. Tess snatched it from her with an evil look.

Joely fingered the medallion at her chest. This was going to be tougher than she'd thought. Still standing, Joely realized she was only a couple of feet from Coach's wheelchair, and she looked at him with curiosity. He didn't look so unaware now. In fact, she could almost swear that he was looking right at her.

"Hi," Joely said softly.

Tess bundled the sheets and pillowcases together and deposited them outside the bedroom door. From the linen closet in the hallway she got a new set, and began to make up the bed again.

Joely edged closer to the man in the wheelchair. It really was sad, she thought, for someone to be so helpless. Unconsciously still touching the St. Christopher medal, Joely looked into Coach's eyes for any sign that there was a living human being in there.

The old man's hand snaked out so suddenly that Joely didn't see it coming until he'd clamped down on her wrist. His withered fingers dug into her skin, and he yanked her to him.

Joely shrieked. She tried to jerk free, but Coach held her with an iron grip. He was smiling at her, his teeth yellowish and crooked, his lips stretched thin as he grinned.

"Tess!" Joely screamed.

Tess was there, prying Coach's fingers back from Joely's wrist, trying to free the panic-stricken girl. Joely kept yanking backwards, and now the only sound she made was an animal-like whimpering.

As suddenly as it had started, it was over. Coach released Joely, and both girls fell back against the bed.

Joely was crying as Tess tried to comfort her. "What happened?" Tess asked, her arms around her sister. "Why did he do that?"

"I don't know," Joely sobbed. "All I did was say hi. I was j-just trying to be friendly. Why didn't you warn me to stay away from him?"

"Because I didn't know he'd do something like that. He's never done it before."

"I f-felt sorry for him." Joely hiccuped. "I was just going to t-talk to him a little bit . . . he didn't have to do that." Joely's sobs subsided, but she still gulped for air.

Tess got up from the bed. Coach was as impassive as ever, his face turned away from them now, the smile gone. It was as though none of it had happened.

"Just a minute," Tess said to Joely. She went to the bedroom doorway and listened. Then, apparently satisfied, she said, "I guess Mrs. Coddington didn't hear you screaming. She's clear on the other side of the house, and she has the library door closed."

"I want to go h-home," Joely whimpered.

"In a little bit. I have a couple of more things to do here."

"No, I want to go *now!*"

Tess began to make the bed up quickly. Joely had to get up for her to do this, but the little girl was careful to keep as far away from Coach as the room allowed.

"You must have done something to stir him up," Tess said as she tucked the fitted sheet in at the corners of the mattress.

"I didn't do a thing," Joely insisted. "He just . . . freaked."

Although she was trying to keep up a brave front, Tess, too, was shaken by the incident, and she hurried through the last of her chores. The sisters were quiet as they rode their bikes away from the house a half an hour later. Tess even agreed when Joely said she wanted to ride over to the doctor's office to see their mother.

"It's almost time for her to get off work," Joely said. "We can ask her to pick up a pizza for supper."

Tess shrugged, sensing an underlying need in the request. "I guess it can't hurt anything. As long as we're together I don't think she'll mind. Remember that—*together.* That means no more disappearing acts."

"You have my guarantee," Joely vowed.

"Yeah, and I know how much that's worth."

They turned their bikes in the direction of downtown. Joely had to stop and wait once when the chain came loose on Tess's bike, but it was quickly fixed and they were at Dr. Kyle's office within minutes, both sweaty from the ride. Tess's hair was limp and stringy, and she almost longed

251

for the air-conditioned comfort of the Coddington house. Almost.

Joely, less bothered by the heat, hopped down from her bike and hurried into the office in search of her mother. It had been a weird day, and she longed for the consolation of Libby's solid presence.

But Libby was already gone. Dr. Kyle himself came out into the waiting room to talk to them.

"She left a few minutes ago with your father," he told the girls. "He came by and said he wanted to talk to her. I think I heard him say something about taking her out to eat."

Tess had come in behind Joely. "Do you know where they were going?" she asked.

Tim shook his head. He looked so miserable that the sisters exchanged looks, then Tess thanked him and pulled Joely with her to the front door. Outside, on the sidewalk, they got back on their bikes.

"Well, that didn't turn out like we expected," Tess said.

"Why do you suppose Dad took Mom out without us?" Joely asked.

"Probably because they wanted to be alone."

"Without *us*?"

"Especially without us." Tess nudged the kickstand with her heel. "Let's go home, that's where Mom's going to expect us to be."

Twenty-four

Libby spoke into the wall phone, one hand over her ear to block out the noise from the restaurant behind her. "Thanks, Francine," she said. "We won't be late, I promise . . . yes, I'll tell you all about it later."

She hung up and walked back through the restaurant to where Brandon was seated, waiting for her.

"Did you get ahold of her?" he asked as soon as she sat down.

Libby nodded. "Francine said she'll go right over to the house and stay with the girls until I get home."

"Did you tell her *why* you wanted her to do that?"

"All I told her was that you and I needed some time alone together to talk." Libby picked up her wine glass and drained the last of the pale liquid. It was only her first glass, but she already felt lightheaded.

"I'll bet that thrilled her," Brandon said. "Francine's not my biggest fan."

"Probably because I confided in her during the breakup."

"Great—aren't there any secrets anymore?"

Libby touched her fingertip to the edge of the empty glass. "Very few, I'm afraid. I was hurt, and I needed someone to talk to."

"But why did you have to talk to that big—" Brandon bit off the last words with an effort. "I don't want us to argue," he said. He reached across the table and caressed the back of her hand. "When I came back here to Cielo, Libby, I told myself it was to see the girls. And it was . . . but that wasn't all there was to it. As soon as I saw you again, I realized how much I'd missed you these past months."

Libby kept her hand on the table, but turned it so it was palm up. Brandon immediately took her hand in his and held it. She didn't look at him, but rather concentrated on the strange sight of their joined hands.

"Missing someone doesn't mean much," she said softly. "We were together for a long time, it's natural that it'll also take a long time to get used to not being together."

"I don't think that's what I want anymore," Brandon whispered.

Libby lifted her eyes to his. "Are you expecting me to fall into your arms just like that? You decide you want me back, and I'm supposed to be so grateful that I forget Greta and all the others?"

"There weren't that many," he protested.

"One is too much."

"You're right." Brandon felt a tug as Libby tried to reclaim her hand, but he held onto it. "I'm asking for your forgiveness."

"I need another glass of wine."

Brandon blew out a little puff of air, but he released her hand and signaled to a passing waiter. They hadn't ordered their meal yet, and when the waiter came back he had pad in hand and was ready to write down their requests.

Libby had no appetite and couldn't pretend. Brandon had appeared at the office shortly before five, and had come right up to her window to talk to her. Tim hadn't been far away, and the tension between the two men had been thick and violent—without saying a word to each other they'd somehow managed to convey a rivalry as intense as between two stags butting antlers in the forest. Libby had felt suffocated by it, and also resentful. She wasn't a prize to be fought over.

Nor had Brandon been subtle when he'd asked her to have supper with him after work—without the girls. She'd tried to protest, giving the obvious excuse of not wanting the girls to be alone, but he'd been so insistent that she'd finally agreed in the hope that it would get him out of the office. But, instead of leaving, he'd planted himself on the long plastic sofa in the waiting area and flipped through a magazine while she tended to the last of her duties for the day.

With Brandon so near, Tim hadn't been able to say much to her. He did, however, manage to touch her cheek lightly as she was getting her purse, and whisper, "Don't go."

"I have to," Libby had whispered back.

She'd left with Brandon, very much aware of the hurt she'd caused Tim.

Now, in the restaurant with Brandon, she knew this situation was going to have to be resolved soon. She couldn't continue to go on stringing both men along. If her own indecision meant she'd have to distance herself from both of them, then that's what she'd do, but that was better than giving them false hope for something that might not happen.

"Don't have too much of that wine," Brandon said after the waiter had brought them each a fresh drink. "It makes you goofy."

Libby smiled, but she barely sipped the drink. He had a point.

He said, "You have a beautiful smile."

"It's not that wine makes me goofy," she said. "I just tend to lose my inhibitions."

"Why did you order it?"

"I'm not sure," she admitted.

He looked like he wanted to touch her again, but Libby sat back in her seat, out of his reach. And she kept her hands on her lap. When he touched her, she tended to forget her promises to herself.

"Remember the time," Brandon said, "about . . . oh, ten years ago, when we were playing table tennis at the MacAllisters' Fourth of July party? You were drinking wine that night."

"I remember," Libby said.

"You got real competitive about that game. You insisted you could beat me two games out of three, and I suggested a little side wager. You lost. Do you remember what the bet was?"

"Yes, I remember."

She'd lost the game and the bet, and they'd ended up making love at midnight on the thirteenth green of their neighborhood country club's golf course, fireworks bursting overhead as they were lost in the passion of each other. The green had been far enough away from the road to be completely private, but it had still been reckless and incredibly exciting.

Libby felt warm, and knew it wasn't caused by the wine.

Brandon stared at her intently. "It's not over, is it?"

She felt her breath catch in her throat in something that was almost a sob, yet the feeling that wanted to burst through her chest was not one of sorrow. "No, it's not," she agreed.

Tess and Joely watched incredulously as Francine walked into their house and announced that she was babysitting.

"We don't need a babysitter," Tess said, outrage in her voice.

"Your mother thinks you do. She called and asked me to come over here. She's, uh . . . she's gone out for a bit."

"Yeah, we know she's with our dad," Joely spoke up.

Francine rubbed her hands together and looked around the living room. "Well, she's old enough to make her own mistakes. What would you girls like to do? We could play some board games, if you have any."

"I don't think we do," Tess mumbled. She looked at Joely and shifted her eyes in the direction of their bedroom. "We didn't clean our room before we left this morning. We'd better do it now or Mom will be mad when she gets home. Come on, Joely, it's your mess too."

Francine looked disappointed. "I guess I could watch TV while you're doing that," she said. "What do you girls want to eat? Is there anything special I should fix?"

"Whatever is easiest," Tess said, and began to move toward the bedroom. "It won't take us long to finish our room, then we'll come out and help you."

"Yeah," Joely said.

They closed the door, and listened for a minute to make sure Francine wasn't hovering around on the other side. When she was satisfied that their privacy was going to be respected, Tess vented her anger.

"I can't believe Mom told Francine to come over here," she raged. "She'll drive me crazy in about ten minutes."

"I thought you liked Francine," Joely said.

"I do most of the time, except when she treats us like we're both about two years old. It's not so bad when Mom's around, because they get talking and she forgets about us, but if she starts pinching my cheek again like she did that time we all stayed with her while we were looking for a house, I'll scream."

Joely sat on her bed. Their room wasn't in bad shape, but even if it had been she had no intention of wasting time on it. There were more important matters at hand. She pulled the bandanna out of her pocket and opened it on her lap.

Tess, who'd been pacing, stopped and looked. "What's that?"

Her voice low with renewed excitement, Joely at last got to tell Tess about the loose brick and its hidden treasure, and she eagerly shared her discovery and the theory she'd formed about it.

"Remember what we heard?" she asked, folding back a corner of the dirty bandanna. "About some kids being killed here in town a long time ago? They never found out who did it, you know."

"Yeah, I know," Tess said. She stood still in the middle of the room, watching Joely closely.

"What if these belonged to those kids? Think about it—four kids were murdered, and there were four different things hidden away in a secret place, like some sort of collection. You can tell this stuff is old. Look at the barrette—no one wears these any more."

"There's only three things there," Tess pointed out.

"Oh, yeah . . . this was in there too." Joely reached inside her shirt and pulled out the St. Christopher medal.

Tess felt she'd made a valiant effort to hold her temper in check, but this was too much. Earlier, she'd been so angry with Joely for running off on her that she'd been planning ways to make her sister's life miserable for as long as possible. But then Coach had grabbed Joely and everything had changed. Joely had been genuinely frightened by that unprovoked attack, and Tess's sympathies had been awakened. It was one thing for *her* to mistreat Joely—no one else had that right.

Now, however, any sympathy Tess had felt for Joely vanished at the sight of those pathetic little items and Joely's unhealthy fascination with forbidden places and ghostly visitations. It was time to put a stop to this nonsense.

Joely, oblivious to Tess's stony expression, babbled on about her theory that the St. Christopher medal had belonged to Martin Stanovich, and that the rest of the things had been taken from those long-ago murdered children.

"Whoever did it must have taken one thing each time he killed," she explained, her voice tense with excitement. "I don't know why he left them there—maybe he really did move on and leave town, like people say. Or maybe he died, and took his secret with him to the grave." Joely was warming to the subject. "Who even says it had to be a man? Maybe the murderer was a *woman.*"

"Give me that." Tess reached out and grabbed the bandanna away before Joely could make a move to stop her.

"Hey!" Joely cried. "That's mine!"

"I'm confiscating it all. I'm going to show this stuff to Mom and Dad as soon as they get home, and I'm going to tell them everything. Give me that stupid medal, too. You shouldn't be wearing that thing—it's probably full of germs and God knows what." She made a move as though to snatch the chain from around Joely's neck, but Joely was prepared this time and scrambled out of reach.

"You can't have it!" she cried.

Tess lunged after her, but Joely was quick and was at the bedroom door in a matter of seconds. She yanked on the handle, yelling at the top of her voice for Tess to leave her alone.

Her feet tangling in the unmade sheets on Joely's bed, Tess fell before she could reach her sister, and tumbled off the bed onto the floor with a resounding crash. She was up almost immediately, cursing and bruised, but Joely was already out the door.

Francine was in the hallway, her face alarmed.

"What's going on?" she cried. "It sounds like you girls are killing each other." Then she squawked as Joely nearly knocked her down going past.

"Stop her!" Tess cried.

Too late. Joely was gone, and they both heard the front door slam.

"Where's she going?" Francine shouted. "I promised your mother neither of you girls would leave this house. Joely, come back!"

Tess reached the front door, but her sister was nowhere in sight. Joely must have ducked into a neighbor's yard almost immediately to have vanished so quickly. Tess had no idea where to start looking for her, and she cursed furiously, using words she'd rarely even heard out loud before, and had certainly never used herself.

Francine, shocked, said, "Young lady!"

Tess ignored her. It was time to bring her mother and father in on this. Joely was out of control, and Tess no longer wanted to carry the burden of responsibility. She was going to tell them everything, as she now realized she should have done from the beginning.

"How am I going to explain this to your mother?" Francine fretted, wringing her hands together. "She trusted me, and look what happened—I wasn't here even an hour and I've made a mess of things."

"None of this is your fault, Francine," Tess said. "I'm going to see if I can find Joely, but whether I do or not I'll find Mom and Dad and let them know what's happened."

Francine grabbed her arm frantically. "No, you can't go too! It's bad enough that I lost one of you, if I lose you both your mother will never speak to me again!"

"Joely isn't lost, and I won't be either. It'll be okay, Francine—Mom won't blame you. I'll make sure she doesn't."

"No, you're not going." Francine tried to sound firm, but she wasn't very good at it.

Tess felt sorry for Francine, but she couldn't waste any more time here. Promising again that everything would be all right, Tess left the house and hopped on her bike. Joely, in her haste to get away, hadn't thought to take hers. That gave Tess a slight edge.

Joely had zigzagged through backyards and under hedges to keep out of sight as long as possible, but eventually she had to come back out into the open. She walked briskly, looking back often over her shoulder in case Tess came after her.

She needed more proof, and the school had to be the place to get it. One old religious medal wasn't going to be enough to convince anyone. There *had* to be more at the school that she could bring back to convince people that she wasn't the world's biggest liar.

"Hey, Gregory—where you going?"

Joely looked up and saw Rachel a half a block away, waving at her. Maria was with her, but while Rachel walked toward Joely, Maria hung back.

Rachel stopped when she noticed that Maria was no longer with her, and the two girls talked for a minute. Joely was too far away to hear what they were saying, but after a minute Rachel shrugged, and Maria turned and ran off in the other direction.

"Boy, she sure is jumpy," Rachel said when she reached Joely. "What did you do to her? Lately Maria gets all weird at the very sound of your name, and just now she took off like a scared rabbit when I said I wanted to talk to you."

"I don't know what's wrong with her," Joely said. She didn't want to talk about Maria. "I'm in a hurry."

Rachel blocked the sidewalk. "Yeah, what's the big rush? Got an appointment at the cemetery?" She laughed, hands on hips, but still wouldn't let Joely pass. "Hey—have the police been to your house yet?"

Joely felt her heart lurch. "W-why would the police come to my house?"

"They're talking to everyone in town. Canvassing, I think I heard it called. A couple of detectives talked to my parents for over an hour this morning, then they asked me a few questions. They're looking for clues."

"Oh . . . no, no one's been to our house yet."

"They will," Rachel said with certainty. "My parents feel better knowing that the town is crawling with police. It's the only reason they let me out of the house at all, but I still have to be home an hour before dark. You never told me what *you're* doing—want to go find Alice and see if she wants to walk around with us?"

"No," Joely said. "I have to go."

"Wait!" Rachel frowned, annoyed. She wasn't used to being given the brush-off. First Maria, now Joely. This was getting to be a trend she didn't care for. "How come you're in such a hurry?"

Joely tried walking away, but Rachel was incredibly persistent, trotting along beside her, firing questions at her and showing no signs of giving up until her curiosity—which was growing greater by the second—was satisfied.

"Okay," Joely finally said in exasperation. "If you really have to know, I'll tell you."

The girls stood in the shade of a big oak tree, and the words spilled out of Joely. Telling Tess had been a mistake, but she still felt the need to share this with someone, so she gave Rachel a condensed version of her recent activities. She did, however, leave out any mention of Martin. Something told her that Rachel would never buy that, just as Tess hadn't. She told Rachel only about going into the old school building, about finding the loose brick and the subsequent discovery of the hidden objects.

When she shared with Rachel her belief about

the origins of those items in the bandanna, the other girl gasped and looked only slightly skeptical. Joely was encouraged. At least here was someone who didn't immediately assume Joely was either lying or crazy.

"So where is this stuff now?" Rachel asked.

"Tess took it," Joely admitted sorrowfully. "I was only able to keep this." She leaned forward to show Rachel the St. Christopher medal.

"Take it to the police," Rachel said.

"They're not going to listen to me. Not with just this to show."

"What are you going to do?"

"I'm going back to the building, and back into that furnace room. There *has* to be something else I can show people. I don't know what—but I'm going to look."

Rachel chewed on her bottom lip. "I'll go with you," she announced after a minute.

Joely was stunned, and not particularly pleased by the offer. She tried to come up with reasons for Rachel to give up on this idea, but, now that she'd warmed up to the idea, Rachel was determined.

"If you do find something," she argued, "it'll be more believable if we can say we found it together. We might get our pictures in the paper."

Joely still protested, but she was weakening. Her biggest concern was how much time had been taken up filling Rachel in. Tess could come around the corner any moment, and this thought filled Joely with such a sense of urgency tha she decided perhaps it wouldn't hurt to have Rachel along, after all.

"Okay, but we have to hurry," she said. "My sister is really mad at me. I don't want to hang around out here in the open anymore."

Together, the girls started walking. Rachel knew about the abandoned building, but she'd never been close to it and for once she accepted the role as follower as she walked along beside Joely. "I hope we do find something," Rachel panted, her excitement growing at the thought of an adventure. "Bloody clothes maybe—or a knife! A big one, with fingerprints still on it. Wouldn't that be cool!"

Joely gave her a look of scorn, but said nothing.

Twenty-five

Tess knew where Joely was headed, but she had no intention of following her sister there. Instead, once she realized she wasn't going to find Joely on her own, she aimed her bike in the direction of downtown. Dr. Kyle hadn't known where her parents were going for supper, but Tess figured there weren't that many restaurants in town, and most of them were within a few blocks of each other. She'd look for her father's car, and if she got lucky she might find them quickly.

Her luck ran out when the chain came off her bike, and Tess was forced to pull off to the side of the road to fix it. She parked close to the curb and stooped down to examine the mutinous chain. A van rushed past Tess, going too fast; she yanked the bike between two parked cars, then dragged it onto the sidewalk. The loss of time infuriated her, making her fingers clumsy as she tried to hurry. She fumbled the job several times before she stood and fought the urge to kick the bike. This was taking way too long. She bunched her fists in frustration.

Looking around, Tess realized she was less than half a block from Dr. Kyle's office. He was probably already gone. Her mother had told her that he didn't hang around the office long after closing time, but Tess longed for a familiar face even if it was only his. Tears threatened to fill her eyes. She was trying to do the right thing, yet everything seemed to be going wrong for her.

Then the front door of the office opened, and Dr. Kyle came out. Keys in hand, he turned to lock the door behind him.

"Dr. Kyle!" Tess called out. Abandoning her bike on the sidewalk, she ran toward him. She was so eager for any port in a storm that she'd temporarily forgotten the look of unhappiness on his face when he'd earlier told her and Joely that her parents were together. All she saw now was someone who might be able to help her.

"Tess, is something wrong?" he asked when she reached him.

"Yes—lots. Joely's run off again and I wanted to find Mom and Dad but my bike broke down and I don't know where they're at. I really have to find them, Dr. Kyle. I know you said you didn't know which restaurant they were going to, but . . ." Here Tess had an inspiration, "could you drive me around until we find my dad's car?"

Tim looked at the frantic teenager. He hadn't yet locked the office door, and now he opened it and motioned for Tess to follow him inside. "I was finishing up some paperwork," he explained. "Otherwise I would have been out of here a long time ago. Instead of driving around town, Tess, it would make more sense for us to call some of the nearby restaurants until we locate your parents. It'll be faster."

"That'd be great," she said, weak with relief. At last, a grown-up to take charge and make things right.

Tim took the Cielo phone book from the top of a filing cabinet and opened it to the yellow pages. He flipped through the restaurant section, running his finger down the page.

"I can eliminate a couple of these right away," he said. "They probably won't be at any of the hamburger or pizza places, so that narrows down the list." He reached over and took the phone from Libby's desk, and handed it to Tess. "Here, I'll give you a number. You call and ask for your parents."

Tess obeyed. The first and second restaurants she called told her that neither of her parents were there. On the third she got a recording saying the number had been disconnected. With the fourth call she made, Tess heard her father's voice come on the line after a short wait.

"Dad!" she cried. She looked gratefully at Dr. Kyle. He smiled and moved discreetly across the room to give her some privacy. "Dad, I have so much to tell you."

Rachel kept up with Joely, and didn't hesitate until they reached the abandoned building. There she hung back, watching as Joely approached the open doorway she'd used on past occasions.

"You've really been in there?" Rachel asked nervously.

"Sure, more than once. I wish I'd brought the flashlight, but I left the house in a big hurry." Joely entered the building, stepping carefully over the debris she knew littered the floor. She didn't look behind her to see if Rachel was following. She would've been just as happy to have Rachel chicken out. The other girl was a burden, and one Joely would have been happy to unload.

But Rachel wouldn't give up. If scrawny little Joely Gregory could go inside that spooky place, then Rachel was going to do so as well. She squared her shoulders and forged ahead. "Wait for me," she called.

Joely walked through the now-familiar hallways, her fist on the medallion at her chest. She could hear Rachel behind her, stumbling but determined to keep up.

Tess waited at Dr. Kyle's office for her parents to arrive. Brandon had instructed her to stay there after hearing an abbreviated—and very strange—story about Joely running away.

Now Tess paced impatiently, even though she knew it had only been a couple of minutes since she'd spoken to her father and it was unreasonable for her to expect them to get here immediately. She kept looking out the front window, fiddling with the blinds until she realized what she was doing and forced herself to stop.

"You don't have to wait with me," Tess told Dr. Kyle when she realized she must be keeping him from going home. "I'll wait out on the sidewalk for them."

"No, I couldn't leave you alone," Tim insisted.

"Really, I don't mind—" Tess started to say, but then she saw her father's car pull up in front of the office. He must have gone through every red light along the way to arrive so quickly. "They're here!"

Tim followed Tess outside just as Libby and Brandon were getting out of the car.

"Dad!" Tess fell into her father's arms, so relieved to have both her parents here that she could almost believe everything was going to turn out all right. Libby became a part of their small circle. All three of them forgot about Tim, who stood near the front door of his office and tried not to watch.

Brandon, when he was able to pry Tess from his chest, held the girl at arm's length and looked into her face.

"What is it you were trying to tell me on the

phone, Tess?" he asked. "None of it made sense—you said Joely went to some vacant building to look behind bricks?"

"I tried to stop her," Tess said. "But she's got so many strange ideas lately. She thinks she's Nancy Drew or something, like she's really going to figure out something the police never could. I know I should have told you about it before, but I—I didn't know—"

Tess was losing it, and Brandon gave her a little shake. "Calm down," he said. "Tell me one thing at a time. And slowly. *Where* exactly has Joely gone?"

"There's an old empty school just outside of town," Tess said, trying to speak slowly so that panic wouldn't again come over her. It was important for her to make them understand, and she knew if she started jumping all around in the story none of it would make any sense. "She went there today, and she found a loose brick in the furnace room, and behind the brick she found an old scarf or something with some things in it. Kids' stuff—a ring and a barrette, I forget what else. I took them from her, and when I did she got mad and said she was going to go back and find some more. She thinks this stuff has something to do with some kids that were killed a long time ago—"

"Wait a minute," Brandon interrupted. "You said she went to the old school?" He looked at Libby. "That building isn't safe, it should have

273

been torn down years ago. It's probably full of rats."

"I was there with her the other day," Tess said before she could stop herself. "We didn't see any rats."

Brandon and Libby both turned to stare at Tess, and she immediately regretted her big mouth.

"*You* went there with her?" Libby said, her voice barely above a whisper. "What in God's name were you thinking of? And why did you wait until now to tell us this?"

"I'm sorry," Tess said.

"You're supposed to be the older one," Libby said. "You're supposed to watch out for your little sister, not *join* her in—"

Brandon put a hand on Libby's shoulder. "We can sort this all out later," he told them both. "Right now the only thing that matters is that we get Joely and make sure she's safe. Come on, we'll take Tess home first, then I'll go to the school for her." He opened the car door and Libby and Joely both got in the front seat.

Tim stood on the sidewalk as they drove away. He watched the car until it was out of sight, then he turned and locked the front door of his office.

"I'm going to drop you both off at home," Brandon told Libby as he drove. "I can get Joely myself."

"Take a flashlight," Tess suggested.

"I'm going with you," Libby said.

They were almost at the house. Brandon barely looked at Libby, who was sitting in the middle, between him and Tess. "No, you're not," he said.

"You can't stop me, and I can't just sit at the house waiting and wondering what's happening."

"Didn't you hear what I said a minute ago?" Brandon said in exasperation. "That building is dangerous."

"Which is exactly *why* I have to go," she said firmly. "Joely is there."

Brandon pulled the car into the driveway. Francine appeared immediately on the front porch, then she came running out to meet them.

"Libby, I made such a mess of things," she cried. "You trusted me with the girls, and I let them both get away." Her eyes rested on Tess and she put a hand on her heart in relief, but then began to flutter nervously again when she realized Joely was not with them. "I'll never forgive myself," she moaned.

"Francine, I need you to stay here with Tess," Libby said to her friend. She didn't have time to try to calm Francine down, and she didn't try. She leaned across Tess to open the door and gently eased the girl out of the car; then she spoke to Francine again. "Brandon and I are going after Joely now, I hope we'll be back shortly."

"Libby—" Brandon began.

She turned on him. "Let's not waste time arguing about this," she told him. "I'm going, with or without you."

He was silent only for a moment. "Okay," he said. "You're the boss."

"That's right," Libby said, and pulled the door shut.

Brandon shifted the car into reverse, and began to back it out of the driveway.

"Wait!" Tess cried. She ran inside the house, then came back out a moment later. "Don't forget this." She held the flashlight out to them.

Libby rolled down the window on her side and took the flashlight. "Don't you leave this house for any reason," she told Tess.

"Don't worry, I won't."

Tess stood on the grass as her parents drove away. Francine, her face flushed and her hair looking as though she'd been running her hands through it, stood beside her. *"This* is exactly why I never had children," she said to no one in particular.

Joely was deep in the heart of the building. Rachel, less brave now in this unfamiliar territory than she had been earlier, began to complain and insist that they leave.

"There's nothing here," she said for the fourth or fifth time. "You're just getting back at me because of that time we left you in the cemetery, aren't you? Maria told me you were really mad about that, but I didn't think you were going to hold a grudge forever."

"Leave if you want to," Joely told her. "I didn't want you to come in the first place."

"Oh, sure, like I could really find my way out of here. You did this on purpose—*eeeh!* What's *that?*" Rachel slapped frantically at her hair, where something small fluttered and became tangled.

Joely went to Rachel and brushed a moth out of the frightened girl's hair. "There, it's gone," she said. "Just follow this hallway, then turn right and that'll get you out of the building eventually," she said. "The furnace room is right through this way, and that's where I'm going."

"No, you have to show me the way out," Rachel insisted. Her face was puckered miserably and she kept brushing at her hair, as though afraid that more flying things would find their way into it. Her clothes were dirty. She'd tripped once, over a length of rusty pipe, and had gone sprawling across the grimy floor.

"Just go on home if you want to," Joely snapped. "But you'll have to find your own way out. I'm going in here."

With that, Joely turned and pushed through the doorway, and was in the furnace room.

She saw Martin immediately. He was standing beside the desk waiting for her, and this time he was pointing at something high on the wall next to the room's only window.

Rachel, too afraid to go off on her own, fol-

277

lowed Joey into the room. "I'm going to get you for this, Gregory. I'm going to tell my father that you made me come in here—" She stopped just over the threshold, her words of complaint frozen in her throat, a look of astonishment on her face.

At first Joely thought Rachel must see Martin. Then she realized that Rachel didn't see him as much as she felt his presence.

"It's *freezing* in here," Rachel gasped. She crossed her arms in front of herself and shivered. "Where is that coming from? It's like being in a refrigerator."

Joely looked at the other girl. "Don't you see anything?" she asked. To her, Martin was clearly visible, waiting patiently in the same spot he'd been at since she walked into the room.

But Rachel was already backing out through the doorway. Her teeth were chattering, and her eyes looked around wildly. "How did you do that, Gregory? You shouldn't be in here messing around with the air conditioning. I'm going to tell!" Rachel spun on her heel and ran from the room. "I'm going to tellll!"

Her last words echoed throughout the structure, her stumbling, awkward footsteps emphasizing each word.

For a moment Joely wanted to follow her. Rachel's panic was contagious, and for the first time Joely felt doubtful about Martin. She shuddered, feeling a chill that, unlike the one Rachel'd felt, came from within her. She might have considered leaving if, at that moment, she hadn't looked at Martin and realized his attention was directed at a group of six or seven small, framed pictures on the wall next to the window. She'd seen those pictures before, though she hadn't paid much attention to them. They were covered with thick dust, the color in the photographs so faded that everything had an orangish cast to it, even through the grime.

The last of Joely's doubts fell away. This was what she had come here for. She'd *known* there had to be something more here that would tell her exactly what it was Martin wanted. All this time, the painstaking first trip to the building—it couldn't all be for nothing. There had to be a reason behind Martin's actions.

Joely stepped closer to the pictures. There was nothing special about any of them. Most were of the school staff, she assumed, people in outdated clothes posing stiffly in front of the building or a long yellow school bus. Joely leaned closer.

The picture with the bus showed a group of a half a dozen men of varying ages. Bus drivers. All had conservatively short haircuts. There was nothing to tell her what year the picture had been taken, and Joely didn't know enough about clothing styles back then to make a guess. She almost turned away. Martin was going to have to give her more help.

Then she took a closer look at the photograph. One young man in the picture looked like he could possibly be a high-school student. He stood in the front, his face half turned away as though unhappy to be having his picture taken. He looked familiar. Something about the square outline of the jaw, the reluctant half smile . . .

"That was me."

Joely screamed, and spun around at the sound of the deep, masculine voice.

Dr. Kyle stood in the doorway, his hands in his pockets, looking as though this was the most ordinary place for them to be.

Twenty-six

Libby thumped the flashlight against her thigh as Brandon drove. "This thing is flickering on and off," she said. "Something's wrong with it."

"Stop banging it around, that might help," Brandon said.

"I think the bulb might be loose." She began to unscrew the head of the flashlight.

"Don't do that." Brandon looked sideways at her. "You're going to break it for sure."

"No, I'm not." Libby removed the protective glass covering, twisted the bulb to tighten it, then put everything back together. She flipped the button up. Nothing happened. "Damn," she whispered.

"I told you."

Libby gave him a dirty look. "It wasn't working right anyway, it wasn't going to do us any good. Why are you slowing down?"

"I can't go any farther on this road. Look—it's a mess."

Brandon had turned the car onto the way leading out to the school, despite the sign declaring that the road was closed. He'd tried anyway, but could see clearly that the pavement was cracked and overgrown with weeds, nearly destroyed by years of disuse. The car lurched painfully ahead, and Brandon winced at the sound of something solid scraping along the underside.

"What are we going to do?" Libby asked. She could see the school up ahead at least another hundred yards, but the way there looked almost completely blocked by wildly tangled foliage.

"We'll walk," Brandon said. He pulled the car over to the side of the road, turned it off and opened the door. "Maybe you should wait here. I'll find Joely."

Libby opened her door and got out. "We'll find her together," she said, and tossed the useless flashlight on the seat.

Dr. Kyle continued to look around the room, his focus turned inward as he examined memories from twenty-five years earlier.

"I used to help out at the school when I was a senior," he told Joely, his manner unhurried. "Driving the bus, sweeping floors—whatever they wanted me to do. I had to save money for college because my parents didn't have any, at least not enough for what I wanted to do. Even after I graduated from high school, I used to come

282

back and work here during the summers and vacations."

Joely stood with her back to the window. She neither saw nor felt Martin. She didn't know when he'd disappeared, but she was now alone with Tim Kyle and she didn't like the blank, unconcerned look in his eyes.

"I—I have to go home now," she said. "My Mom will be worried about me."

He looked directly at her for the first time. "Your mother lets you run around loose far too much," he said.

"Yeah, well, I doubt if I'll be doing it anymore."

"It started when I was still in school myself," Tim said, switching subjects so suddenly that for a moment Joely was confused. "The first time I didn't mean to," he continued. "It just happened—some stupid, spoiled little girl who got no supervision at home, whose parents didn't really care what she did. I probably helped her. She would've grown up to be undisciplined trash—I saw to it that that never happened."

He'd come a little farther into the room, and Joely shifted her eyes around, searching for some exit other than the door. He was still blocking the way out, and there seemed no possibility of her getting around him.

"Then there was a boy," Dr. Kyle said, "and that time I went looking. The first time had been so easy, I wanted to see if it would be as easy again. It was. He was a little boy I'd seen around the school often, I'd even driven him on the bus a few times. I don't know what made me choose him, I just knew he was going to be the next one. I grabbed him practically out of his own backyard."

Joely couldn't stop herself. "His name was Martin, wasn't it?" she said.

Dr. Kyle looked at her. "Was it? I don't remember, it wasn't important to me. After that one, though, I knew I was going to have to be more careful, and I stayed away from the local children from then on. When I was away at college I stopped for a while, but after a couple of years the pressure began to build up inside, and I knew there was only one source of release for me. I was always cautious, though, and I'd drive to another city to do what I had to do."

Joely had stepped to one side as the doctor slowly came closer, and now she realized he was looking at the picture on the wall. What memories did it evoke for him? She didn't think she wanted to know. The only thing that concerned her now was that, as he came closer to the picture, the open doorway behind him became more accessible to her. Joely tried to stay small and invisible as she edged cautiously toward freedom. Whenever he glanced in her direction she would freeze in place, but he didn't seem to be paying much attention to her. He was caught up in his own twisted thoughts, feeding on the telling of past horrors, trying, incredibly, to justify his actions.

"I shouldn't have come back to Cielo," he said, his back almost to Joely now. "I thought it was the right thing to do at the time, but being in that house again has made me weak. I've made mistakes . . . careless. I should have stayed away from the local kids. Too late now. I don't seem to be able to stop myself . . . where are you going?"

He turned abruptly and glared at Joely. She screamed and lunged for the doorway, but Dr. Kyle was upon her before she could escape. He grabbed her shoulders, his hands digging into her flesh as Joely struggled, trying to bite, kick— anything that would make him release her.

"My sister knows I'm here," she screamed up at him, wiggling furiously. "She's going to come after me pretty soon."

"They all know you're here," Tim said calmly. "Tess told your mother and father everything, even about those things of mine you stole from this room. I don't blame you for that—it was foolish of me to take something from those first children, but at the time I had some lofty notion of saving something from each one. I stopped that practice almost immediately when I realized it could be dangerous to me—I even forgot all about that bandanna until I heard Tess talking about it a little while ago. Then I knew I had to get here quickly, before your parents arrived."

"My mom and dad are coming here?" Joely asked hopefully. "Than you'd better let me go."

"No—I'd better hurry up and do what I have

to do." He put one hand on Joely's throat and began to lift her, by the neck, off the ground.

Something Joely had been taught long ago came back to her suddenly, in that moment when she knew her time was running out. Her father had once told her what to do if a man ever grabbed her.

Before her feet completely left the ground, and while she still had a little leverage, Joely brought one knee up with all her strength into Dr. Kyle's groin. The results were immediate. He gasped and released her, doubling over in surprised pain.

Joely stumbled backwards but didn't fall. Then she spun around and ran for the doorway. He was on her almost immediately. She hadn't hurt him badly because she hadn't been able to put enough power behind the thrust of her knee, and now he grabbed at the back of her blouse. Together they struggled out into the hallway, falling onto the filthy floor.

Joely was up first, and she took off down the hallway—in the opposite direction of the way she'd come in, but in her panic she wanted only to put as much distance between herself and Dr. Kyle as possible.

She could hear him pounding behind her as she ran. It was darker in this direction, and the way more littered with debris. Joely nearly tripped more than once, banging her shins painfully and once almost knocking herself out on a low-hanging pipe, but she staggered on ahead, too terrified of what was behind her to stop. Only when she'd turned a corner and left him somewhere behind did she dare stop for a moment to catch her breath.

Joely was completely unfamiliar with this part of the building. Besides being darker, it was also more decayed. The walls were caved in in spots, pink insulation hung from spaces in the ceiling where tiles had fallen out. Even the floor felt unstable beneath her feet, and Joely began to pick her way carefully, aware of the trouble she would be in if she broke through some rotten floorboards and got stuck. She'd be trapped like a fish in a barrel, just waiting for Dr. Kyle to find her and do whatever he wanted.

She could hear him somewhere behind her, but he was far enough away that Joely began to feel she might give him the slip after all. She didn't even have to get out of the building right away, she realized. All she had to do was avoid him long enough for help to arrive.

She didn't see the broken coatrack until she tripped over it. Joely put her hands out instinctively to catch herself, and felt her glasses fly off her face and clatter somewhere ahead of her. Expecting to hit hard, dirty floor, she fell instead onto something soft and cushiony that saved her from more injury, and Joely lifted up, groping with her hands to determine what it was that had broken her fall.

She found herself staring directly into the face of Rachel Fletcher. Even without her glasses, with her vision blurred, Joely could see that Rachel's eyes were half open, looking off at nothing. The other girl's lips were parted delicately, their perfection marred only by the blood gathered at the corners. Rachel's neck was nearly black with bruising, the only part of her that seemed truly violated.

Joely shrieked and threw herself backwards. She'd been almost nose-to-nose with the dead girl, and the screams that tore from her throat were an explosive reaction to the horror of those unseeing eyes.

Scrambling to her feet, Joely clamped her hands over her mouth, but it was too late. She'd given away her position, and she could hear Dr. Kyle's footsteps coming closer, turning the corner now that would bring him almost to her.

She looked back over her shoulder and saw him bearing down on her. With no time even to search for her glasses, Joely got up and, unable to bring herself to step over Rachel's body, ran in the only direction available to her—through a wide, unblocked doorway to her right. She immediately found herself in a huge, open room with a ceiling so high she could only sense it somewhere above her.

It was the school's gym, and Joely didn't know if there was going to be another way out on the far side. She had no choice but to go straight ahead, even though the openness of the room meant there would be no place here for her to hide.

Joely was halfway across the gym floor when she felt it begin to give beneath her. Stopping, she barely breathed as she waited to see what was going to happen. Still almost blind, Joely squinted. There was a sound of creaking, rotted wood that threatened to collapse if strained any further. It held her as long as she didn't move, but Joely felt certain the whole works could give way with very little encouragement.

"Come on out of there, Joely," Dr. Kyle said. She looked back over her shoulder and saw him standing in the doorway.

"There's no way out of here and you're about to fall through," he said softly, no hint of menace in his voice. "Come on, Joely. Be careful where you put your feet, I can see the weak spots." He held a hand out to her encouragingly.

Joely took a tentative step forward. The flooring groaned but held. She continued, putting space between herself and him slowly, an inch at a time.

"Now, Joely," he coaxed, "you aren't going to get anywhere that way, and you can't even see the rotten boards . . . can you? Come on back, I'll help you find your glasses."

"Yeah, sure you will," Joely mumbled. Arms out for balance, she slid first one foot forward and then the next, not even lifting her feet any more now because she was afraid of putting even the slightest weight down.

Looking up to see how much closer to the far end of the gym she'd gotten, Joely gasped. She squinted again, unsure if her weak eyes were playing a cruel trick on her.

They weren't—Martin was up ahead, almost at the wall, about thirty feet in front of her. His blurred, wavering shape was familiar to her even in her near-blind condition, and she was sure she could sense encouragement from him. He was leading her to the other side of the gym—he was telling her that there was a way out there.

Emboldened, Joely walked a little faster, still being careful about where she stepped but not so afraid anymore. She was almost to Martin when she heard movement behind her. She looked back over her shoulder and saw that Dr. Kyle was taking slow, cautious steps toward her, deeper into the gym.

And the floor seemed to be supporting his weight.

"Go away and leave me alone!" Joely shouted at him.

Libby and Brandon fought their way over the cracked road, the school tantalizingly close but still separated from them by an almost solid path of weeds and brush.

"Ow!" Libby tripped and would have fallen if Brandon hadn't grabbed her arm and held her. She'd twisted her ankle on a pothole, and the pain shot through her clear to her hip. With Brandon still holding her up, she reached down to massage the ankle.

"Look, this is going to take too long," Brandon said. "Why don't you wait here and I'll go on ahead. I'll be back with her in a few minutes, I promise."

"No way," Libby gasped. To prove her point, she straightened up and put her full weight on both feet. "It's not that much farther, I can make it. We'll just follow these tracks here that should make it easier."

"Tracks?" Brandon looked down at the road, and saw that there were, indeed, a double row of thick tracks where a heavy vehicle had recently flattened the weeds.

"Somebody else drove on this road," Libby said. "We should have driven closer in, too. It would've saved us some walking."

"A car came this way not long ago," Brandon said. He'd bent down to examine the crushed foliage, and saw that it was already beginning to spring back up. "What the hell—"

Libby watched in astonishment as Brandon bounded on ahead, leaving her behind to wonder what was going on. She hurried to catch up with him, ignoring the pain in her ankle.

She nearly bumped into him.

The tracks had left the road and veered off to the right side of the road. They could both clearly see now that a car had been driven off the road and hidden in the tall bushes there. They both recognized the dark gray BMW.

"That's Tim's car," Libby said. "What's he doing here?"

Twenty-seven

With Dr. Kyle coming toward her, Joely felt trapped once again. There was no way out of the gym on this side, as far as she could see. She'd ventured in, trusting Martin to show her a way out, but now she knew she'd made a mistake. She was cornered, and if Dr. Kyle continued to step carefully, he was going to reach her in a matter of moments.

To make matters worse, Martin had disappeared. She'd been abandoned, and Joely wanted to scream out at the unfairness of it.

Testing each step before putting his weight down, Dr. Kyle smiled at Joely in an almost friendly way. The gap between them narrowed. Joely was frozen in place, unable to risk any sudden movement that might further jeopardize her own precarious position on the rotted floorboards.

"They'll catch you!" she cried out. "You won't get away with it anymore. You'll go to jail!"

Dr. Kyle stopped as a board beneath his foot creaked loudly, the sound like a groan in the cavernous gym. For a moment Joely thought he was listening to her words, but then she realized he was only testing the strength of the floor, and avoiding those boards that were obviously too weak to support his weight. She might as well have been shouting into the wind. He had only one goal at this time, and that was to reach her and put his hands around her neck again. Joely began to understand that nothing was going to stop him until he'd accomplished this, and despair swept over her. Tears streamed down her face as she looked frantically around for any means of escape.

There was none.

He'd circled around an especially rotten patch of boards, but the trip hadn't taken him far out of his way. Grinning in triumph, Dr. Kyle looked up at her and again began coming toward her.

Joely longed for a weapon—a stick, a rock, anything. With only her bare hands with which to defend herself, she knew she wouldn't last two minutes once he finally reached her.

Brandon no longer waited for Libby to keep up. He began running toward the school building, the implications of Dr. Kyle's car in the brush only too clear.

Not far behind, Libby ran as though her ankle wasn't sending needles of pain through her leg.

Like Brandon, she hadn't puzzled for long over the sight of Tim's car. Whatever his reason for driving here, it couldn't be good, and as she ran, a portion of Libby's brain began to piece together sections of a puzzle that, looked at as a whole, revealed a terrifying picture. Joely was in that building, and Dr. Kyle, for reasons of his own, was after her. Libby's fear gave her a speed and strength she otherwise wouldn't have known she possessed.

Brandon reached the building first, and yanked open the first door he came to. It opened easily, the locks long since rusted into uselessness. Libby came right up behind him. He didn't try to persuade her to wait outside. He knew she wouldn't, anyway.

Together they made their way down a darkened hallway, both wishing for the flashlight as they stumbled over the obstacle course of broken furniture and abandoned equipment.

"Which way?" Brandon asked, stopping momentarily to get his bearings.

"Call her," Libby whispered.

"No. If she's hiding, and she answers us, it might lead him right to her."

Libby stood stock-still, ears strained for any revealing sound. Her head whipped to the right as she tensed, listening. "I heard something," she whispered. "Over this way."

"Wait," Brandon said.

He was too late. Libby, her eyes having adjusted to the gloom quicker than his, had already gone down the hallway and turned a corner ahead. He had no choice but to follow and hope that he could catch her before she got too far ahead. He wanted to be in the lead. He wanted to be the first one to reach Dr. Kyle and get his hands on the man.

Turning the corner Libby had disappeared around, Brandon tumbled to his knees when he tripped over a small stack of boards. Cursing, he brushed himself off and hauled himself back to his feet. He looked around, straining to distinguish the odd shapes and darker patches here and there. The hallway branched out into two separate passageways, and both were deserted. Libby was nowhere in sight, nor did he hear her anywhere ahead. He'd lost her, but he didn't dare announce his presence by calling out to her.

He had to make a choice, so Brandon took a deep breath and took the hallway to the left.

Libby kept going in the direction from which the sound had come, even though she no longer heard anything other than her own pulse pounding in her ears. She could see well enough to hurry, now that she'd been in the building for a few minutes, and she stepped over and around any obstacles with ease. She was vaguely aware that Brandon wasn't with her, but she didn't take the time to wonder what had happened to him. Her only thought was to reach Joely, to find her daughter before any harm could come to her.

Somewhere along the way, Libby had picked up a board that was narrowed on one end and fit snugly in her hand. It wasn't much of a weapon, but it was better than nothing and she was prepared to use it on anyone who tried to come between her and her child.

"You'll go to jail!"

The voice was Joely's, and Libby heard clearly. She wasn't far away, somewhere up ahead and obviously not alone. Holding the board tightly, Libby headed in that direction.

At first she thought the shape on the floor was nothing more than a bundle of rags. She'd almost reached it and was about to step around it when she realized it was a body.

Libby gasped. The sound escaped from her before she could stop it, shock making her suddenly light-headed. For one awful moment she thought the dead girl was Joely—then she recognized Rachel Fletcher and her relief was so great that she couldn't even be horrified at herself for being happy that someone else's child was dead.

"Stay away from me!"

This was Joely's voice again, so close this time that Libby knew exactly which doorway to go through. Turning away from the sight of Rachel, she pushed her way through the wide double doors and found herself in a space so wide and open that it took her a moment to realize she'd entered a gym.

Tim Kyle was several yards in front of Libby, his back to her. Joely was there also, even farther away but facing Libby. At the sight of her mother, Joely cried out in joy.

"Mom!"

Tim turned and frowned. "Libby, you're making this more difficult than it has to be," he scolded. "This has nothing to do with you."

Libby held the board out menacingly in front of her. "Get away from her," she said. She took a step forward, and felt the floor protest.

"Don't come in here," Tim warned her. "It's not safe."

"I'm taking Joely home with me."

"No, I can't let you do that."

"You're not going to hurt her."

He tilted his head to look at her. "You're suddenly very concerned, but where were you earlier, when she needed you? You were with your ex-husband while your children were running around loose. Besides, she's been snooping into my business."

"He did it, Mom," Joely shouted from across the gym. "He killed those kids. He told me so—and he killed Rachel, too."

"I know," Libby said. She kept her eyes on Tim, prepared to react to any sudden movement on his part. She was only a few feet away from him now, but the floor beneath her feet felt so unstable that she was afraid to go any farther. She wouldn't be able to protect Joely if she fell through the floor herself. "Joely," she said, "walk slowly along the wall in this direction. Stay away from the middle of the floor."

"No," Tim said.

Joely obeyed. The flooring did seem stronger near the walls, and she began to work her way toward her mother, keeping her eyes on Dr. Kyle at the same time. She didn't trust him.

Tim watched her progress for a minute, then he returned his attention to Libby. "You shouldn't have come here."

He said the words so calmly that Libby was unprepared for his sudden lunge in her direction. He grabbed the board and wrenched it out of her hand, leaving splinters deep in her palm. Libby cried out more from outrage than pain, and threw herself at him, her fingernails going for his eyes.

They grappled like two wild animals. Tim dropped the board and held Libby's wrists, trying to protect his face from her fury. She bit the back of his hand, sinking her teeth into his flesh until she tasted blood, but he didn't release her. They stumbled backwards, their feet tangling in each other as each tried to drive the other down.

Joely screamed. Still several yards away from them, she could see her mother and Dr. Kyle fighting almost in the middle of the gym. To her it looked like they were going to tear each other apart, and her mother's strength amazed her.

Libby got one hand free and struck out at

Tim with her fist. She connected solidly with his jaw but it hardly slowed him down. He was trying to get his hand on her throat, and she brought her shoulders up and tucked her chin in, to protect that vulnerable spot. She kicked at his shins with her shoes, tried to stomp on his toes—anything she could do to inflict pain on him. His strength seemed to have no limits, and Libby knew hers was only going to last so much longer.

At first Joely didn't understand why there seemed to be three people there in the middle of the room, then she realized Martin had returned and was standing just behind Dr. Kyle.

Martin was there, and even from this distance Joely saw the rage on the little boy's face. He reached a hand up toward Dr. Kyle's shoulder.

"Mom!" Joely screamed.

Libby tumbled back as though she'd been shoved. She didn't know what had happened, but managed to keep her footing and looked up in time to see an expression of pure terror come over Tim Kyle's face. He turned around and threw his hands up as though to protect himself.

Joely saw Martin touch Dr. Kyle just as her mother fell back. Martin's hands connected solidly with the doctor, and by the expression Joely saw then on the man's face she could only imagine what he was experiencing. She herself had once had only the briefest contact with that cold, empty space that Martin occupied—and it had been enough to leave her shaken and unwilling to repeat the experience. Dr. Kyle was being assaulted by the small figure, and though he put his hands up and seemed to be trying to break free, Martin had swept his arms around him so that they'd merged into one writhing mass.

Libby wasn't sure what she was seeing. Crawling backward, she scooted towards the gym door, putting space between herself and Tim Kyle. He had begun to scream, an unearthly sound that ripped itself from his chest even as his arms flailed at some unseen enemy—it echoed throughout the cavernous gym, reverberating off the rafters, driving Libby farther back. She covered her ears with her hands, but couldn't take her eyes from the sight before her.

Tim, still screaming, fought desperately to escape. He twisted and almost fell, his face momentarily turned toward hers—and Libby screamed then too, because his face reflected a hell she hoped to never see.

Crawling on her hands and knees, Joely made her way to her mother, then she grabbed Libby's arm and tried to haul her to her feet.

"We gotta get out of here!" Joely shouted.

Libby was frozen in place, but Joely understood what was happening and she used all her strength to pull her mother away from the terror before them. Finally Libby seemed to understand, and she held onto Joely as they made their way through the doorway.

Brandon reached them at that moment, drawn to the gym by the sound of Tim Kyle's continuing shrieks. Brandon's face was pale, but he looked immediately relieved to see both Joely and Libby safe and together. He'd found the body of a little girl out in the hallway, and his worst fear had been that a similar fate had befallen Libby or Joely. Holding them both against his chest, he looked over Libby's head into the gym, and said, "What in God's name is happening to him—"

The rotten flooring collapsed beneath Dr. Kyle then. He fell through, to decades of broken boards and sharp edges, and his scream was cut off as suddenly as if a plug had been pulled. The silence was so sudden and so complete that the three survivors could only cling to each other for a moment before the reality of what had happened began to sink in.

Brandon recovered first. He released Joely, then Libby, and made a move as though to go to the dark gap in the middle of the floor.

Libby held him back. "Don't go in there—it won't hold you."

"But he might be alive—"

"He's not," Libby said, her fingernails digging into his arm through his shirt.

Brandon still hesitated, and Joely joined her mother in convincing him that they had to leave the building so they could notify the authorities, that there was nothing more they could do here.

Tim Kyle was beyond their help.

Twenty-eight

Joely led them out of the building into late-afternoon sunlight that surprised them all. It seemed as though they'd been in that dark place for hours, when in actuality it had been less than twenty minutes since Libby and Brandon had entered the building in search of their daughter.

They spoke only once as they walked wearily to where they'd left the car.

Libby asked, "What happened to him back there, Joely? What made him let go of me so suddenly, and . . . it almost looked as though there was someone else *there*."

"Did you see anyone?" Joely asked.

Brandon broke in. "Wait a minute—there was no one else."

"Did you see anyone?" Joely repeated, stopping to look at her mother. They were standing in the middle of the road; having gotten through the worst part of the weeds, the car was only a few feet away now.

"No," Libby said. "I mean . . . I'm not sure. I . . . *almost* thought I saw someone just before the floor caved in. Someone small . . . like a child." She shook her head as though to clear it. "No, that couldn't be. Tim just went crazy, that's all. He was crazy anyway . . . he had to be, to have done what he did. He must've just gone completely over the edge, finally."

"Yeah, I guess that's what happened," Joely agreed.

She didn't say any more about it, but her mother's troubled silence told her that Libby was still puzzling over that last, brief glimpse she'd had of Tim Kyle fighting to protect himself from the vengeance of a little boy who'd waited twenty-five years for that opportunity.

Martin *had* been there. Joely had seen him clearly, and she knew Dr. Kyle had gone through a torture during their struggles that must have made his eventual death a relief. He and Martin had been wrapped in each other's arms like doomed lovers when the floor had collapsed—then they'd both been gone, and even though Dr. Kyle was dead now Martin hadn't shown himself to Joely again before she and her parents had left the school.

She wasn't going to be seeing him again, ever.

Joely was certain of this, and a small part of her felt sad over the loss. Martin had finally attained his goal—he'd gotten the man who'd murdered him all those years ago, had found the satisfaction that'd kept him tied to Cielo for over two decades. By leading her to the school and showing her the things hidden behind the loose brick in the furnace room, he'd used Joely to make his revenge possible. Maybe Martin had even known, somehow, of her connection to Dr. Kyle, and had recognized her usefulness to him.

Joely knew she was never going to have the answers to most of her questions. She could speculate for years, but that's all it ever would be—speculation. All else was now buried forever, with Martin Philip Stanovich.

Brandon opened the car door and Libby and Joely fell heavily inside.

Libby closed the door on her side. Joely was sitting in the middle, and Brandon went around to the other side and got in behind the steering wheel.

"Guess we'd better head to the nearest phone," he said. "I sure the hell wish there was some way we could just walk away from this. It's going to be a mess—and we'll be tied to it from now on. People will never forget that we were involved, no matter how innocently."

"I know," Libby said. "We can't possibly stay here in Cielo."

Brandon turned to look at her. So did Joely.

"What do you mean, Mom?" she asked.

"This town is too small. Your dad's right—people will never forget, and I can't stand the thought of being stared at and whispered about every time I step out of the house. In the city it'll be easier to blend in, and one scandal is forgotten as quickly as another takes its place."

"We're going home?" Joely was almost afraid to hope for such a miracle.

"Well . . . We're going to give it some serious thought. Come on, Brandon, we'd better go call the police so we can get this over with as soon as possible."

"Right," he said, and turned the steering wheel of the car sharply around to aim them back out the way in which they'd come.

Twenty-nine

Tess took the white envelope that Mrs. Coddington handed to her. She opened it and looked inside, then gasped at the sight of the check.

"That's a lot more than you owed me for my last week of work," she said.

Mrs. Coddington's expression softened, but she waved a hand in dismissal. "Call it a bonus then. You did good work during the short time you were here, Tess. I'm going to miss having you around, and I'm afraid the young girl I've hired to replace you doesn't display your sense of responsibility. Coach will miss you, too, I'm sure. He did love to have you read to him."

Tess could only nod. Goodbyes were so difficult, even though she was deliriously happy to be leaving Cielo before the new school year started. She'd be back with her friends soon, and would be starting school with them in a few weeks almost as though she'd never been away.

"Did you say goodbye to Coach?" Mrs. Coddington asked.

"Yes, just a minute ago. I think . . . I think he looked a little sad when I told him."

"I'm certain he did, dear. I know you found being around him difficult at times, but I assure you he understands and cares about everything that goes on around him. If you think about it, write to him why don't you? I'll read the letter to him."

"I will," Tess promised.

Together they walked to the front door and Tess prepared to leave this house forever. She wasn't sorry to be going, but neither was she sorry she'd had the experience of working for the Coddingtons. Like everything else that had gone on during this summer, it was sure to shape her life in some special way.

The news of Dr. Kyle's many sins had hit Mrs. Coddington especially hard, because she'd worked for him for a year without suspecting anything sinister beneath the false surface of goodwill and sanity. The fact that she, who'd considered herself an expert at judging others, had been fooled by him was secondary to her horror at the thought of the number of local children who'd been in contact with the doctor—children she cared for almost as much as she did her only son.

The guilt Mrs. Coddington felt for praising Tim Kyle around town had only partly prompted her generosity with Tess's final paycheck. She

307

truly wanted to do something to help the girl, and this was the only way she knew how.

It wasn't enough, but it would have to do.

A few minutes later Tess was walking swiftly toward her own house, the check from Mrs. Coddington safely in the back pocket of her jeans. It would buy her school wardrobe and more.

The two weeks since Dr. Kyle had died in the old school building seemed a nightmare from which they all wondered if they'd ever awaken. The police, the FBI, just about every law enforcement official imaginable had descended upon them to ask questions, the same questions over and over again until Tess had wanted to scream at them all to just leave her and her family alone.

She hadn't done that, of course. She'd endured it as best she could, and had even tried to understand why it was necessary. People had died, after all—a lot of them. Andrea Polzer, William Overby, even Rachel had only represented the tip of the iceberg. An investigation of Dr. Kyle's background, along with Joely's testimony as to his admission of the facts to her, had quickly tied him to the deaths of seven children for sure, and the list was growing as his years in college and his practice in San Francisco were also brought to light.

His house, too, had revealed a darkness previously unsuspected. Dr. Kyle'd talked often of renovating the old house his mother had left to him when she'd died, yet the house was untouched, a demented tribute to the twisting of a young mind. Tim Kyle's bedroom still sported faded, childish wallpaper of cowboys and Indians, and the bedspread on his twin bed was a similar, youthful print. Toys lined the shelves, propped up by mildewed books. All of it was old to the point of crumbling, yet he'd slept in that room without, apparently, making any effort to change any of it.

Whatever secrets lurked there would probably remain hidden. There was no one left to answer any of the questions.

Less than two blocks from her house, Tess saw one of her neighbors, out watering his lawn, turn his head away and pretend not to see her.

"Hi, Mr. Vincent," she called out as she walked past.

He looked at her and managed a smile. "Oh, hi, Tess. Hot day, isn't it?"

"Like always," she agreed. She could feel his eyes on the back of her neck as she continued on her way.

Her mother had been right—the town would never forget. Sometimes Tess felt like a freak in a sideshow, the way people gawked. Yet none of them had done anything wrong. Her mother had worked for Dr. Kyle, the now-infamous serial killer, and Joely had been his last target and the only one to escape with her life. Tess's involvement had been even less than theirs, but she still received her share of furtive glances and rude questions.

Tess turned the corner onto her street and saw the house ahead. There was a big orange U-Haul parked in the driveway, already mostly loaded up. They'd be leaving within a matter of hours, putting Cielo and all that had happened here behind them.

Joely came bounding through the front door and down the porch steps as Tess reached the front yard.

"It's about time you got here," Joely said by way of greeting. "I need your help with those big boxes we filled this morning. They're the only thing left in our room to be put on the truck."

"I had some things to take care of," Tess told her. "I wasn't gone that long."

"You shouldn't have gone at all. We're busy around here."

"Well, I'm back now. Come on, let's get those boxes."

They went into the house together and found it an empty shell. All the furniture was already out, closet doors hung open, the carpet was trampled down by a long day of busy activity.

In their bedroom, once so crowded with furniture that they could hardly move around in it, Tess found the emptiness strangely disquieting. Only a few big boxes were stacked against one wall. Tess took a moment to look around the room and tried to remember the last two months here. It had been such a short stay—would she forget it entirely with time? She hoped not, be-

310

cause although she was happy to be leaving, something had happened here that had changed her forever.

For one thing, she was no longer as impatient with Joely as she had been. She was far too aware of how close she'd come to losing her sister permanently, and she didn't want their time together to be ruined by petty arguments and rivalries. It wasn't always easy, but when she felt on the verge of saying something sharp or sarcastic to Joely, she forced herself to remember that day when Joely had tried to tell what was going on, and she'd not only ignored her sister but had treated her so badly that she'd been driven to go back to that old school by herself to try to find the proof to back up her words. Tess knew she'd always carry the guilt of that day with her.

Joely was struggling with a heavy box, and Tess went to her. "Wait a minute, I'll get the other end," she said. Shoulders straining under the weight, she lifted her half of the box from the floor and together they walked slowly out of the room. "What's in this thing?" Tess asked. "Rocks?"

"Don't you remember—your stereo and tapes, some books, all our photograph albums."

"We should have divided this stuff up more efficiently." Tess stopped and shifted the load. She noticed that Joely, on the opposite side of the box, was still wearing the St. Christopher medal around her neck. From the beginning she'd made clear her intention of keeping that thing, even going so far as to omit any mention of it during their interrogation by the police. She'd admitted to finding the brick at the school, and the bandanna with the other objects in it, but she'd said nothing about the medallion having been part of it. Tess was the only other person who knew about it, and, following Joely's lead, she'd also kept her mouth shut. She didn't know if that had been an especially wise thing to do, but she'd been wanting to do something for Joely, so she'd remained silent.

"I see you're still wearing it," she said, nodding her head at the now-polished medal that hung on the outside of Joely's blouse.

"It's all I'll ever have to remind me of Martin," Joely said. They'd gotten through two doorways and were now carrying the box down the front steps. "I'm going to keep it forever. You said you had some things to do today—"

"That's right."

"So did I. I went to the cemetery."

Tess put the box down on the grass. "You didn't."

"I had to," Joely said. She looked across their yard to the garage. They could hear their mother banging around in there, gathering together rakes, spare tires, and whatever else in there that belonged to them. "I couldn't leave without saying goodbye to him, even though I knew I wouldn't see him there. He was just a little boy, Tess, but he suffered for such a long time. None of what happened was his fault, not even the part about Rachel . . ."

Joely dropped her head and looked at the shiny medal, its surface glinting in the sun.

Tess went to her sister and put an arm around her shoulder. "I know," she said softly. Joely had her own guilts to contend with, Tess realized.

And did she believe in Joely's ghost? Although she told herself she didn't, Tess had to admit there was a small part of her that sometimes, late at night, wondered. Joely'd wisely said nothing to the police about him, but she still obviously believed, and most of the time Tess just hoped their getting away from Cielo would allow Joely to put all of this—Martin included—behind her forever.

Libby came out of the garage, a roll of garden hose looped over one arm and trailing on the ground behind her. Her hair was pulled back into a ponytail and there was a smudge of dirt on her cheek, but she looked, for the first time in weeks, happy.

"We're almost done, girls," she announced, "and then we'll be on the road. We'll be in our new house before bedtime tonight."

"Our new *rented* house," Joely pointed out.

Brandon emerged from the garage. He was pushing their lawn mower in front of him. "Hey, it was the best I could do on short notice," he said. "Don't knock it—it's got a bedroom for each of you and it's in your old school district."

"I'm not complaining, Dad," Joely said. "I

wouldn't care where we lived—as long as it's not here."

"Me, too," Tess said.

"Then we're all in agreement." Brandon stood beside Libby, their arms almost touching. He looked down at her and winked.

For all of them, the move was going to be a period of adjustment. Brandon wasn't going to move into the house with them. He was going to keep his apartment for the time being, but he and Libby were going to have some long, in-depth talks about their future together, and so far they agreed that his moving back in with them eventually was not out of the question.

The girls were aware of this, having been made part of most of the discussions, and they were both hopeful that their family would again be together.

The transition from resentment to optimism hadn't been as difficult for Tess as she'd expected. She found she couldn't harbor a grudge against her father's past mistakes when he was obviously trying so hard now to make up for them—and that he made her mother happy was a fact Tess couldn't ignore.

Joely, on the other hand, accepted his eventual return as though it were already an established fact, and no one tried very hard to caution her from expecting too much.

"What's left to load up?" Brandon asked, rubbing his hands together.

"Some big boxes in our room," Joely told him.

"That's it?"

She nodded.

"Then let's get them. I don't know about you guys, but I'm ready to go."

"So am I," Libby said. She stood on her toes and impulsively kissed Brandon's cheek.

Tess nudged Joely with her elbow. Joely stifled a giggle, but looked delighted.

A few minutes later they'd brought the last of the boxes from the house and had wedged them into the back of the U-Haul. The house, completely empty now, was already becoming a distant memory that reflected nothing of the fragmented family that had occupied it for a short while.

Only Joely stopped to look back one last time, her eyes sad behind her glasses until Tess came to stand beside her.

"Time to go," Tess said, her voice gentle. "We have to forget what happened here, Joely. None of it was good, and we'll be better off leaving it all behind."

"Not all of it," Joely said, her fingertips touching the St. Christopher medal. She looked up at her sister. "I want to remember Martin—because if I don't, maybe no one else will, and he deserves that much from me. But we won't ever be back here, will we, Tess?"

"Probably not," the older girl agreed.

Then, their arms around each other's waists, the sisters walked to where their parents were waiting for them.

HAUTALA'S HORROR — HOLD ON
TO YOUR HEAD!

MOONDEATH (1844-4, $3.95/$4.95)
Cooper Falls is a small, quiet New Hampshire town, the
kind you'd miss if you blinked an eye. But when darkness
falls and the full moon rises, an uneasy feeling filters
through the air; an unnerving foreboding that causes the
skin to prickle and the body to tense.

NIGHT STONE (3030-4, $4.50/$5.50)
Their new house was a place of darkness and shadows, but
with her secret doll, Beth was no longer afraid. For as she
stared into the eyes of the wooden doll, she heard it call to
her and felt the force of its evil power. And she knew it
would tell her what she had to do.

MOON WALKER (2598-X, $4.50/$5.50)
No one in Dyer, Maine ever questioned the strange disap-
pearances that plagued their town. And they never discussed the eerie figures seen harvesting the potato fields by
day . . . the slow, lumbering hulks with expressionless features and a blood-chilling deadness behind their eyes.

LITTLE BROTHERS (2276-X, $3.95/$4.95)
It has been five years since Kip saw his mother horribly
murdered by a blur of "little brown things." But the "little
brothers" are about to emerge once again from their under-
ground lair. Only this time there will be no escape for the
young boy who witnessed their last feast!